D1389000

PET IN PERIL

PET IN PERIL

Marie Celine

This first world edition published 2016
in Great Britain and the USA by
SEVERN HOUSE PUBLISHERS LTD of
19 Cedar Road, Sutton, Surrey, England, SM2 5DA.
Trade paperback edition first published
in Great Britain and the USA 2017 by
SEVERN HOUSE PUBLISHERS LTD

Copyright © 2016 by Marie Celine.

British Library Cataloguing in Publication Data
A CIP catalogue record for this title is available from the British Library.

ISBN-13: 978-0-7278-8647-7 (cased)
ISBN-13: 978-1-84751-749-4 (trade paper)
ISBN-13: 978-1-78010-813-1 (e-book)

All Severn House titles are printed on acid-free paper.

Severn House Publishers support the Forest Stewardship Council™ [FSC™],
the leading international forest certification organisation.
All our titles that are printed on FSC certified paper carry the FSC logo.

MIX
Paper from
responsible sources
FSC   FSC® C013056
www.fsc.org

Typeset by Palimpsest
Falkirk, Stirlingshire, Scotland.
Printed and bound in Great Britain by
TJ International, Padstow, Cornwall.

ONE

'**F**red and Barney are depressed.'

'That's the silliest thing I've ever heard,' Kitty said. Fran was her best friend and all but what was she thinking? Kitty served them each a plate of eggs and sausage at the kitchen table. OK, so it wasn't *real* sausage. It was soy and quinoa sausage and Fran hated the stuff. She'd made that clear on more occasions than Kitty cared to remember. 'Eat before your food gets cold.'

Fran kept up her monolog while generously pouring tons of ketchup over her breakfast because when it came to faux meat of any kind, Fran wasn't a fan. Not even a faux fan. She said the faux sausage tasted like the recycled cardboard box the stuff came packaged in.

She said that often, too. The woman wasn't one for holding back her feelings.

'Animals can be quite emotional.' Fran stabbed at an egg and took a bite. 'I don't know why you insist on paying extra for cage-free, free-range eggs when the eggs from the egg factory are cheaper. They all taste the same to me.'

Kitty nibbled at her food. 'I feel bad for the chickens. They ought to be free.'

Fran rolled her eyes. 'The next thing you'll be telling is that we're only going to be buying our eggs from chickens that have been home-schooled as well.'

'Very funny. You did just say that animals have emotions. Chickens are animals too.' Fran liked to tell people she had a Type A personality. Kitty liked to kid her that it was more a Type B personality – B as in blabbermouth.

'And they do,' Fran said between mouthfuls. She might have complained constantly about the food but it hadn't yet stopped her from eating it. 'And you have to pay attention to their emotions.' She jabbed her fork in Kitty's direction for emphasis.

Kitty wolfed down her food and stood, dropping her plate in

the sink. 'I don't have time to discuss the emotional needs of my pets right now, Fran.' She wiped her hands on her apron. 'I have a business to run.' The nature of Kitty's gourmet pet chef business meant that she was up at the crack of dawn six days a week. On the seventh she was glad to sleep in late, if the cat let her. The dog took a much more live-and-let-live attitude and allowed her to sleep in as late as she liked.

Fran turned to face Kitty at the stove. 'You've got to listen to them. Every wag, every purr tells a story.'

This from a woman who'd never had a pet, not so much as a goldfish. Kitty was juggling various pots and pans. Every burner was ablaze. 'You know I love Fred and Barney. They're like children to me.'

She cracked open the kitchen window to let some air into the apartment. According to her weather app it would be a haze-free day in Los Angeles with the high climbing into the nineties. Kitty grabbed a clean wooden spoon and began stirring it slowly around in a steel saucepan, watching the gravy turn golden brown. Kitty was baking a large meatloaf that would be sliced into smaller portions and distributed to several of her clients' pets later that day. While she used to love the meatloaf her mom made with ketchup on top, Kitty knew her clientele would like the beef gravy better.

'I'm just saying,' replied Fran, not one to back down. She'd gone on a sudden bead kick, purchased a bucketful of recycled kona wood hair beads and woven them into her long black locks. When she whipped her head from side to side it made a sound like a soft rain falling through leafy trees. 'Fred is in a funk. Barney, too, if you want to know the truth.' Her green eyes fluttered as she scrunched up her pouty red lips to shoot Fred an air kiss.

Kitty peeked in the oven window. The meatloaf looked about done. The overpowering smells of meats and veggies brewing together in the small space was beginning to overwhelm her – almost as much as this conversation.

'Now you're going to tell me you know what *my* pets are thinking?' She wiped her damp brow with the corner of her apron then pushed the window up the rest of the way. Kitty glanced appraisingly at Fred and Barney. Fred was the sleek black Labrador Retriever that she'd adopted from a local rescue organization. Barney was a frisky tuxedoed stray cat that had followed Kitty home one day when she was out for a stroll and had since more or less adopted her.

Were they looking a bit forlorn?

'Maybe I should make an appointment with the vet.'

'The vet?' The New York faction of Fran's accent grew stronger as she grew more strident. 'They don't need needles and shots or to have an ice-cold thermometer shoved up their tender nether regions.' Fran Earhart was part German on her father's side and all Jamaican on her mother's. She'd spent the first years of her life in NYC, then the family had moved to Kingston, Jamaica in her father's effort to give his family a better life.

Later, Fran, hoping to make a living as a makeup artist, had struck off for Miami on her own, then LA. Fran eventually landed a job at Santa Monica Film Studios, which was exactly where Kitty was now working part-time as well. The two had met a couple of months back when Kitty had shown up for her initial meeting with the producer of a possible cooking show for pets. Kitty had got the job and a new bestie and roommate in the bargain.

'You asked my opinion and I'm giving it to you, girl,' Fran continued.

Kitty refrained from correcting Fran. She had definitely *not* asked for Fran's opinion about the state of her pets' mental health.

'Fred and Barney are in a funk. It's time you took them to see a shrink. The vet.' She snorted. 'Katherine Elizabeth Karlyle, I cannot believe you even said that. Shame on you.'

Kitty shook her head firmly. 'I am *not* taking my dog and cat to a pet psychologist. That's crazy.' Kitty replied. 'No pun intended.'

Katherine was her given name but everybody called her Kitty. When she was a mere babe her parents had owned a silvery Siamese named Princess. Every time her mom called 'Kitty, kitty, kitty,' to attract the cat, baby Katherine had come running – or crawling to be more precise – thinking that her mother was calling her. Thus, a nickname was born. Princess, on the other hand, never came running unless the kibble bag was shaking.

'I think it is exactly what you, Fred and Barney need. Right, Fred?'

The Lab raised his head at the sound of his name.

'Don't you dare answer, Fred.' Kitty waved her spatula then

turned her attention to the two-quart saucepan on the back burner. She was making up a batch of her popular liver and oatmeal bran dog biscuits. 'Psychologist, please. I am not about to go all Hollyweird like my clients.' She didn't mean that in a bad way. Kitty ran a struggling gourmet pet chef business out of her house and relied on the wealthier members of Los Angeles society whose pets she created meals for on a regular basis. Her clients were quirky but harmless for the most part.

Of course, all that was changing now with the new TV show, *The Pampered Pet*, coming to TV in a few months. They'd already shot and aired a pilot and were well into the first season's batch of episodes, with three shows 'in the can' as Greg Clifton, the show's director, liked to say. Now that she was a newbie TV cooking show host she wasn't struggling quite so much these days. Except with her roommate's rantings.

Kitty was still waiting not so patiently for her first real paycheck from the show. She'd been hounding the show's producer who continually promised the check was on its way, but somehow the money hadn't made it into her slim checking account yet.

Fran had suggested she hire an agent to represent her. That was one suggestion of Fran's that she might be right about. Fran had given her the names of a couple good-sized local agencies and Kitty was considering talking to one of them soon.

'Why not see a psychologist?' Fran said, not letting go. She dipped her index finger into the big yellow mixing bowl on the counter between them then licked it clean. 'Not bad. Could maybe use a little more salt.'

'Hey, those are for my clients' pets.' Sure, the girl wouldn't eat tofu but she had no problem eating pet food.

'Oh, you mean those same clients that take their precious little poochies and kitties to pet psychologists?' Fran folded her arms and taunted her roommate. 'In fact, girl, didn't you tell me that you actually got one of your client's pets that way? You know, that magician guy whose wife I met.'

'The Fandolfis,' Kitty muttered as she popped a tray of doggie bones in the oven above the meatloaf.

'What was that?'

Kitty slammed the oven shut a little harder than necessary. 'I said the Fandolfis.' Her voice held a note of resignation. It was true. George Newhart, a pet psychologist in Beverly Hills, had referred a pet or two her way. He'd spotted her business cards tacked to a bulletin board at a local health food shop, grabbed several and handed them out to his clients, several of whom had apparently expressed a need to do even more for their precious pets than the already outrageous act of taking them for pricey weekly sessions with a pet psychologist.

Kitty cast a nervous glance at the ceiling. The rattling of the stove, not to mention Fran's booming voice, might raise the wrath of her upstairs neighbor, Mirabelle Stein. It didn't take much to get that wrath in gear. The Widow Stein was a deceptively demure-looking elderly woman of French–Jewish descent who lived directly upstairs from Kitty. If the Widow Stein had been manning the Maginot Line the Germans might never have invaded France.

Mrs Stein typically could be found wearing a black frock with white piping and smelling of rosewater. She also quite typically had a tart countenance – like she spent her days sucking on sour, hard lemon candies – at least, she looked that way every time Kitty ran into her around the apartment complex. An occurrence she always dreaded and did her best to avoid at almost any cost.

The widow's one joy in life seemed to be complaining about Kitty and her pets to the building's manager, Jerry Frizzell. While she had rarely seen Jerry, she had often heard him – usually when he was demanding the rent or when he was relaying one of Mrs Stein's latest complaints against her. Sometimes he put those complaints in writing and delivered them to her in the much-dreaded form of written notices. Kitty had a stack of them in the back of her bureau, buried behind her underwear – where they belonged.

At least rent hadn't been a problem of late. With Fran as a roommate to share expenses with Kitty's finances weren't as bad as they'd been the past couple of years. And though the money had not yet been very forthcoming, with the new gig as host of *The Pampered Pet* on the CuisineTV network on top of her somewhat sketchy career as a gourmet pet chef – a job she loved despite its hardships, lack of security, meager pay and Hollyweird clientele – her credit rating had improved, if not her aforementioned checking account. Fortunately Santa Monica Film Studios was giving her a small advance against her CuisineTV contract money.

Sure enough, three resounding bangs rattled the overhead lights. *See what you did?* mouthed Kitty.

Fran snorted and launched her boot at the ceiling. It struck heel first. 'Keep it down up there, Mrs Dingbat! Some of us are still trying to get our beauty sleep!'

The black leather boot clattered to the kitchen floor and Fred dutifully retrieved it for her, albeit a bit slobbered up, but Fran didn't seem to mind. 'Thanks, Fred. Good boy.' She glanced up at the ceiling. 'Somebody's going to kill the old dingbat one day.'

'Must you?' Kitty asked. The boot had left a three-inch long curved scuffmark on the ceiling. How was she ever going to explain that to the landlord the next time he came to inspect the place?

'What? What did I do?'

Kitty shook her head. 'Come on – help me load this stuff up.' She glanced at her watch. 'We're going to be late as it is and you know how Steve gets.'

As Kitty backed the car out of its slot she caught a glimpse of Mirabelle Stein dressed in shaggy pink slippers and a matching housecoat, coming up the walk and heading for Kitty's front door. Her gray hair was done up in a haphazard knot atop her diminutive head. Kitty hadn't heard the end of the boot-throwing incident.

TWO

'You're late,' were the first words out of Steve Barnhard's thin-lipped mouth the minute they rolled into the parking lot of Santa Monica Studios. 'Half an hour late,' Steve growled, 'to be precise.' He tapped the big Rolex wrapped tightly around his wrist like a princely cockalorum. 'We're behind schedule.' The next words out of his mouth were, 'And what is *that* thing?' He pointed accusingly at the poor, helpless pooch darting between Kitty's legs.

'I'm only twenty minutes late,' Kitty retorted, throwing open the tailgate of the Volvo and grabbing her purse and chef's backpack. 'We'll be right in.' The backpack had been a present from her parents when she'd graduated from culinary school. The sturdy black pack was a top-of-the-line model with a removable knife insert that held all her knives, a compartment for a laptop and plenty of pockets for all her extra gear.

'Tick-tock.' The producer tapped his watch once more. 'I'll see the two of you inside. We have things to discuss.' Steve stomped off in a huff, leaving behind a subtle whiff of some fancy cologne with its woody, leathery, three-hundred-bucks-a-bottle aroma.

'And *that*,' Kitty hollered as he retreated, 'is my dog, Fred!' In a moment of weakness and guilt she had let Fran talk her into bringing Fred along to the day's taping. Barney would rather face down a raging bull elephant than have to get in the car and go for a ride.

'I'd like to discuss the back of my hand with his face,' muttered Fran. She helped lug Kitty's gear to the soundstage.

Kitty grabbed a cup of coffee from the pot in the corner of the makeup room and fell down into the chair at the brightly lit makeup table, waiting for Fran to work her wonders.

'Muffin?' offered Fran, holding up a gooey and sinful-looking pecan-and-icing-topped pumpkin spice muffin the size of a small cantaloupe that she'd grabbed from the crafts table on the way in.

Kitty shook her head. 'No, thanks.' The holidays were just around the corner and she was trying to lose weight. 'How's my hair?'

Fran fluffed a few strands of Kitty's fine, long brown hair. 'Depressed, like your pets.'

Kitty groaned. Apparently Fran wasn't done badgering her about the pets. 'I am not taking them to a psychologist.' Kitty scowled, looking at her reflection in the mirror. She had her mother's fine features and fair complexion and her father's strong nose and blue eyes, though the bags under them this morning were all hers.

'Trust me,' Fran was saying, 'I know such things. I'm a bit psychic, you know.'

Kitty mumbled under her breath, 'Psycho, more likely.'

'I heard that,' harrumphed Fran, grabbing a hairbrush and

running it through Kitty's hair a little too viciously for Kitty's taste and pain receptors.

'Scoff all you like but it's true.' She patted the top of Fred's head. 'And I know what a neglected dog looks like, too. Don't I, you cute thing? After all, I've been neglected more than once myself.' Fran had recently broken up with her latest boyfriend – one who had some neglect issues himself – like having neglected to tell Fran that he was still married.

'Can we focus on hair and makeup for a minute? We've got two shows to tape and I've still got my food deliveries to make.'

'If you don't believe me, go see a shrink.'

'I do not need a shrink,' Kitty said, putting her coffee cup down carefully on the wobbly tray table by her side.

'Not you. I'm talking about your pets.' She motioned toward Kitty's Fred, who'd collapsed in a heap in the corner with his head resting on his paws.

'Tell me you're kidding. Tell me you're just trying to give me a hard time this morning. Tell me – please tell me, Fran – that you are simply taking some sadistic pleasure in yanking my chain this morning.'

'Not at all.' She deftly pulled Kitty's hair into a ponytail and twisted a black tie around the clump. 'I can't believe you of all people are saying that. You were the one who told me about that guy—' Fran snapped her fingers several times while staring at the ceiling. 'What did you say his name was again?'

Kitty frowned. 'Doctor Newhart.'

What a mistake it had been to tell Fran about the Beverly Hills psychologist whose practice specialized in treating the so-called psychological issues and ailments of pets. Pets whose owners were rich beyond belief and often indulged – over-indulged in Kitty's opinion – their cute little four-legged members of the family. Some even scheduled regular visits for their 'children' with pet masseuses, life coaches, trainers and psychics.

Not that Kitty was complaining. After all, it was those same owners who were her key clientele. Without them she'd be working in her parents' restaurant or slogging hash somewhere on Sunset Strip instead of doing what she loved. She definitely would never have had her own TV show.

'I don't know,' said Kitty. She shot a concerned look toward

Fred and nagged at her lower lip with her front teeth. She had been really busy, and her next-door neighbor, Sylvester, seemed to be spending more time with Fred and Barney than she was lately. Luckily she could always count on Sylvester to check in on her pets when she was overwhelmed with work, which seemed to be happening more and more frequently. As a struggling young musician he had more time on his hands than he would have liked and was always happy to pitch in. Kitty suspected he might have a little crush on her.

Between the day job and the show Kitty was suddenly being pulled in a hundred directions at once – not to mention that Jack, her adorable fiancé, was always complaining that she never had time for him. Was that a look of depression on Fred's face? Was Barney feeling neglected and unloved?

Should she make an appointment with Dr Newhart at his Beverly Hills office?

As if reading her mind, Fran announced, 'Don't worry, I'll call the doc's office and set up an appointment for the three of you. Maybe he'll give you a group rate.'

Kitty laughed nervously. 'Maybe we should invite Jack to come then, too. Make it a foursome.'

'Hey, couldn't hurt, could it? What man couldn't use a shrink?' They both laughed. Fran grabbed a can of hairspray. 'Hold your breath.' Fran hit her with a cloud of citrus-scented spray.

'I agree,' said a voice from behind.

Kitty's head spun. 'How long have you been standing there?' It was Steve Barnhard, looking as sourpussed as ever. Steve had been an assistant producer at Santa Monica Film Studios when she'd first had the misfortune of meeting him. He was a slim fellow with wavy ginger hair, a light trail of freckles running from cheek to cheek, boyish features and a man-sized irritable disposition. Only in his thirties, he had now been promoted to producer of Kitty's pet cookery show. Not that his father being head of the network had anything to do with it. No, of course not.

Kitty got the feeling that Bill Barnhard, Steve's dad and head of the CuisineTV network that owned the show, had put him in charge of her TV show just to irk her.

'Long enough to concur, for once,' Steve said, shooting a

steely look at Fran, 'with her that you ought to have your head examined.'

Fran grumbled, 'Tell me about it.'

Kitty jumped out of her seat. 'Hey whose side are you on? I took you in.' Albeit reluctantly, all had worked out pretty well so far.

'I'm just saying.' Fran put a hand on each of Kitty's slender shoulders and eased her back down. 'Actually, I was telling Kitty how she should take her dog and cat to a shrink.'

Steve beamed. 'Oh my God. That's a wonderful idea. Just splendid.'

Kitty's eyes grew to the size of tea saucers. 'You have got to be kidding?'

Steve folded his arms across his chest. 'I'm not kidding at all.' He snapped his fingers. Fred's ears perked up. 'Who is this man or woman and where can I find them?'

'Some pet psychologist with an office in Beverly Hills. His name's Newhart—'

Kitty cut Fran off. 'Hey!'

'Perfect,' said Steve. 'I'll have my assistant phone his office straight away.' He stopped in the doorway. 'Now, we're very, very late. I suggest you slap a final coat of paint on Kitty and hustle her out to the set. The crew is waiting. And I don't have to tell you how much their lollygagging around is costing us.'

Kitty punched Fran in the arm.

'Ouch.' She rubbed her arm. 'What did you do that for?'

'For not keeping your big mouth shut,' Kitty said, leaping from the makeup chair and stomping out the door. 'I am not talking to a psychologist. And, if you think I'd even consider it, then you're the one who ought to have her head examined.' She turned. 'Come on, Fred,' she said, clapping her hands. 'We've got a show to do.'

Kitty stopped dramatically in the doorway, hands gripping the doorframe. 'No psychologists. Get it out of your head.'

Fran raised her arms in surrender. 'Your mommy's crazy, you know that, Fred?' She was looking at the Lab and rolling the hairbrush around in circles orbiting her left ear like a lunar lander looking for a good spot to touch down. 'Maybe we should get a psychiatrist for you.' She twitched an eyebrow in Kitty's direction.

Kitty opened her mouth then shut it again. Fran was simply being Fran. What was the point in arguing?

Fran waved her brush. 'Have a good show. Break a veggie chicken leg!'

THREE

'Hello, Doctor Newhart,' Kitty mumbled with a forced smile and a barely stifled sigh of defeat. 'It's so good to see you again.' She'd been ambushed by that smarmy, sneaky, irritating, ugsome and condescending Steve Barnhard. Realizing she was grinding her teeth, Kitty forced herself to stop before something snapped. Probably a molar. Worse yet, a canine. She might not eat meat but that didn't mean she didn't like to sink her teeth into something satisfying now and then. Like right now, for instance, she could use a fresh, flaky pastry.

She glared across the room at Steve. There just weren't enough adjectives to describe her producer. Had she mentioned short-tempered and evil?

'Hello, Ms Karlyle.' The doctor bowed ever so slightly. In a navy-blue pinstripe suit, brilliant white shirt and matching blue-and-violet paisley silk tie, the petite doctor barely came up to Kitty's chin – even with those lace-up shoes with the one-inch heels. A dapper man in his early sixties, the doctor possessed a square jaw and inky blue pools where his irises should have been. Kitty imagined those were just the sort of puppy dog eyes that real puppy dogs liked to get lost in and tell their doggy troubles to. Maybe that's what had made him such a great pet psychologist with one of the leading practices in the area all these years.

And no, he wasn't the only pet psychologist in the LA phone book – Kitty had checked.

Of course, having a bunch of folks with too much money and too little sense, as the saying goes, within a twenty-mile radius of his luxury-appointed Beverly Hills office hadn't hurt. He and Kitty both catered to the pets of the deep-pocketed in their own way. Kitty catered to their stomachs and Newhart their psyches. The doctor, at least, was making a pretty good living from it. She had a feeling he had gained some pretty deep pockets of his own in the process of helping his troubled clients' troubled pets.

They'd finished taping the first show and Kitty was thanking the audience out in the bleachers when Steve had come prancing onto the kitchen set that provided the backdrop to *The Pampered Pet* show. The guy might have been one of Santa's lead reindeer in another life. He had Dr Newhart in tow.

'Congratulations on your television show.' The doctor extended a pale, liver-spotted hand.

She was about to reach for it when, out of the corner of her eye, she noticed what her producer was holding. 'What is Barney doing here?'

'He's a handful, isn't he?' grunted Steve. The producer was clutching Barney while desperately attempting to keep her cat from tearing a paw-wide swath through his lavender polo shirt. Barney's sharp claws struck the producer's stomach as the cat lashed out in what looked like a life or death struggle with Steve. He yelped and held the cat out as far as possible.

Kitty couldn't blame the poor cat for putting up a fight. She'd struggle if Steve was trying to hug her, too. The only man with those privileges was her future husband, discounting relatives and close friends, of course. 'What are you doing with my cat?'

'I brought him for Doctor Newhart. You know, so he could examine him as well. After all, your dog is already here.' Barney reached back and nipped Steve's fingers. 'Ouch.' He extended the squirming cat toward Kitty. 'You didn't want this guy to feel left out, did you?'

Kitty snatched Barney away. 'But how did you get him?' She had left Barney safely locked up in her apartment. She petted his head and whispered sweet nothings, like what a jerk Steve was.

Steve shrugged. 'I found your purse in makeup and gave your address and keys to one of my assistants. She fetched him for me.' Steve frowned. 'She's still cowering in the ladies' room. I think she's been traumatized by that beast.' He was pointing at Barney.

'You went in my purse?'

Steve shrugged once more. 'I don't know why you're making such a big deal out of this, Kitty. I did it for you.'

'For me? You broke into my purse,' she huffed, 'and my apartment? And it was for me?'

'And for your pets. You should be thanking me,' Steve sniffed.

Doctor Newhart looked about uncomfortably. 'I fear you're upsetting the animals, dear.' He pulled at his silk tie.

Kitty wondered if the good doctor would mind if she borrowed his tie for a moment – just long enough to strangle Steve. Kitty opened her mouth to respond and spotted Fred cowering under the kitchen table, looking at her with those big brown eyes of his, tail drooping. Was Fran right? Did every wag or lack thereof tell a story?

And Barney . . .

Well, Barney was struggling to be put down. So he could no doubt run away – far, far away. Like Kitty felt like doing.

Perhaps the little tuxedo cat knew a nice feline getaway where all three of them could go hang out, have some drinks and tapas under a striped beach umbrella thrust foot deep in the golden sands of some exotic island.

From the corner of her eye, she spied Fran hiding behind one of the cameramen. The big chicken. 'Sorry, Doctor Newhart. You're right, of course.' To show them all what a good mommy she was, she stroked Barney vigorously. He struggled to free himself from her tight grip but she wasn't about to let him loose. The studio was a maze of hot lights and live wires. No place for a cat to be running around on the loose. Who knew what mischief he might cause to the equipment or injury he might do himself?

Besides, she was trying to prove a point here. Why couldn't Barney cooperate? Take it like a man? Or at least a cat. Kitty grabbed Steve's sleeve, pulling him aside. 'When am I going to get my own dressing room?' Kitty said. 'With a lock on the door.'

'I told you that you could have Gretchen's old office but you said you didn't want it.'

Kitty shivered visibly. No, she most definitely did not want Gretchen Corbett's old office. Too much bad juju there.

'So,' said Steve, glibly, 'you'll simply have to wait until another office opens up.' He made a show of straightening his sleeve. 'Sonny did offer to share his office with you.'

Ewww, thought Kitty. Double bad juju there. And potential cooties.

The two of them were still arguing when Greg Clifton butted in. 'OK, are we done here?'

Kitty jumped. 'Sorry, you startled me.' It wasn't just Gretchen Corbett's old office that spooked her. Despite all the workers scooting about and all the bright lights, the soundstage gave her the jitters, too. Some nasty things had gone down here. And she hadn't been able to forget them yet.

'Excuse me, Kitty, but we need to get moving. Let's save the drama for in front of the camera.' He cupped his hands together and brought them to his lips. 'Come on, people. One down, one to go. Let's get ready to roll cameras!'

He hollered for the AD – that meant his assistant director. Greg was a normally affable, trim fellow in his fifties with long, graying black hair that he kept in a ponytail most of the time. He got loud when he was in director mode. His style in clothes reflected his casual, laidback attitude. Today he was wearing a spotless black T-shirt and jeans. He was in a relationship with the AD, Julie McConnell, a thin young woman with light brown hair and soft chestnut-brown eyes. Julie preferred pantsuits to jeans and today's outfit was no exception: a charcoal two-piece, tailored to show off her girlish physique.

'What's up?' Julie said, clipboard in hand and a sharpened pencil stuck behind her ear.

'This is Doctor Newhart – our special guest.' Greg waved toward the psychologist.

'Hello, Doctor.'

'What's going on?' Kitty asked warily.

Steve grabbed Kitty by the elbow and dragged her over to the kitchen table on the set. 'Doctor Newhart has agreed to be our special guest this morning. Did I forget to tell you?' He turned to the psychologist and waved him over. 'Have a seat, Doctor.'

'Let's clear the set!' commanded Greg. He clapped twice and people and equipment began moving and whirring.

Kitty's head started spinning. Steve immediately stopped talking and hustled off to the side of the stage. Kitty only wished she could get him to listen to her on cue like that.

Show time, Kitty told herself.

She put on her game face and waved to the audience brought in for the filming. Kitty had prepared a family-style salmon-and-veggie dish for this next show. She had designed the meal for a family with multiple cats. Quite a clever idea, if she did say so herself.

Midway into the program they cut for an interview with Dr Newhart where Kitty asked some questions that had been prepared for her by Steve and his staff. All very softball in nature, but then CuisineTV was all about good food, good friends and good times – this wasn't the place for hard-hitting news or investigative journalism, and that was OK by her.

She and Dr Newhart then fielded questions from the audience. She always enjoyed speaking with members of her audience and answering their questions. Still, she was relieved to bid the pet psychologist farewell and get back to the cooking. That was what she knew and did best, after all. Being a talk-show host had most definitely not been in the job description.

'Kitty,' said Steve, running over and tucking his cell phone in his front pocket. 'Great, great show.'

'Uh, thank you, Steve.' Wow, that was so out of character. Usually he came armed with a litany of notes on his tablet for things she should do better next time.

'And I've got great news.'

Kitty eyed him with suspicion. He was throwing a lot of *greats* around. Too many for her taste. This was never a good sign. 'Yes?' she asked reluctantly. 'What is it?'

'I've got you booked into the Little Switzerland Resort and Spa. You leave in the morning.'

'A resort? Tomorrow?' Kitty made a face like she'd just chomped down on a lemon and shook her head no simultaneously. 'No way, Steve.' She waved her hands in front of her. 'I've got a business to run and pets to feed.'

Not to mention her fiancé, Jack, who could also use some TLC. He wouldn't be happy about her suddenly leaving town. He'd been complaining that they hadn't been getting much quality time together these days. Kitty thought part of that was due to the fact that his father had passed away in the last year and his mother was still having a difficult time coming to terms with his death. Jack's father had died in his sleep. His mother had never had a chance to say goodbye. She'd also regretted all the things the two of them had never had the time to do together but had always planned on doing one day.

One day had never come.

Steve's voice broke into her thoughts. 'What? We'll do the show from the resort and your pets will be accompanying you. Don't worry about your business. We'll take care of it.'

'No,' insisted Kitty, puffing a lock of hair from her eye. There wasn't a hairspray out there that seemed to hold up to the steam rising off a cooking pot. Steve would take care of it? No way she was leaving her business in the hands of Steve. She'd either come home to a dead business or a slew of food poisoned pets. Probably both.

She cursed herself for letting Steve include Dr Newhart on the program. It was the psychologist who had talked about this crazy spa and resort for pets nestled in the southern California hills somewhere.

Worse still, Newhart had told Kitty, Steve and company that the upcoming weekend at Little Switzerland would be perfect because they were hosting a New-Age/New-Pet Festival with all sorts of holistic pet-centric events. Oh, brother, thought Kitty.

While she had politely nodded and said she would consider taking Fred and Barney there for a little quality time, she had no intention of actually following through on the idea. Now Steve thought he could muscle her into actually going? No way. 'Forget it, Steve. I am not interested and I don't have the time. I don't even have time for this conversation.'

'What's all the hubbub?' Greg asked.

Steve explained and, by the expression on Greg's face, the director seemed to be liking the idea. 'You heard Doctor Newhart – he said you should pamper your pets like the name of your show implies.'

Steve raised a pallid finger – he'd probably never done a day's worth of hard labor in his life, thought Kitty. He'd been born with the proverbial silver spoon in his mouth. How hard could it be to lift a silver spoon?

'To quote,' continued Steve, '"after all, that's what your program is all about, isn't it, Ms Karlyle?"'

Kitty had reddened then and she reddened now.

Greg was nodding enthusiastically. 'Road trip,' he cooed, squeezing the hand of his young squeeze.

'No road trip.' Kitty was fuming like hot soup left too long on the stove. She forced herself to keep a lid on the pressure cooker that her head had become. It wouldn't do to make a scene in front of the lingering audience or the crew. She picked up Barney and whistled for Fred. 'Now, if you don't mind, I have meals to deliver. Where's Fran?' She was supposed to be helping her out today. And why wasn't she here backing her up against these two?

'Please reconsider, Kitty,' begged Greg.

Steve was glaring at her but she stared him down. 'Never. Not in a million years.'

FOUR

K itty set her handbag down on the cold granite counter with a sigh. A million years went by quicker than she would have thought.

'Welcome to the Little Switzerland Resort and Spa,' beamed the crisply uniformed clerk behind the front desk. He flashed teeth so white the color could only have come from a dentist or one of those weird whitening booths popping up in shopping malls. 'Checking in?'

'Yes, thank you.'

'Name, please?'

'Karlyle.' Kitty turned to Fran. 'I can't believe that weasel called his father,' Kitty complained under her breath. No sooner had she and Fran returned to the makeup room after the taping than the red phone on the wall had rung. It had been Bill Barnhard on the line, Steve's father and head honcho of the CuisineTV network. A few words from him and they were packing their bags for Little Switzerland. It was a good thing her clients were so understanding of her having to cancel their pets' meals for a few days – and on short notice.

Kitty had thumbed through one of the resort's brochures on

the drive down while Fran spelled her at the wheel. The place
boasted both an indoor pool and a heated outdoor pool and about
a dozen hot tubs – all pet friendly. If the rest of the dogs
were anything like her Fred, they'd spend more time drinking
the pool and tub water than swimming in it. The resort also
included a pet/people obstacle course and play area complete
with a pet-friendly jungle gym. Was there anything at this place
for *actual* children to play in or on?

Fran shrugged at Kitty's comment. She didn't look too upset
by the turn of events. In fact, Kitty could swear she was smirking.

'What are you going to do, Kitty? Besides,' said Fran without
waiting for an answer, 'look at this place. It's adorable. And all
expenses paid.'

'I suppose so.' And Jack hadn't given her a hard time at all.
He'd been very supportive.

'Do you realize how close Little Switzerland is to Calabasas?'

'So?'

'So?' exclaimed Fran, cupping her hands around her mouth.
'We might see some movie stars.' She shook herself. 'I hear a lot
of them hang out in Calabasas to get away from all the paparazzi
and drooling fans.'

'Like you?'

'Hey.' Fran planted her hands on her hips. 'I don't drool.'

'You're hopeless,' replied Kitty, taking a look around. It had
been a long drive and she was exhausted. It wasn't so much the
miles as it was the LA traffic, which she was glad to be out of.

The sprawling resort was tucked up along the low mountains
at the edge of the town of Little Switzerland itself and within
easy walking distance of the town's many shops and restaurants.
Little Switzerland looked like a replica of an authentic Swiss
village – not that Kitty had ever been to Switzerland – but it
looked exactly like all the pictures, or at least the Disney version.
Kitty figured the tourists must eat it up.

The resort maintained that same Swiss style. The chalet-
inspired main building was no exception with its grand V-shaped
roof and extended eaves. What set this place apart from the
typical hotel resort so far was that there seemed to be as many
pets as there were people running around and nobody seemed to
mind. A gold-lettered sign on an easel beside the entry to the

formal dining room even stated *People are welcome, only if accompanied by a pet.*

The crowded lobby carried the sound of laughter and barking. There was a humongous two-sided limestone fireplace near the center of the lobby that Kitty estimated she could easily walk through without so much as bending a knee. Comfy sofas and chairs of both people and pet varieties formed a loose circle around it.

They made their way through a small crowd that had formed around the registration booth for the New-Age/New-Pet Festival. Fran wanted to check it out but Kitty said they had enough things to handle on this trip and that the New-Age/New-Pet Festival was not one of them. Kitty and Fran were running solo at the moment, because the minute they had arrived at the spa/resort Fred and Barney had been expertly hustled off by a white-gloved attendant in a red uniform with black buttons and a vintage doorman's hat. He explained that the pets would be attending a pets-only orientation.

Fran was busy ogling a three-tiered stone fountain with a small herd of bronze-cast deer positioned around it. One fawn dipped its head repeatedly at the base of the fountain as if drinking. A brace of live ducks floated lazily along the surface of the water. Not watching where she was going, Fran crashed into the back of a tall, sandy-haired gentleman in a tweed sport coat and khakis. Even from the rear, he had a noticeably athletic body and the broad shoulders to match.

The man spun around, his blue eyes flashing as if preparing to launch heat-seeking missiles. His face was tan and taut. He'd been tossing a gold object up and down in his hand.

Kitty now saw that it was a ring. He trapped it shut in his palm as it landed. She was reminded of a Venus flytrap. Two tall white poodles with poufy, furry pompoms atop their heads shared a leash at his side. Diamond studded collars adorned their necks. Another man stood to his left. 'I beg your pardon?' he growled.

'Sorry,' said Fran, holding up her hands. 'I didn't mean to bump into you like that.'

He locked eyes with her, his frown turning to a smile so fast Kitty thought somebody somewhere might have remotely flipped his switch.

'Oh!' Fran took a step back.

'No need to apologize, my dear.' He slurred his words. His eyes seemed to be taking her all in like a snake sizing up a tender mousy morsel. 'In fact, now that I'm facing this way, what say we try it again?' He wriggled an eyebrow and stretched out his arms. A bit of thick gold chain peeked out from his open shirt collar.

He was obviously tipsy, thought Kitty. She sniffed. He reeked of alcohol. His eyes were bloodshot. Kitty also spotted a dark ring below his right eye that appeared to have been covered with makeup. What was that all about?

The man's companion shrugged after making eye contact with Kitty in a universal gesture that she interpreted as saying, 'Hey, what can I do? We don't pick our friends, they pick us.' Kitty knew the gesture and the sentiment well – after all, she had Fran, didn't she?

'Come on, Vic. I think you've had enough.' Vic's friend was also athletic with similar fine, sandy hair and mischievous blue eyes. A pair of soft leather gloves hung out of the back pocket of his chinos.

Standing over six foot, the man was only a tad shorter than the man named Vic but just as handsome, though in a less cold, more boyish sense. His firm, light-toned face was clean-shaven. The two men could have been brothers. Maybe they were.

'Nonsense, John.' He shook off his friend. 'The young lady and I were just about to get to know each other. Weren't we?'

'I know you already, buddy,' Fran quipped.

'Oh?'

'Yeah, and I've squashed bigger cockroaches than you.'

Vic leaned back and howled in laughter. The dogs looked up at him as if uncertain how to take it. 'I like you, Miss—'

'Miss kiss my—'

Kitty pulled Fran's sleeve. 'Let's go, Fran. I'm exhausted. I could use a nap before dinner.'

'Bed is what I have in mind,' said Vic with a flashy smile. 'Shall I join you or will you be joining me?'

Kitty couldn't believe how arrogant this guy was. If his head swelled any bigger all he'd need was a gondola and he could offer hot air balloon rides. They'd better leave before Fran said or did something they'd both regret. She physically hustled Fran away.

'Call me if you change your mind!' hollered Vic. 'Victor Cornwall. Ask for me at the desk!'

More like *cornball*, thought Kitty.

Fran turned at the bank of elevators and called out, 'Drop dead, jerk face!'

'Please,' said Kitty. 'Everybody is watching. You're making a scene.'

'I don't care,' snapped Fran, whipping her hair around and coming within a literal hair's width of clipping Kitty's nose.

'Well, I do.' Kitty was not big on scenes. Or confrontations, for that matter.

As she allowed Kitty to hustle her into the elevator, Fran said, 'Boy, for such a handsome guy he's sure got one heck of an ugly personality. Am I just imagining it,' she said, theatrically wiping down her arms, 'or am I covered in green slime?'

Kitty couldn't suppress a giggle. The man did have a rather snakelike personality. She was about to punch the button to the third floor. 'Darn.'

'What's wrong?'

'I don't have my purse.'

'What happened to it?'

Kitty frowned. 'I must have left it at the front desk. I'll have to go back and get it. You can go on up to our room if you want to.' She handed Fran a keycard.

'Nah, that's OK. I can't leave you to face that slimeball all by yourself.' She started in the direction of the lobby. 'I'll come with you and run interference if I have to. Heck, I'll dump him in the fountain with the ducks if need be.'

But there was no sign of Victor or his companion in the lobby. Fran excused herself to run to the ladies' room while Kitty retrieved her purse.

They were approaching the silver-sheathed elevator doors once more when Kitty spotted something flashy on the carpet. 'Hey, what's that?' She bent down and picked up a heavy gold ring. She rolled it around in her fingers. It looked sort of like a high school or college ring but wasn't.

'That looks like the ring Victor the slug was wearing,' said Fran.

'Yes, it does.' Kitty turned the ring around in her fingers. There was a large deep-blue oval gemstone in the center and some writing around the finely scrolled edges.

'What's it say?'

'BKA Championship,' Kitty replied. 'And the year.' She squinted as she inspected the inner band. The name Manchester was etched inside. 'Eighteen-carat gold.' This was one valuable ring.

Fran shrugged. 'Toss it. In the fountain. If it belongs to Victor Cornwall he can jump in after it.' She made a grab for the ring but Kitty pulled her hand back. 'I'm hoping he can't swim.'

Kitty slid the ring over her finger. Definitely too big for a woman and too manly. It did look like the ring Victor Cornwall had been playing with. 'We should return it to him.'

'What?'

'You heard me. Come on, we'll ask for his room number at reception.'

'Have you lost your mind?' Fran yelped as she ran after Kitty. 'I'm telling you – toss it. Throw it in the fountain. Throw it in the trash. Throw it in his face. Better yet, let me do it.' She yanked Kitty to a halt a step from the front desk. 'But do not give it back to that dirt bag.'

The receptionist watching them had an uneasy look on her face. Kitty feared the woman had already labeled them as *trouble* guests.

Kitty took a breath and approached. 'We found this.' Kitty held the ring out in the palm of her hand. 'I believe it belongs to our friend—'

'Huh!' Fran snorted from behind.

'Our *friend*, Victor Cornwall.' Why did the name sound familiar the more she said it? 'But I'm afraid I've forgotten his room number.'

The receptionist glanced at the ring. 'I saw you two talking to your *friend* earlier.'

Was that a look of mockery on the woman's face? wondered Kitty. Nonetheless, the woman's hands ran over the keyboard as her eyes scanned the computer screen. 'Mr Cornwall is in suite 304.'

'Thanks,' said Kitty. That should only be a few doors down from their own room.

'My pleasure,' replied the receptionist.

OK, that time Kitty definitely noticed a mocking tone. But she didn't have time to deal with that. They would return Victor

Cornwall's ring and make nice. Surely he'd be grateful. The ring must hold a lot of sentimental value to him if it was a real championship ring of some sort. And he probably wasn't such a bad guy after all. They'd just gotten off on the wrong foot.

She'd show Fran. If you simply act nice and are willing to rise to every occasion, you can bring out the best in anyone. Even Victor Cornwall. 'Come on,' she said sternly. Kitty edged past a well-stocked housekeeping cart in the hallway and stopped outside suite 304. Their own suite was around the corner. 'This is it.' She knocked and waited. 'Mr Cornwall?'

'No one's home,' Fran said. 'Let's go. Leave the ring outside the door if you must but let's get out of here.'

'Wait,' said Kitty. 'I think I heard something.' She pressed her ear to the door. 'I thought I heard a whimper.' She knocked harder. 'Mr Cornwall? It's me, Katherine Karlyle.'

'He doesn't know your name.'

'Oh, right.' They hadn't actually been introduced. Kitty tiptoed over to the housekeeping cart. There was a keycard attached to a coiled red rubber key ring hooked over the handle of a feather duster. 'Bingo,' she whispered.

'What are you doing?'

Kitty shushed her and pointed at the open door across the hall. No doubt the housekeeper was inside. Kitty lifted the key ring and slid the keycard over the lock to Vic's room. There was a satisfactory click as the unseen bolt drew back. Kitty smiled and slowly pushed open the door.

'Mr Cornwall? It's Kitty Karlyle.' Kitty stepped inside and Fran followed. The dimly lit room was expansive and well-appointed, with a small marble tiled foyer. Kitty hoped their own room was this nice. The bathroom was to the left. The door was ajar and the room was empty. At least she didn't have to worry about catching him in the tub.

Louvered closet doors hung open, revealing several shirts and a couple of jackets on hangars. A brown suitcase sat on the ground in the near corner.

Kitty froze. 'Did you hear that?' It was a weird whimpering sound and it was coming from the other side of the wall.

Fran nodded and followed closely behind Kitty as she turned the corner into the bedroom. The shades were pulled tight. A bedside lamp with a buttery-yellow shade was turned on, giving off a soft glow. Victor Cornwall lay atop the king-sized bed, his feet dangling over the edge. The covers were pulled back. Four king-sized pillows leaned against the headboard, two per side. Oddly, one was missing its white-and gold-striped pillowcase.

Vic's shirt was untucked from his slacks and his shoes were on the floor below his feet. Vic's massive poodles stood atop the bed hovering near his face. Their combined four eyes followed the women as closely and carefully as they were watching the pair of dogs. Were they vicious or gentle as proverbial poodles? Time would tell. Kitty hoped that time wouldn't include a trip to the ER to have stitches laced up her calf.

'Man, you are one freaky dude.' Fran shook her head.

Vic's left hand seemed to be clutching at the bed sheets. His right hand was clenched around a very expensive-looking pen.

'I don't think he can hear you,' Kitty whispered.

'What do you mean?' Fran crossed her arms over her chest and frowned.

'I mean, I think he's dead.' Something definitely did not look right.

Fran leaned in closer, her brow furrowing. 'Dead?'

Kitty tiptoed as close as she dared. 'Victor? Mr Cornwall?' The big dogs shuffled their paws and sniffed in her direction. His shirt was unbuttoned down to his navel. His belly button was an innie and then Kitty wondered why, at a time like this, she'd even made note of it. Kitty then noticed that his neck was all splotchy and purple. And wet. Kitty inched closer still.

'Be careful, Kitty. You don't know what the man or those dogs will do.'

The dog on the right growled as if on cue.

'It's OK, big guy,' Kitty replied, putting forward a placating hand. 'I just want to check on your master, OK?' She leaned over Victor. His eyes were half-open but Kitty was pretty sure he wasn't looking at anything, at least not of this world.

'Better call an ambulance.' Kitty sighed and took a step back. A wave of nausea hit her like a slap and she sensed that her lunch was about to make a repeat visit to her mouth. 'And the police,' she instructed Fran. 'I believe Victor Cornwall has been murdered.'

FIVE

'Oh, this is so not good,' squeaked Fran.

'Certainly not for Victor Cornwall,' Kitty agreed. Seeing herself reflected in the mirror above the dresser, Kitty realized she was looking almost as bad as Victor.

'No.' Fran shook her head in disbelief. She looked as pale as Kitty, as if all the blood had drained to her toes. 'Don't you see?' Fran said, her voice sounding squeezed. 'I told the sleaze to drop dead – in front of witnesses!'

'But, Fran—'

'And now he *is* dead.' Fran was wringing her hands. 'What are people going to think?'

'Relax,' said Kitty, taking Fran's trembling hands. 'People aren't going to think anything. Besides, you've been with me the whole time.' She scanned the room. There was a magazine spilled open on the floor beside the night table and a half-empty glass on top of it. An open black leather-bound checkbook was on the desk with the corner of a torn check remaining on the open page.

Near Victor's bed were two plush dog beds, six foot in diameter, that appeared to be upholstered in real mink. If not, it was a very good imitation. Several gold-leaf bordered white china dog dishes lay on a mat near the kitchenette consisting of a built-in mini-fridge, microwave, sink and coffee maker.

'Is it my fault he's dead?' asked Fran. 'Did I put some sort of curse on him?'

'Of course not,' replied Kitty. 'Don't be ridiculous. You're not some kind of witch doctor.' Fran was from the Caribbean. Birthplace of witch doctors, according to all the cheesy old movies on late-night TV that Jack liked to watch. But telling someone to drop dead didn't make it happen. Did it? No, people would be falling like flies. Besides, Victor Cornwall hadn't simply dropped dead. Kitty was sure he'd had help.

Kitty dug into her purse, looking for her cell phone. Something loud, a cough or a sneeze, broke the gloomy atmosphere like a sudden clap of thunder. Fran shouted and the dogs started barking. Kitty spun on her heels. 'That sounded like it came from over there.' She pointed toward the heavy brocaded black curtains.

Fran nodded. Her eyes had transmogrified into big white golf balls.

Kitty shushed the dogs and stepped to the curtains. 'H-hello?' she said tentatively. There was a scraping metallic sound in response. She rushed to pull back the drapes, her hand trembling. Peering out, she discovered there was a large balcony with a seating area outside that housed two chairs and a square table. Kitty placed her hand on the sliding glass door, partly to steady herself and partly because she knew she was going to have to go out there.

The door slid open easily. It hadn't been locked.

The balcony was deserted. Kitty didn't know whether to be disappointed or relieved. But at least there were no more dead bodies.

The chill evening air wrapped around her like a blanket left out overnight. The resort grounds were reasonably well lit but there were plenty of dark places where a person or persons could hide. All of the balconies on this side of the building jutted out and were attached to each other. One of the chairs on Victor's balcony was pushed up with its back against the right-side railing. Kitty stepped up on the chair and carefully leaned over to get a better look at the room next door. The patio was a mirror image of this one. The room appeared unoccupied – at least, no light spilled out from the cracks in the curtains. Its occupants could be out to dinner. She found the same thing on the left side.

Could Victor Cornwall's killer have escaped this way?

'Katherine Karlyle,' hissed Fran, 'what are you doing? Get in here.'

'I'm coming.' Kitty scanned the grounds once more then reluctantly turned back. 'Fran, I think somebody – like a murderer – could get away from this room by leapfrogging the balconies.'

Kitty stepped inside. 'It might be dangerous, but I'll bet that's what—' She froze. A young woman in a gray housekeeping uniform with white trim was standing inside the door. Several plush white towels were draped over her left arm. Long, straight blonde hair fell below her shoulders. She looked like somebody's trophy wife more than a maid. And with that creamy Nordic skin of hers, she reminded Kitty of someone she would rather not be reminded of.

'What are you doing?' The young lady scrunched up her face. Definitely a northern European accent.

'Please, you don't want to come any closer.' Kitty held up her hands as if to ward her off. The woman ignored her and stepped around the corner, taking in the dogs and the body of Victor Cornwall. The housekeeper's horror-film-caliber scream set the dogs to howling in unison once more. Were Victor Cornwall's dogs always this touchy?

Sheesh, thought Kitty, why hadn't they howled like this when their master was being murdered? Or had they? But then, wouldn't someone in one of the other rooms have heard something? Not necessarily, Kitty supposed. As she'd discovered, the rooms on either side might be vacant or their occupants out. The resort did seem to have thick walls and doors. It was a luxury spa, after all, and would, by its design, be filled with potentially loud pets. There was probably a lot of soundproofing between the conjoining rooms.

Victor could have cried for help and never been heard.

The poodle scream-and-howl fest was all it took to set Fran off again because she was screaming at the top of her lungs, too. And with all those beads shaking in her head, it sounded like a horror movie on a dark and stormy night.

Kitty's head throbbed as she urgently jabbed at the numbers on her phone.

'Please step away from the body.' Stern basso words cut through the air like a sharp-edged saber.

Kitty looked up, startled. She didn't realize she had been standing so close to the body. Victor Cornwall's left hand was close enough to reach out and caress her legs. The very thought of it made her skin crawl. Not that he'd likely be doing any reaching out and touching. Unless he was part zombie.

The muzzle of a gun pointed at the space between Kitty's eyes. She took an immediate and exaggerated step to the left. Guns sort of had that effect on her.

She held up her hands, one clutching her phone, the other Victor Cornwall's ring. 'OK, OK. Everything is all right.' Well, sort of. She guessed that depended on one's point of view. Victor Cornwall might have another opinion on the subject. 'In fact,' she wiggled her phone in the air, 'I was just going to call you. Well, the police.' Though this guy was dressed in a tan-and-black uniform and shiny black lace-ups, he looked more like the private security variety rather than the officially sanctioned police type. She should know – she was engaged to a cop.

Speaking of which, Kitty wished Jack was here. The house-keeper had fled and Fran was standing as stiff and stern as a library entrance statue – no use at all.

The security guard spoke into a small black walkie-talkie he'd unclipped from his shirt. 'Hey, Penny. This is Howie. You'd better call the police and an ambulance pronto. And tell Mr Ruggiero.' He clicked off and shook his head. 'Boy, he's sure not going to be happy.'

Kitty wasn't feeling so happy herself. 'Would you mind putting that thing away – or at least not pointing it between my eyes?' This guy looked a little skittish. One false move and she could be toast. No, make that Swiss cheese.

'Oh, sorry.' He glanced at his weapon, looking suddenly rather abashed. He lowered the handgun to his side.

Kitty raised her eyebrows in Fran's direction.

Fran shrugged almost imperceptibly. 'Yes, don't shoot her. After all, it's my fault he's dead.'

'Fran!' Oh, sure, now she decides to talk – and stick her foot in her mouth. And possibly get them both impulsively shot down as likely murder suspects.

Kitty took a step forward. Not a good move. She stopped as the guy once more sighted his gun on her then Fran, wavering between the two of them as if unsure who to shoot first. 'She's kidding. Well, not kidding exactly.' Kitty managed a smile that she hoped would keep the two of them alive long enough to clarify the situation. She took a calming breath and started again. 'Look, let me explain. It's like this. That guy,' she pointed to the dead man, 'was acting like a jerk.' She just realized what an awful thing she'd said about a dead man. She'd always heard you never speak ill of the dead. 'I mean, no disrespect or anything, but he kind of was acting like a jerk.'

'Kitty—' Fran started.

'No, no.' Kitty gestured with her hands for Fran to stop interrupting. 'Let me finish.'

She turned back to the security guard with a renewed smile.
'Anyway, Fran said he should drop dead and—' She gestured
grandly toward the bed and the body of Victor Cornwall. Was it
possible that he was looking deader by the minute? 'Well, you
can see for yourself. This is how we found him. We came to
return his ring. He dropped it.' Kitty held the ring out in her
open hand. 'See? This ring.'

The security man chewed his lips a moment as he cautiously
leaned in to get a better look at the ring.

What? Kitty thought. Did he think it was a bomb or
something?

'Yeah, all right.' He lowered the black menace. 'You mean
he's really dead?' He turned two shades paler than he already
had been.

'I-I think so,' Kitty gulped. 'We'll have to wait for the
paramedics or a doctor to tell us for sure.' The poor guy. He'd
probably never seen a dead body before. Despite having pulled
a gun on her, he didn't seem like a bad fellow. He was of average
build and average height with brown eyes and medium brown
hair that fell onto a slightly sloping forehead.

Altogether a rather ordinary and harmless-looking man – when
he wasn't training a deadly weapon on you. He had a wide, flat
nose and broad cheeks. Scraggly sideburns appeared to be struggling to grow out and down his jaw. A plastic black nametag
attached to the left side of his shirt had his name, Howie
Patterson, in white block letters. Kitty estimated him to be in
his early thirties and, judging from his accent, she figured he
was from the Midwest somewhere, maybe Toledo or Detroit.
Howie Patterson wasn't wearing a wedding band so he was
probably single.

'And listen,' he said, his eyes imploring them in what Kitty
thought was a rather odd turn of events as the sounds of many
running feet approached them from out in the hall, 'please don't
tell anyone, especially Mr Ruggiero, that I pulled my gun on you
ladies. Management doesn't like it when I pull it out of its holster.'

'Well . . .' began Kitty, rather unsure what to say.

'But I like to keep it with me,' he confessed, patting the tan leather holster at his left hip attached to a matching leather belt. 'There are a lot of animals around here and you never know when one might become dangerous.'

Kitty and Fran shared a smile. 'We promise,' Kitty said. The security guard would owe her. He could become her eyes and ears. Something told her she was going to need an extra pair of each.

Howie seemed uncertain what to do.

'Really, we won't tell,' Fran said.

'OK.' Howie dropped his eyes to the ground. 'It's not a real gun anyway. It's a tranquilizer pistol, see?' He aimed the barrel at Kitty's eyes and she ducked. What was it with this guy always aiming that thing between her eyeballs?

'I see! I see! Please,' she said, motioning with her hands, 'put that thing away.' She had thought the gun looked different somehow but hadn't been able to put her finger on it. Despite Jack being a member of the police department she knew little about weapons and planned to keep it that way. Jack had taken her to the shooting range once despite her resistance and she'd cringed every time a gun went off. Kitty had refused to try shooting no matter how much Jack insisted it was safe. He argued that she might need to defend herself someday. She argued that it was his job to make sure that need never arose.

Howie slid the pistol back into its holster. A moment later Victor Cornwall's hotel room filled with police and emergency medical personnel.

SIX

K itty woke with a start. Somebody was banging on the door. She reached from under the covers and twisted the face of the hotel alarm clock in her direction. It was nearly seven-thirty. She hadn't slept in this late since . . . well, she couldn't even remember since when.

Her arm fell over the edge of the bed. Fred immediately covered it in slobber. Somewhere in the distance she heard Barney mewl.

They were looking for their breakfast. Her pets rarely ate this late. Pets have internal clocks that tell them precisely when their supposed 'masters' should be feeding them their royal breakfasts. Kitty's dog and cat were no exception.

She said good morning to Fred, told Barney to hold his horses – probably an impossibility for a cat – and rolled over on her side. Fran was snoring away. Kitty could only marvel. She'd tossed and turned all night. How did Fran manage to shut out the world like that? And could she teach her the trick?

Kitty fought to free her legs from the tangle of covers that had snared her in the night. The banging had started up again. Good grief.

A quick glimpse of her reflection in the mirrored closet door elicited a 'Yikes!' Her hair looked like she'd spent the night with her head thrust out the window of a fast-moving commuter train. The bags under her eyes looked large enough to hold groceries for a family of four. Her Garfield pajamas were rumpled and sagging. Perfect. She ran a finger through her hair just for fun and shuffled to the door. The banging picked up as if whatever fool was out there had sensed her approach and was leading the orchestra to its crescendo.

Whoever it was had succeeded in giving her a throbbing headache and Kitty was going to give them an earful for their trouble. She hurried to undo the chain and slowly pulled open the door. 'You!' She was gripping the door handle so hard she feared either the handle or her fingers would break. 'What are you doing here?'

'I told you we'd start filming this morning. Don't be such a fusspot.' Steve abruptly pushed in, dressed in a yellow-and-black gingham shirt with the top three buttons undone and a pair of charcoal-gray slacks.

Kitty went tumbling backward, barely managing to maintain her footing. Good thing the edge of the dresser had been there to slam into her tailbone, saving her from possibly falling on the soft and dangerous carpet. Pain shot up her spine and stars circled her eyes and nose.

She was about to let loose on Steve when Greg Clifton, the director, Julie McConnell, his assistant and lover, a cameraman whose name she kept forgetting, some new woman holding a long pole from which extended two bright lights, Artie, the sound recorder, and one of the Santa Monica Film Studios gofers all came bursting into the room as one.

Yikes again.

Kitty gasped. 'What is going on? What are you people doing here?' A bloodcurdling scream came from behind and Kitty instinctively turned.

Fran was sitting up, wearing a well-worn gray short-sleeve Bob Marley T-shirt that she often slept in. She took in the scene, dived under the covers and pulled a pillow over her head. 'Go away!' she hollered. Smothered by the pillow, she might as well have been whispering in her sleep for all the effect her words had.

Kitty thought Fran might have also muttered something about not even having her extensions in yet but she couldn't be certain. An exploratory trip to the bathroom would clear that up. Fran liked to drape her hair extensions over the towel rack back home in their shared bathroom. There was no reason to think she wouldn't be doing the same thing here. Fran considered all space her personal space.

In any case, no one was leaving their room despite Kitty's demands.

'Somebody pull open those draperies,' ordered Greg. 'I'm not getting enough light over here. Kitty's face looks terrible.' He was in full director mode now. 'Where's my meter? Get me a light reading!'

Kitty was about to vehemently object to that last statement when she caught another glimpse of herself in the mirror over the refrigerator. OK, so he was right about her face. The young gofer, a timid woman in a blue peasant dress, whom Kitty had seen around the studio, hurried to obey Greg. Bright light coming in from the east seared Kitty's eyes before she could argue against opening the curtains. It was like somebody had just dropped her eyeballs into a frying pan full of hot canola oil. 'Ouch!' She covered her eyes with her fingers.

Fred barked.

'Please, Greg,' Kitty implored. 'Not now. Turn off the lights and that camera.' She pointed angrily at the camera operator, who did not so much as flinch. Apparently he was well aware that the only person he had to answer to was Greg.

'What's the problem?' asked the director. He looked genuinely puzzled. 'I mean, we're here to film. That's what this whole trip is all about.' He looked to Julie for support and she nodded vigorously.

She would, thought Kitty sourly. Even Fred was bobbing his head up and down. 'Traitor,' growled Kitty. Fred wagged his tail happily. He was a hard one to insult. She tried pleading with Greg. After all, he always seemed so level-headed – certainly more so than Steve. 'Please, Greg, this is not a good time. There was a murder here last night. Around the corner from our room. Fran and I found the body. We were up all night being interrogated and answering endless questions.'

'I know. I heard about that. Who hasn't? It's big news.' Greg was grinning. 'Isn't it great? Talk about your luck. I mean, it's too bad and all, but still.'

'Greg,' Kitty repeated slowly. 'A man was killed last night.' Had he not understood?

'Yeah.' He rubbed his hands together. 'Think of the ratings boost!'

'Julie, can't you talk some sense into him?'

Julie shrugged. 'It's never worked for me in the past.'

'OK, folks, that's all for now. Let's get moving,' interjected Steve. 'Kitty's got a cooking demonstration at ten o'clock.'

'A cooking demonstration?' gasped Kitty. 'Are you crazy? I'm not prepared to do a cooking demonstration.' Kitty pulled at her pajamas. She heard Fran mutter a muffled something about please getting all these people out of here followed by a string of curses that she might have picked up from Jamaican pirates. Even they might have blushed at some of her words.

'Haven't you looked at your itinerary?' Greg asked.

'Itinerary?' Kitty's brow furrowed.

Greg snapped his fingers. 'Somebody hand Kitty a shooting schedule.'

The gofer grabbed a folded sheet from her purse and thrust it in Kitty's fingers. Her eyes quickly scanned the typed paper. 'I can't possibly do all this.' This schedule was packed. It barely gave her time to breathe. 'I'm supposed to be here spending some quality time with my pets. Remember?' She turned on Steve. 'This was your idea.'

Steve nodded. 'I know.' His finger thwacked the schedule in

Kitty's hand. 'Look, you and the beasties are scheduled for a session with Doctor Newhart at nine.'

'Doctor Newhart is here, too?'

Steve tapped his Rolex. 'Better get moving, Kitty.'

'Did I hear someone call a Kitty?' a voice boomed from the right.

Kitty's jaw dropped. 'Mom? Dad? What are you doing here?'

'Hi-ya, Kitten.' Her mother and father stood shoulder to shoulder in the narrow doorway. In his left hand her father was clutching a dozen white roses. He never visited without bringing a dozen, always white. And he always called her Kitten. He and he alone. 'Steve invited us.'

'Yes, Mr Barnhard was gracious enough to ask us to come and we've been given such a lovely room. Thank you, again, Mr Barnhard.' Kitty's mom, Paula, was curvy and vivacious, with bouncy light brown hair that curled forward from her ears. She had an easy smile and rarely raised her voice.

Paula Karlyle was the perfect person to run the front of house at Newport Bistro, her mother and father's fine-dining establishment located in what was known as the dock and dine area of Newport Beach.

Steve beamed. 'My pleasure.'

Kitty groaned. If she could get Steve alone somewhere dark and quiet – away from witnesses – she had some thanking she'd like to do to him herself.

'Greg, I expect some great material out of this,' Steve said. 'We're only here for a couple of days and the budget on this is astronomical, despite the spa's generous comps. So I expect results. I'm off to brunch with Roger and the babies.'

Oh, great. Steve had brought his smarmy French *ami*, Roger Matisse, with him. But who were the babies?

Fran jumped from her bed, tugged her T-shirt down to protect her image and grabbed her suitcase from the corner near the window. She started yanking open dresser drawers and throwing clothes inside. Half of which weren't even hers.

'What are you doing?' demanded Kitty.

'Going home,' cried Fran without stopping. 'This is not the vacation I signed up for.'

'Oh, no you don't.' Kitty slammed the drawer shut and locked her fingers around the handle of Fran's suitcase. 'If I've got to be here then so do you. After all, it's your fault we're here in the first place.'

'My fault?' Fran's hands flew to her chest.

'Yes, your fault. Who else's fault could it be? You're the one who insisted Fred and Barney were unhappy – that they needed some kind of therapy. And, Miss Big Mouth, you went and mentioned just that to Steve Barnhard of all people.' She threw her hands in the air. 'And look what you've gotten us into!'

Fran took the opportunity to snatch back her suitcase. 'Yeah, well. Tell me all about it when you get home. We'll throw back a couple of margaritas and put this all behind us. Have a good laugh.'

There was no reasoning with Fran when she was in a dither and not thinking rationally. Kitty had seen it before. It was time for her ace in the hole. 'I don't think the police would like it if we left.' Kitty folded her arms across her chest. 'Do I have to remind you what the police chief said?'

Fran groaned and squeezed her eyes shut. Kitty smiled, knowing she'd won. 'Mom, Dad, I'd like you to meet Fran Earhart. She's the woman I told you about who's my new roommate.'

Her parents expressed their pleasure in meeting Fran. Kitty took the flowers her father brought and stuck them in the melted remains of the ice bucket. 'Fran's spending the weekend here with me and the pets, too.'

Fran limply shook her parents' proffered hands and flopped into a burgundy-colored pleated velvet wingback chair near the sliding door.

'Come on down to Newport Bistro sometime. Lunch is on the house,' said Mark Karlyle. Her father, despite having been a chef and restaurant owner, had managed to maintain a slim, wiry physique. He kept his walnut-brown hair never any longer than two inches and he was more comfortable in his chef's clothes than anything else. He'd been known to wear his chef pants and jacket lounging around at home on his days off. While he was known to be temperamental in the kitchen, away from the heat of the ovens and grills he was a pussycat.

The offer of a free meal seemed to have lifted Fran's spirits.

'Give me a few minutes to get dressed,' Kitty said. 'Then we can meet for coffee in the lobby.'

Her parents agreed and waved goodbye. Kitty grabbed some fresh clothes and headed for the bathroom. 'I need a shower,' she said. 'I need to wash the nightmare that was yesterday off me.'

'Understood,' said Greg. He motioned for the crew to follow. As a unit, Artie the sound engineer, the cameraman and the woman working the lights squeezed through the bathroom door behind her.

'Get out!' ordered Kitty, her voice echoing over the bathroom tiles as the three crew members spilled quickly back out the door as if the force of her voice had pushed them back like the wall of a category-two hurricane. 'This is *not* a reality show!'

SEVEN

'**M**iss Karlyle?'

Kitty turned. 'Yes? Can I help you?'

A swarthy middle-aged man with a razor-sharp crew-cut circling his crown and an impeccable goldenrod brown suit had timidly tapped her on the shoulder. 'I am Richard Ruggiero – Rick to my friends.' He tugged at a checkered tie with the resort logo. 'I am the manager of the Little Switzerland Resort and Spa.'

Kitty smiled as she shook his hand. He seemed pleasant enough. All that hair that should have been on his shiny pate seemed to have relocated to his eyebrows. And though he had a bit of a paunch, it didn't look like anything that a few pushups and a regular jog around the expansive grounds wouldn't cure.

'We hope you are enjoying your stay.' He hesitated. 'Despite the unpleasantness.' His midnight-blue eyes darted side to side then stopped, honing in on her like the twin barrels of a Remington side-by-side shotgun.

Unpleasantness? The first thing that came to Kitty's mind was the invasion of her room that morning. Then she remembered. 'Oh, you mean the murder.'

The manager pumped his hands up and down. 'Yes.' He looked about nervously. The lobby was filled with guests. 'The unpleasantness. I hope it won't interfere in any way with your cooking program.'

'I shouldn't think so,' Kitty reassured him, her voice automatically lowering a notch. 'We're enjoying being here at your resort as a special location for *The Pampered Pet*. And while Mr Cornwall's death is tragic, I don't expect it to interfere with our plans.' Truth be told, if Steve and Greg had their way it would become a key component. But Kitty was not about to let that happen.

The manager nodded. 'I'm happy to hear it, Miss Karlyle. We are honored to have you. I and my staff shall do our best to see that you are allowed to film undisturbed.'

Kitty shrugged and smiled lightly. 'I appreciate that.'

'And we shall do our very best to keep the overly inquisitive press from disturbing you and your crew as well.'

'I don't expect any reporters will be bothering us. A cooking show for pets is hardly front-page reading.'

'Of course. It's just that with the dead man being somewhat of a minor celebrity himself, it seems the murder has taken on extra significance to the news hounds.' He rubbed his hands together with satisfaction. 'I've instructed security to keep them out of the hotel and off the property completely.'

'Minor celebrity?'

'Didn't you know, Miss Karlyle? Mr Cornwall was a speaker and author. He had written several financial and self-help books and starred in a number of infomercials some years ago.' Mr Ruggiero frowned. 'Until he went to prison, that is.'

A light bulb slowly came to life in Kitty's head. So that was why the name sounded familiar. Victor Cornwall. She remembered now. He had been one of those self-proclaimed financial and self-help gurus that dot the late night and early morning TV landscape. There had been some sort of scandal but she couldn't remember the details.

A young woman at the front desk called the manager's name. He held up a finger. 'I'm afraid I am needed.' He clasped Kitty's hands in his. 'Please let me or my staff know if there is anything at all that we can do for you. We wish your stay here to be happy and successful.'

Kitty promised she would. 'Don't worry, Mr Ruggiero,' she said, 'I'm sure the police will get the mystery of who killed Victor Cornwall wrapped up quickly. I don't suppose they have made an arrest yet?'

He shook his head in the negative as he dropped her hands and marched toward the front desk. 'I'm afraid not. And please,' he shouted over his retreating backside, 'call me Rick.'

'S'cuse me.'

Somebody tugged at Kitty's sleeve. She was tired and hungry and being pulled in so many directions at once that she felt like she was being drawn and quartered. After all, she'd had barely half a cup of coffee with her mom and dad at a small coffee shop off the lobby. The only other nourishment since the night before had been the cherry Danish she and her mom had shared in their few moments together.

Low blood sugar sometimes made her irritable. Or it could be that her current simmering irritation stemmed from the fact that she had had no desire to be away from home in the first place, let alone dragging the crew of *The Pampered Pet* along with her on location. She turned, prepared to snap at whoever was bothering her now.

'Oh, it's you. Good morning.' It was the security guard who had caught Fran and Kitty standing over the dead Victor Cornwall in his suite the night before. He was dressed in the same uniform he had been in then.

'Good morning, ma'am.'

'Hi, Howie. I'm afraid I'm running late. I'm meeting my pets for a session at nine.' She glanced at her watch; it was a minute or two till nine now.

'I understand, ma'am.'

'Call me Kitty.'

'Yes, ma'am.' He looked at his shoes.

Kitty waited a moment longer, trying to hide her impatience, then said, 'Was there something you wanted?'

'Well,' he stammered as his feet shuffled side-to-side across the plush wool carpet, 'I saw you speaking to the manager, Mr Ruggiero, and I was wondering—'

Now she understood. 'No,' she said with a broad smile, 'don't you worry. I did not tell your boss that you pulled your tranquilizer gun on me.' She raised his chin with her forefinger. 'I made a promise, after all. And I keep my promises.'

'Thanks,' he breathed.

'No problem, Howie.' Though looking back on last night, maybe she should have let him shoot her – begged him to shoot her. One good shot from a tranquilizer gun and she would have had a far better night's sleep than she'd gotten without it. That was something to keep in mind for the next time. Shoot first, ask questions later.

She turned to leave then put on the brakes. 'Say, have you heard anything? About the murder, I mean?'

Howie shook his head. 'Nah. The police are stumped.'

'No fingerprints?'

'Bunch of them all around the room. Dog prints, too. But none they seem to be able to make heads or tails of.'

Kitty ignored the unintended pun. 'There were very pronounced red marks around his neck,' Kitty replied. 'As if he'd been strangled.'

'Yeah, I noticed that too. But Chief Mulisch says there was also a lot of dog slobber around his neck. So I guess that's messed up their chances of getting any good DNA like you hear about on TV.'

'Why do you suppose his dogs didn't protect him?' After all, Kitty would like to think that if she was being murdered good old Fred would come to her rescue.

Howie shrugged. 'It doesn't make any sense. Maybe they knew the killer. They might not have realized that their master was being offed.' He pulled an open pack of spearmint gum from his pocket and offered her a stick. She declined.

'Besides,' Howie said, peeling back the wrapper, 'I've seen those dogs around the past few days now. They're a couple of real pussycats,' he said with a boyish grin. 'They wouldn't hurt a fly.'

She considered the security guard's words for a moment. 'Howie, do you think you could get me into Mr Cornwall's room?' She batted her eyelashes.

He scrunched up his forehead. 'Now, why would you want to do that?'

She smiled as harmlessly as she could imagine. 'I'd just like a look around. That's all. See if I notice anything.'

'I don't know, Miss Karlyle—'

'Kitty, remember?'

He nodded and appeared to be caving. 'I'll see what I can do. Mind you, I'm not promising anything. It won't be easy. Chief Mulisch and his team have got that suite locked down. Mr Ruggiero says it's off limits to everybody else. Even the house-keeping staff has been ordered to stay out.'

'Thanks, Howie.' Kitty patted his arm. 'You're a sweetheart.'

'You realize that being late to a therapy session with your pets is a sign of disrespect?'

'I'm very sorry, Doctor Newhart. It's been a difficult morning.' She smiled and wiggled her fingers at Fred and Barney. Fred was ensconced on an overstuffed tan sofa against the window basking in the morning sunshine. Barney was snoozing on a small pillow in the inglenook that was bathed in equally warm light. Fred was pretty far gone himself. 'A difficult night, to be honest.'

Why did Dr Newhart always make her feel so defensive? Why did she always feel like she was having to apologize for the way she treated her pets? She was a good owner. Fred and Barney got love, warm beds and good food – great food. She had nothing to apologize for.

'You should be apologizing to Barney and Fred, Miss Karlyle, not me.' The doctor's suite had a separate sitting area complete with a gray stone-faced gas-burning fireplace. Maybe she should ask for an upgrade. Everybody's rooms seemed a tad nicer than hers.

'Oh, right. Sorry.' Kitty groaned and squeezed her hands like she was draining the very essence from a couple of Lisbon lemons. Ugh. She'd apologized again. She really couldn't help herself.

She spent the next thirty minutes playing with Fred and Barney on the floor while Dr Newhart directed the action and made occa-sional comments meant to be insightful and informative. Kitty tried not to roll her eyes, at least not in Dr Newhart's line of sight.

She and her pets were rescued by a knock at the door. It was the show's gofer, Lucy something, announcing that it was time for her ten o'clock cooking demonstration and Fred and Barney's grooming session. 'Sorry, guys,' Kitty said, giving them each a pat of farewell, 'looks like we've all got busy days ahead of us.'

Kitty raced after Lucy while a second young woman, a member of the Little Switzerland staff, escorted Fred and Barney to their next appointment.

'Wait up!' Kitty cried as Lucy quickly turned the corner of the long hallway. The main building was a maze of corridors and easy to get lost in.

Strong arms reached out and grabbed Kitty from behind, locking around her waist and pulling her back. She screamed and kicked.

'Whoa!'

The arms suddenly let go and Kitty dropped to the ground, prepared to run. 'Jack!'

He was grinning. 'I'd ask if you were surprised to see me but that seems rather obvious.' He leaned back and laughed.

She punched him in the arm. 'Don't do that.'

'Sorry,' he snickered.

'What are you doing here? Have you come to help?'

Her fiancé rubbed his upper arm where she'd punched him. 'I told you we might stop by on our way out of town, remember?' Jack shook his head.

That's when Kitty noticed Elin Nordstrom standing to the right of Jack and a step behind. The annoyingly beautiful Elin Nordstrom could have been a runway model and, in fact, had apparently done some modelling in her early days. Not that she was old now. Probably no older than Kitty.

Her teeth were too white, her hair too blonde. Her lips too full and pouty. What wasn't there to hate about this sexy Swedish import?

The lieutenant flashed her perfect white teeth and said hello. Eyes the color of blue topaz sparkled in smug amusement. She was Jack's new boss, much to Kitty's dismay. So the two of them were spending a lot of time together. Again, much to Kitty's dismay. She'd thought that problem had been solved when Nordstrom started seeing one of Jack's colleagues, but that had ended abruptly. Kitty had heard the guy had relocated to Portland. Was that to escape Nordstrom?

'Of course,' replied Kitty. Jack had said something about having to attend a law-enforcement conference in Sacramento. Had he added that Elin was driving up with him? She couldn't remember and hid her frown. 'What about Libby?' Libby was Jack's black Labrador Retriever.

'Staying at my mom's place.' Jack squeezed her arm. 'Boy, you really don't listen to a thing I say, do you?'

'I'm sorry,' Kitty said. She pushed a stray lock of hair from her face. 'It's been rather hectic today. In fact, I'm supposed to be doing a cooking demonstration that the show has arranged in about—' She checked her watch. 'Now.' She groaned. Steve and Greg were going to kill her.

'Sure,' Jack said lightly. 'We only stopped to say hi. Don't let me keep you.'

'Yes, don't let him keep you,' echoed Elin. Was she mocking Kitty now?

Kitty took a step toward Elin but Jack stepped between them and smoothed back his hair. 'Hey, I forgot to tell you: we stopped by your room. I spoke with Fran. She filled me in on what happened last night. I saw the story on the news this morning but I didn't realize that the two of you had been involved. I spoke briefly with a Chief Mulisch on the phone,' Jack went on. 'Victor Cornwall has quite a checkered past.'

So Kitty was beginning to learn. 'I wouldn't say we were involved,' answered Kitty. 'More like unfortunate bystanders.'

'Interesting that you found the body.' Elin cocked an eyebrow.

'Yes, interesting.' Kitty glared at Elin. 'Don't you have someplace to be?' She really wanted a minute alone with her fiancé. She'd give anything for a few moments alone with Jack, snuggled warmly in his arms. Over by the fireplace or, better yet, someplace quiet and secluded. Someplace without Swedish imports.

'Yes, in fact, we do. Sacramento.' Elin looked down at Kitty. 'Come on, Jack. We don't want to be late and it's a long drive.'

The two of them alone in a car for the next four or five hours. Oh, great, thought Kitty, her thoughts wandering in directions she would rather they didn't.

'There you are,' Lucy said, bursting among them like a firecracker. 'Come on, Kitty. Greg's fuming. We've got to get you to the demonstration.'

Jack and Kitty kissed quickly. 'Can't you stay?' Kitty whispered

in his ear. 'I could use your help. The police questioned us half
the night.'

'Don't worry, Kitty. The police are just doing their job. Trying
to find a killer.' His finger touched her nose. 'So let them do
their job. You concentrate on your job. Understood?'

Kitty nodded.

'There's nothing I can do here anyway. Little Switzerland is
far out of my jurisdiction. I hear Chief Mulisch runs a pretty
tight organization. I'll be home in a few days.'

Kitty said she understood. Emotions tugged at her heart as Lucy
dragged her away.

'Stay away from dead bodies and try to have fun,' called Jack.
'And keep out of trouble!'

Kitty promised she would. But trouble had other plans.

EIGHT

Elin turned to Kitty on parting. The look on her face was
one of triumph.

'You wouldn't be smiling long if I had a tranquilizer
gun in my hands,' muttered Kitty, thinking how pleasant it would
be if Elin spent the whole time snoring like a freight train in the
passenger seat next to Jack the entire way to Sacramento.

'What's that?' Lucy asked. She hustled Kitty up the aisle of
a people-and-pet-filled room, at the head of which was a temporary but well-fitted kitchen.

'Nothing,' murmured Kitty, hoping that Jack took his own
advice and stayed out of trouble too.

Greg was glaring at her. 'It's about time,' he whispered harshly.
Fran ran over to apply a fresh coat of makeup to Kitty's cheeks.
'Never mind that,' said the director. 'It's show time.' He escorted
Kitty to the center of the stage.

Steve introduced Kitty to a chef from the resort. 'He'll be
assisting you during the show.'

Fran, ignoring Greg's pleas to stop, busily dusted Kitty's face
then the chef's.

'I am Chef Henri Moutarde,' the man pronounced – rather grandly in Kitty's opinion. Was she supposed to bow or something?

'A pleasure to meet you,' she said, dodging her head in an attempt to see her reflection in the toaster. There wasn't enough makeup in the world to make up for the way she looked.

'I am the chef de cuisine.'

Kitty nodded.

'I am from Brussels, Belgium. You know the muscles from Brussels?' He flexed his arms. It really wasn't much of a sight.

'Well, I am the Mussels from Brussels,' he quipped. 'Get it? Mussels!' He scooped up a slimy blue mussel with his fingers and pressed it under Kitty's nose.

Oh, brother. Mussels were not even supposed to be on the menu for the day's cooking demonstration. Did this guy keep a bucketful around as a prop for that lame joke of his? Or was he trying to change her menu?

She'd have none of that. They would be sticking to the script whether the Mussels from Brussels liked it or not.

'Did you say mustard?' Fran dipped her makeup brush. 'Chef Mustard?' She chortled.

'Not mustard, you idiot, Moutarde,' he snapped at her.

Fran rolled her eyes out of the line of the tightly wound chef's vision. 'Sor-ry.'

Greg dragged Fran away before she could do any more damage. Kitty was forced to continue to listen to the chef de cuisine's nattering all by her lonesome while she tried to explain what they'd be preparing for the morning demonstration. The man was pompous and conceited. Steve probably adored him.

'But I don't need an assistant,' Kitty had argued, pulling Steve aside.

'You're getting one. It's called public relations. The hotel is providing us with all sorts of guest services and accommodations,' Steve shot back. 'The least we can do is be accommodating back. The manager asked if his head chef could possibly be part of the show. Am I supposed to tell the man no?'

Kitty hated it when Steve was right. Fortunately, it wasn't often.

Kitty walked back to the irksome chef, determined to make

things better. She extended her hand. 'I appreciate you lending your assistance today.'

He looked down his decidedly long and bent out of shape nose at her fingers as if they were a tangle of poisonous asps waiting to strike. 'Well, it is not my pleasure at all.'

'Excuse me?'

'I am the head chef. It is not my place to be here. Besides, I have more important things to do.'

'I-I don't know what to say—' So much for Steve's theories.

'Patty Kakes, that's Kakes with a K,' he rolled his eyes round and round, 'was supposed to be here. But no, the woman decides to take maternity leave.'

'Patty Kakes? That's funny.'

'I do not make a joke. Of course, her real name is Sherry Schwartz. Her father is a cardiologist on Long Island.'

'I-I see.'

'The woman fancies herself the *chef de pet*.' He wrapped his words in air quotes. 'She prepares the meals for the animals. I,' he boasted, 'cook for people. I don't know what Ruggiero was thinking giving the woman a job.' His fist landed on his bony hip. 'And a title. Now I must fill in for her.'

'So she's having a baby,' Kitty said, trying to find a more pleasant subject, something that wouldn't set him off further than he already was. 'That's nice.' After all, who didn't like babies? And pets?

'Delivered yesterday.' Moutarde fumed. 'She knew this demonstration was today. She couldn't wait a day?'

'Some people can be difficult.'

The chef nodded. 'Tell me about it.'

Kitty shot the AD a pleading look. Thankfully, the woman understood her silent cry for help.

Julie jumped to the front of the stage, said a few words to the audience then introduced Kitty. No sooner had she started her demonstration when a burly police officer came quietly up the side aisle. He whispered something to Lucy, who pointed him to Julie, who pointed him to Steve.

Steve uttered a few words then pointed to Fran who was sitting quietly in a molding plastic chair against the wall, her eyes half-shut. Probably dreaming about sitting on a warm Jamaican beach in a leopard-print bikini, sipping an icy margarita. Kitty hoped she'd ordered two.

Fran's eyes shot open when the burly officer leaned over and whispered in her ear. Kitty fumbled for words and dropped her spatula in a pot of boiling turkey gravy as she watched the officer escort Fran out a side exit.

Kitty could only wonder what was going on. There was an audience watching her every move. She'd prepared two dishes – one for cats and one for dogs. Stopping to field occasional questions from the audience, she forced herself to concentrate on the job at hand. It wasn't easy. Why had Fran left with a police officer? After nearly slicing her thumb off with a paring knife, Kitty felt a jab in her shoulder coming from Chef Moutarde.

'You must wear the disposable food prep gloves.' He shoved an open box of gloves at her chest.

'Ouch.' Kitty reddened and turned to the audience. 'I prefer to feel my food in my hands, beneath my fingers,' she explained, mashing the meat in her bowl.

The chef was having none of it. He shoved the box at her again. She noted he was wearing gloves. 'I am certain not everyone shares your passion for filth. In my kitchen,' he said, puffing up his chest, 'I insist that everyone wear gloves when preparing food. Even when preparing food for dogs,' he'd added rather cattily, giving his own gloved hands a snap each.

Kitty's nose twitched under the assault of the skunky odor emanating from the gloves. As much as she'd wanted to take one of those flimsy gloves and slap him with it, she smiled broadly and turned her attention back to the turkey meatloaf in her mixing bowl. She could hear the chef fuming behind her and felt an odd tingle between her shoulder blades, as if her flesh could sense that he was dreaming of drilling a long steak knife through her back to her ribs.

'Thank you, everyone,' Kitty said as she wrapped up the show. 'Please watch for episodes of my new cooking show, *The Pampered Pet*, on CuisineTV!' She finished up to a moderate round of applause and the audience began to filter out. Moutarde tossed his gloves in the trash and went off in a huff. Kitty raced after Steve who was on his way out the door with Roger Matisse. Did Steve think he was going to get away that easy?

Roger had a pair of Pembroke Welsh Corgis yipping happily at his Italian leather heels. Kitty adored Corgis. They were a beautiful breed, sable in color with white markings and a peppering of black. These pups were no exception and she would have been content to spend the day with them. Roger, on the other hand, she could live without. He was only a rung above Steve on her list of least favorite people. Maybe that was because he worked as Barbara Cartwright's personal assistant. Ms Cartwright was the celebrity chef and TV host from Great Britain who had very nearly taken Kitty's place as the new host of *The Pampered Pet*. Kitty suspected Barbara Cartwright could still be angling for the job though she had nothing concrete to base her nagging suspicions on.

Tall and slender, Roger's wavy brown hair was brushed to one side and his cheeks looked freshly shaven. When he spoke, his voice oozed a French far more accentuated than was probably natural. He and Steve were an item.

'Kitty, you remember Roger.'

'Of course, it's nice to see you again.' She bent down and gave each of the Corgis a fair scratch behind the ears, which they dutifully ate up, craning up to lick her fingers. Then again, they probably smelled turkey gravy and Chef Moutarde's mussels under her fingernails. 'Beautiful dogs you have, Roger.' So these were the babies Steve had mentioned having brunch with. She should have known.

'Thank you.' He beamed like a proud daddy. 'Care to gather up your own babies and join us for lunch?' He favored Lacoste polo shirts and Guess jeans. Today was no exception, the shirt color *du jour* being mauve.

Steve looked aghast and Kitty would have accepted if only to stick it to him but she had more important things to do. 'Sorry, I can't. Some other time, OK?'

Steve sighed with obvious relief. 'Well, if you really must—' He grabbed Roger's arm and started his escape.

'Wait a minute. What's going on?' She pulled at the back of his shirt. 'What did that police officer want with Fran?'

'I've no idea,' Steve said petulantly.

'You must know something. I saw him talking to you.'

'The police officer? He merely asked me to point out Fran

Earhart. And I did.' He shrugged. 'After that, I simply have no idea.'

He left before she could say another word. Kitty grabbed Julie. 'Do you know where Fran is?'

Julie didn't. Neither did anybody else on the crew. Kitty pulled out her cell phone and dialed Fran's number. She didn't pick up so Kitty shot her a text, which likewise went unanswered.

There was no sign of Fran back in their suite either. There was no sign of her anywhere on the resort grounds. She ran into Howie outside the main entrance patrolling aimlessly, his hands in his pockets.

'Howie. Did you see my friend, Fran? You know, my roommate. The woman you found with me in Mr Cornwall's room?'

'Sure, I saw her.' He scratched an inflamed pimple at the corner of his temple then pointed. 'I saw her get in a police car and head that way.'

Kitty's nostrils flared. Howie was chewing something minty, practically caustic. 'A police car? Do you know where they were going?'

'To the police station, I imagine.'

'Can you tell me how to get there?'

'It's up toward the center of Bern Street – you really can't miss it. Bern's one of the town's two main streets. It isn't far. You could walk there if you wanted.'

Kitty didn't want to walk.

She wanted to run.

NINE

'Is Fran Earhart here?' she asked, bursting through the door of the Little Switzerland Police Department.

A willowy brunette who'd likely seen a good forty summers stood behind a counter that faced the entrance. The tag pinned to her snug uniform identified her as a sergeant. She held a baby-blue watering can whose contents she was steadily applying to a two-foot-tall variegated Schefflera on the bookcase in the corner. Kitty was fond of the Schefflera plant, or umbrella tree as it was sometimes called, but being poisonous to cats she wasn't able to keep one in her apartment.

The sergeant set down her empty watering container and looked Kitty over. Kitty wasn't sure that she looked so good and that the results would tally in her favor. Lack of sleep, lack of food, racing a mile on foot in low heels to the LSPD. She imagined she made quite a sight. And not a pretty one. 'She's with the chief,' the woman replied, sitting back down at the chair and placing her hands on the counter. 'Anything I can help you with, ma'am?'

'I—' What should she say? Should she demand the police let Fran go? The sergeant obviously wouldn't listen. Kitty bit her lip. In her race to the rescue she had not given a moment's thought to what she would do or say once she got to the station. And now, here she was. She went for the truth. 'Fran Earhart is a friend. I heard she was at the station. I wanted to check on her.'

The sergeant pointed to a pair of simple steel chairs near the window. 'Have a seat. I expect Harry won't keep her much longer.' She cast a quick look at the door behind her; its glass was stenciled with the name Harry Mulisch, Chief of Police, then locked eyes with Kitty. 'Unless he's planning on tossing her in the clink.'

Kitty gasped.

'Relax.' The sergeant waved her hand. 'Just a joke. Sorry. Have a seat.'

Great. Little Switzerland police were also standup, or in this case, sit-down comedians. Not that there was anything funny about Fran getting arrested. It was bad enough that she'd been hauled downtown. Even a downtown as quaint and charming as Little Switzerland, California.

Kitty sat. The chair was hard and cold. In a town like this, she half-expected they'd have kept with the theme and provided some bench seating designed to look like a ski lift. Maybe have a hot toddy nook set up in the corner for guests.

Running out of thoughts, she stared out the door at the tourists walking by, dressed to suit the bracing fall weather. She jiggled her feet and bit her fingernails, only quitting when the woman behind the desk caught her doing it. Sure, thought Kitty, you try sitting here waiting impatiently and worriedly for your best friend to come out from being interrogated by the police – the chief of police, no less. See if you wouldn't be biting your nails, too.

'Fran!' Kitty pushed out of her chair, sending it bouncing off the cinder block wall. The sergeant shot her a dirty look but said nothing.

Fran slumped out looking tired but managing a light smile. Her clingy blue dress looked a little more wrinkled but there were no signs of her having been strapped to the rack, doused with burning oil or water-boarded.

'Are you OK?'

Fran said she was. 'What are you doing here?'

'Checking on you, of course. I saw the police take you away.'

'Yeah, they had a few questions for me.'

A stern-looking man had followed her out. This had to be Chief Harry Mulisch. He handed a bent manila file folder to the desk sergeant and hooked a thumb inside his black leather belt.

Like the desk sergeant, he wore dark slacks with billowy cargo pockets, a royal blue shirt and a blue, red and white striped polyester tie, all wrapped up with a thick black leather holster around his middle. The holster held a veritable arsenal including a small black club and a very lethal-looking black-and-chrome pistol.

Black epaulets highlighted his shoulders. The only noticeable difference between the two officers was the increased number of medals and patches on the chief's larger shirt. It was all very Switzerland, in Kitty's opinion, and probably done with a nod toward the tourists that kept this town alive. At least they weren't forced to wear lederhosen. Or was that German?

'I don't get it,' Kitty said, getting back on point. She'd let the uniform distract her. 'Why down here at the police station? And in the middle of taping our segment?'

She looked from Fran to the chief of police. The police chief looked like a former college football player, big but slowly going to fat, with a pleasant face and intimidating eyes. 'Why not ask you back at the resort when we had some time? Besides, what could you possibly tell the police that you – we – haven't already told them?'

Chief Mulisch hadn't been present last night when they were questioned but surely the officer that had done the questioning had asked everything that could possibly be asked. Wouldn't he have filed a report or verbally filled the chief in afterward on what they'd told him?

'Well . . .' Fran's eyes took a sudden interest in the flat blue-gray carpet.

'Is everything all right? Should I call Jack? He could help, I'm sure of it.' Kitty faced the chief. 'My—' She cleared her throat and stuck out her chin. 'My husband, Jack, is a state police official.' OK, a slight exaggeration there.

'But Jack isn't—' started Fran. Her face betrayed her confusion.

'Isn't here, yes, but I'm sure he wouldn't mind driving up.' Kitty finished Fran's sentence for her. OK, so she'd revised it some. 'He could be here in an hour.' Of course, that would take a supersonic jet or a time machine but technically it *was* feasible.

'Hold on a second.' Chief Mulisch's ears had perked up. 'Your husband is named Jack? Jack Young?'

Kitty said it was.

'That's funny.' He scratched the side of his ski slope-like nose. 'I spoke with a Jack Young a bit earlier.'

'You talked to Jack?' Kitty felt her face heating up. 'My Jack?' Her mouth went dry. Jack had said he'd called the department. How could she forget?

He nodded. 'Sure did. He called my office this morning. And he didn't say anything about the two of you being married. Only said his fiancée was staying at the Little Switzerland Resort and Spa and saying how he'd heard about the murder and was wondering what was going on. He asked me to fill him in as a professional courtesy.' Chief Mulisch stared flatly at Kitty. 'He told me he was a detective down in Los Angeles.'

'Well, you see, what I meant was . . .'

Chief Mulisch waved a broad tanned hand, shooing them toward the door out to the street. Kitty noticed a plain gold wedding band on his finger. 'I think we're done here. Miss Earhart.' He turned to Fran. 'Don't forget what I said.' Fran nodded once.

'And you,' he said, turning to Kitty. 'I'd be extra careful if I were you.'

'Extra careful?' Kitty said, her hand on the door. 'What do

you mean?' Was that a threat of some sort? Was he thinking she might be involved in Victor Cornwall's murder?

'Because,' he glanced at the desk sergeant and there was an unmistaken twinkle in his crisp blue eyes, 'if you are married to Jack Young, I'd be very careful that his fiancé doesn't find out about you.'

'His fian—'

Chief Mulisch broke into laughter. He sounded much like her Lab, Fred, when he barked at the squirrels in Griffith Park. 'Yeah, I hear she's staying at the resort, too. I'd hate to get a nine-one-one call to break up a cat fight between the two of you.'

Kitty stormed out the door, her face vivid red. Fran raced after her. 'Boy, that was something,' Fran said, falling into step beside Kitty.

Kitty stopped on the sidewalk and looked pointblank at her friend. 'What was that all about, anyway?' She gestured toward the police station and saw that Chief Mulisch had his nose pressed against the glass and appeared to be smirking. Kitty spun Fran around. 'Let's keep walking.'

Fran let herself be pushed down the street until a metal sign caught her attention. 'Food!' she called, pointing to an incongruous-looking English pub-styled restaurant with indoor/outdoor seating. 'I need nourishment. And drink.' She dropped down at an empty table outside without waiting for a hostess to seat them. 'Mostly drink.'

Fran waved to a sprightly young waitress in a white shirt and black skirt that was a little too short in Kitty's opinion. But then, if she'd legs like that she might have worn something just as short. With her peroxide-blonde hair, the waitress looked like a Hollywood refugee but her accent leaned more toward Valley Girl.

'Now,' said Kitty, laying her hands on the tabletop once their food had arrived, 'do you want to tell me why the chief of police had you pulled out of my cooking demonstration and dragged down to headquarters, Fran?'

Fran toyed with her half-empty beer mug and snatched up a chip. 'You're not going to like this.'

Kitty stabbed at her salad, coming up with a cucumber slice. 'So far, there isn't much that I'm liking about this trip so I don't think anything you have to say now is going to make things any worse.'

She was wrong.

TEN

'The police think I might have had something to do with Victor Cornwall's murder.' She downed the rest of her beer and waved for another.

'But that's crazy.' Kitty signaled for their waitress to ignore Fran's request. Two beers were enough for lunch. She needed Fran to keep her wits about her. 'You were with me the entire time. Besides, what possible reason could you have for killing Vic? We saw the guy for two seconds in the lobby – you called him a jerk and we left. End of story.' Kitty's head was wagging but she stopped when she saw the look in Fran's eyes. 'Fran?' she drew the word out. 'What is it that you aren't telling me?'

Fran took a heavy breath. 'I've never told you much about my family, have I?'

'No, not really.' Kitty had never met Fran's mother and father and only knew the basics. She hadn't known Fran that long.

'Dad had a printing business in Kingston. Mom helped with it.'

'What's all this got to do with Victor Cornwall?'

'Mom and Dad never had much.' She smiled sadly. 'But my father, boy, he really wanted to make good.' She lifted her eyes. 'You know, live the American dream for us kids.'

'What happened?'

'Victor Cornwall happened.'

'You knew Vic?' Kitty's hands locked against the side of the table. This was not good, not good at all.

Fran nodded. 'Not personally, but you know he had all those infomercials, get-rich schemes. Books about how to improve your life, make good investments. He ran a real-estate invest-ment club. He dubbed its members Vic's Victory Club.

'Of course, it was all a fraud. A flimsy house of cards. After it all came out and Vic was exposed as the crook he was, the news started calling all those poor investors the Vic's Victims Club. Like it was some sort of joke.' Her voice was husky with sadness. 'My parents had mortgaged the house and the business and put all the money they had in one of Victor Cornwall's timeshare investments near Tampa.'

A tear fell from Fran's eye and down the edge of her nose, which she dabbed with her napkin. 'There was no resort. Nothing. Only an empty lot of swampland, better suited for alligators than timeshares.' Fran heaved a sigh. 'My parents lost everything.'

Fran explained how Victor's schemes had finally caught up with him and blown up in his face. As she spoke, Kitty had vague recollections of hearing some of the stories in the news. Cornwall had defrauded an untold number of innocent people who'd bought into his cons, bilking them of millions of dollars. Wow, the guy was quite a piece of work. No wonder somebody had murdered him. Kitty was surprised it hadn't happened sooner.

'Oh, Fran. I'm so sorry.' Kitty reached across the small table and squeezed Fran's hand.

'They never recovered. My dad got a night job working at a donut shop in Coconut Creek and Mom—' Fran hesitated. 'Well, Mom just sits at home. The shock and pain of losing everything was all too much for her.' She laced her fingers and squeezed. 'I told her I'd be home for Christmas. Now I'm not so sure. I could be in jail.'

There was a moment of awkward silence as Kitty digested her friend's words. 'It still doesn't make sense that the police would think you might have murdered Vic.' There were probably millions of victims of Vic's larceny who might like to see him dead, and she said so.

'Plus, you and the police are forgetting – you were with me the whole time.' Kitty smiled. 'You could not have possibly killed Vic.' In an effort to lighten the mood she banged her fist on the tabletop and said, 'Your honor, my client is innocent. The proof is clear and undeniable and I rest my case.'

But even as Kitty spoke Fran shook her head, as if to erase

the effects of her friend's smile. 'No. No, I wasn't.' Fran polished off her burger and pulled her soggy napkin across her lips. 'Don't you remember? You forgot your purse.'

Confusion spread across Kitty's face.

'You went to the front desk to fetch it. I went to the ladies' room.'

'So?'

'So, I didn't go to the ladies' room.' She hesitated, looking down at her empty plate. 'I went to Vic's room,' she confessed softly.

Kitty practically fell from her chair. 'You went to Vic's room? Why didn't you tell me?' Kitty lowered her voice. Heads were turning their way. 'What happened? What did you do?'

'I didn't do anything,' Fran whined. 'I knocked on his door.' She pulled apart her napkin. 'I was so angry, thinking about what he did to Mom and Dad.'

'So what happened?'

'Nothing. He didn't answer. That's all. I swear.'

'How did the police find out?' Had Fran told them?

'It was the housekeeper. You know, the one who caught us in Vic's room.'

How could she forget?

'She was working in the room across the hall and saw me knocking. She told the police.'

'But she didn't see you actually enter Mr Cornwall's room?'

'No, but it looks bad for me.'

Yes, it did. 'Fran, what were you thinking?' Kitty's mind raced through a million scenarios and outcomes. None of them good.

Fran shrugged. 'I wasn't thinking, OK?' she said as more tears poured down her face, taking her carefully applied mascara with them. 'I wasn't thinking,' she repeated. Then she rose and pushed back her chair. 'Excuse me.'

Kitty watched Fran speak briefly to their server, who pointed out the door to the ladies' room, behind which Fran quickly disappeared. Kitty's breath caught in her throat. Poor Fran. Fran had been gone only five minutes but that was long enough to kill Victor Cornwall. That made her a suspect. And with her family's history with Vic it made her a very good suspect at that.

Fran returned to the table, her face puffy but makeup repaired. 'Sorry about that.'

'Nothing to be sorry about. Don't worry. We'll figure this thing out.' Kitty would call Jack. He'd know what to do.

'Thanks, I— Hey, there's that guy again.'

'What guy?'

'That guy. Look,' Fran hissed as Kitty's head swiveled around and then back again. 'No, don't look. He seems to be following me – us, around.' This whole murder business appeared to be making Fran even more emotional than normal.

'I don't see anybody.' At least, nobody special. There were fifteen or twenty people spread out among the indoor and outdoor tables. Some couples, a few families. A toddler in a red jumpsuit was rooting around under a four-top. What was Fran going on about?

'That guy over there,' Fran explained, barely moving her jaw. 'At that small table to your left. Wearing glasses.'

Kitty lifted her purse and set it on her lap. She pretended to be fishing around while surreptitiously trying to get a good picture of Fran's supposed stalker. He looked harmless enough. In fact, he was rather handsome and couldn't have been much older than either of them. He had his nose buried in the paper he was clutching, a copy of the *Little Switzerland Gazette*. Kitty had seen their news stands outside the resort and at several kiosks along the street.

'I saw that same guy at the resort,' Fran said.

'So?' The man was wearing a tweed coat over a cream-colored sweater and a loose-fitting pair of dark jeans. He had an oval face and a wave of dark brown hair swept back from his forehead. With his black-rimmed glasses he looked a little bit like Clark Kent. Was he wearing tights beneath those jeans?

'So why is he following us around? I'd swear I saw him coming out of the police station as I was going in, too.'

'Fran, slow down. So what if you saw him walk out of the police station? This is one of the busiest streets in town. Maybe he stopped to ask for directions. He probably walked up from the resort like I did. Maybe he decided to do some window shopping and stopped here to get lunch the same as we did.' Kitty set her purse back down by her feet. 'All perfectly normal.'

'I still say it's no coincidence,' grumbled Fran, staring at her empty beer mug. 'And he looks like the killer type.'

'He looks harmless.'

'Exactly.' She gasped. 'Oh, no!'

'Now what?'

'He's coming this way,' she whispered a little too loudly.

Kitty turned. Sure enough, he had risen, folded his newspaper, which he left lying on the table, and was heading toward them. She shut her eyes. How embarrassing. She held her breath as his shadow passed over her. Hopefully he was merely leaving the pub and hadn't noticed them spying on him. The messes that Fran got her into . . .

'Good afternoon, ladies.' He stopped at their table and laid a smile on them. Kitty looked up. He certainly was handsome. There was mischief and charm in those green eyes. She was surprised Fran was suspicious of the guy rather than fawning over him – after all, that was her usual response to a good-looking man. Most men never stood a chance with Fran. She was that kind of woman, with a certain sexual chemistry that men seemed to find irresistible once she set her sights on them. Kitty had witnessed it firsthand. Fran would bowl an unsuspecting guy right over and ply him like warm, wet potter's clay in her hands. He'd never know what hit him.

'I'm Ted Atchison.' He stuck out his hand, first toward Kitty, then Fran. 'I hope you don't mind me interrupting. It's just that I'm staying at the resort, the Little Switzerland Resort and Spa?'

Kitty nodded. His hand was quite warm for such a cool afternoon. And no wedding band.

'Anyway.' He smoothed back his hair. 'I've seen you two ladies around and the resort and thought I'd say hi.'

Kitty and Fran said hello, though Fran wasn't hiding her feelings and looked rather put out. 'Who are you here with?'

'I'm afraid it's only me.'

Kitty's brow formed a V. 'No pet?' The Little Switzerland was a resort for pets. Would they even accept a guest without one?

He looked confused for a moment, then spoke. 'Oh, my dog, of course. Yep, got my dog with me.' He grinned from ear to ear. 'I can't forget him, can I? I thought for a minute you meant somebody two-legged.' He marched two fingers through the air.

Fran rolled her eyes and opened her mouth but before she could say anything rude, Kitty said, 'Are the two of you enjoying your stay, Mr Atchison?'

'Sure,' he extended his arms, 'it's like living in a postcard around here. What's not to like?' He grew serious. 'Except for the murder, of course.' His eyes locked on Kitty's.

'Yes.' Kitty shuddered visibly. 'That was horrible.'

'I read all about it in the paper. To think, we're all staying at the resort. I hear the police haven't caught the killer yet. He could be staying right there with us.'

'True,' Kitty said. Not a pleasant thought.

Ted Atchison rested his hands on the back edge of an empty chair. 'Do they have any leads?'

Too many, and all pointing in the wrong direction was what Kitty wanted to say. Instead, she replied, 'Nothing specific as far as we know.'

'Hmmm.' His finger tapped his lips. 'I guess we'd all better be careful then. There could be a vicious killer roaming the halls.'

'I don't think so,' replied Kitty. 'At least I hope not.'

'How do you mean?'

Kitty explained how the murderer was very likely somebody that Victor Cornwall knew and maybe had badly ended business dealings with in the past.

Ted wiped his glasses with a napkin then returned them to his nose. 'That makes sense.'

Kitty waved to the empty chair between her and Fran. 'Won't you have a seat?'

'There's no time for that,' interjected Fran. 'We have to be going.' She rose, the legs of her chair scraping across the stamped concrete. 'Got to keep to the schedule, remember? We don't want Greg and Steve dropping the hammer on us.'

Kitty sighed and rose. 'I suppose you're right. It was nice meeting you, Mr Atchison.' She laid some cash on the table, enough to cover the bill and a generous tip.

'Please, call me Ted.' He stepped back from the table, glanced at Fran then turned to Kitty. 'I was wondering if you might like to have dinner with me tonight.'

Was he blushing?

'Thanks but I'm afraid I couldn't.' Kitty was flattered but she was also engaged to be married.

Ted looked crestfallen. 'If you change your mind . . .'

ELEVEN

A fter dropping Fran off in their suite to nap, Kitty stepped out to the gardens near the pagoda and dialed Jack's cell phone. The call went straight to voicemail. Darn. How irritating. Where was he when she needed him? Fran needed him. She was hoping he could drop what he was doing and drive back down to Little Switzerland. There was nothing unreasonable about that, was there? He was a policeman, after all. Even if Little Switzerland was outside his jurisdiction there must be something he could do to help.

Of course, best-case scenario, he'd leave Elin Nordstrom in Sacramento. The lieutenant could hitchhike home for all Kitty cared.

She left a wordy message, hoping he'd call back soon, then went to fetch her pets. She unfolded the day's schedule that the hotel had provided for the guests' pets. Why was it that everybody and every pet seemed to have a schedule around here? This was supposed to be a relaxing spa resort pleasure trip, not boot camp. She ran her finger down the list of items on the itinerary. Fred and Barney should be wrapping up their *mani-petty* and grooming session in a few minutes.

Rick Ruggiero was standing beside the fountain giving an impromptu history lecture on the fountain's mallard ducks to a family of five. The youngest was a handful and chased gaily after the ducks. The ducks didn't seem to mind. In fact, a particularly aggressive iridescent green-headed male mallard seemed to delight in chasing the youngster back.

Kitty interrupted the manager long enough to ask for directions to the grooming salon and soon found herself wandering down a long, broad hall past the heated indoor swimming pool, whose signage indicated that it was for pets and their guests. A lone collie paddled about while its probable owner slurped an icy drink. She hurried past the rear of the kitchen and then out to an atrium off which were a hair salon for people and a pet grooming parlor. Inside the parlor, Barney sat like the supreme ruler of all he surveyed atop a wooden table that looked like it might have been an authentic Chippendale. He was licking his paws the way he did after a particularly fine meal. Lunch must have met his royal approval.

Fred was resting, comfortably by the look on his face – drooping eyelids and a lolling tongue – in a claw-foot tub on the travertine floor. An olive-skinned woman with generous curves snapped off a pair of elbow-length latex gloves and rested them on the side of the tub.

'Can I help you?' She sniffled and plucked a cotton handkerchief from her pants. Rows of lotions and potions lined the glass shelves behind her. There were little bottles of resort-branded shampoos and conditioners for pets.

'My name's Kitty Karlyle. I'm here to pick up my pets. These guys,' she said with a grin. 'Though I'm not sure the two of them are ever going to want to leave the way you're treating them.'

The woman grinned back, wiped her nose then sprayed a soft warm jet of water over Fred's back and haunches. 'Yes, of course. I'm Lina.'

Kitty nodded. Sure enough, the woman's nametag read Lina Dolofino. The name sounded Greek and by the look of her she could be of Mediterranean descent with that gorgeous skin and thick, dark wavy hair parted down the middle – as wavy as Kitty imagined the Mediterranean Sea to be on a windy day – with large hazel eyes, thick lashes, voluptuous lips and a pronounced nose that on her looked regal, like she could have been a Greek goddess. A diamond pendant hung from her neck on a slender gold chain.

'They'll be ready in a minute. I need to give Fred a good dry. You can take a seat there and wait if you like.' She sniffed again and indicated a plush wingback chair in the corner. 'Sorry, I'm allergic to the chamomile in the shampoo.'

Kitty scooped up Barney and rested him in her lap. She was going to give the guy some love and attention whether he wanted it or not. Wearing black pants and a black shirt, Kitty couldn't begin to guess how the groomer kept her clothing hair-free. 'Fred sure seems to be enjoying himself.' She watched Fred lick at

Lina's fingers. She would have said something but Lina didn't seem to mind.

'Believe me, I enjoy it as much as the animals do.' She grabbed a plush white bath towel with the hotel's name in red letters running the length of it and proceeded to rub Fred down.

'Hey,' Kitty spotted two large poodles stretched out on a rug in the next room, which seemed to serve as an office, 'aren't those Victor Cornwall's dogs?' The collars were different – simple but sturdy Little Switzerland Resort and Spa bands of red and blue – but the poodles sure looked identical.

'Yes.' She made the sign of the cross. 'I heard about his death. I was giving a Shih Tzu a teddy-bear cut when one of the waitresses popped in and told me. There was quite a commotion, though the manager tried to keep the news quiet.' She shuddered. 'I was horrified.'

'Tell me about it,' Kitty replied.

The groomer's brow went up.

'I found the body.'

She gasped. 'Are you all right? I'd be mortified.'

Kitty shrugged. 'I'll be OK. I mean, I'm doing better than Mr Cornwall.' She pointed to the poodles. 'They seem to be holding up and they were hovering over the body when I – that is, my friend Fran and I – found the body.'

'That's Mercedes and Benz.' The groomer rolled her eyes very slightly but Kitty hadn't missed it. 'I'm taking care of them until his wife shows up.'

Lina took a look at the damp gloves at the edge of the tub and spotted a hole through which she ran her pinkie. 'I go through a thousand of these a day, it seems.' She tossed them into a trash bin where they joined several previous pairs of castoffs. 'Latex and cat claws don't mix.'

The groomer grabbed a bright green, bristly rubber mitt and, to Fred's delight, gave him a firm rubdown.

'Victor Cornwall was married?' She hadn't even considered that. He didn't seem the marrying kind. At least not the reliably faithful kind. And his behavior toward her and Fran had strongly backed up that opinion.

'Yes. I mean, that's what I heard around the resort.' Lina grabbed a spray bottle and spritzed the Lab with something citrusy, then snatched a blow-dryer from the counter. 'Not that you'd know it by the way he hounded it up around here.'

'I take it you didn't care much for the man.'

Her smile was elusive. 'He was a guest. One never speaks ill of a guest.'

Kitty nodded. Of course.

A twinkle flashed in the groomer's eyes like twin flashbulbs. 'But just between you and me, he was a real shmendrik.'

'A what?'

'A jerk. King of all jerks, actually.'

Kitty laughed. 'Sounds like the right title to me.' King Shmendrik. She liked it. From what little she'd seen of the man – alive – the title fit like a glove or, in this case, crown.

The groomer turned the blower on Fred. He woofed at the warm air the way dogs always seemed to do. Barney, on the other hand, stiffened. 'Again,' she cleared her throat, 'just between you and me,' she said, waving the blower at Kitty, 'I hear she's a real piece of work.'

'I hope she likes dogs,' Kitty quipped, struggling to calm Barney as the warm air wafted over them.

'Me, too,' said Lina, snapping off the blow-dryer. 'All done.'

Kitty reached into her purse. 'How much do I owe you?'

Lina shook her head. 'It's all included in your stay.'

'At least let me give you a tip.' Kitty pulled out her wallet.

Lina laid her hand atop Kitty's to stop her. 'No, really. That's not necessary.' She leaned closer. 'To tell you the truth, I'd pay to do this job. I love the animals. They are so special . . . so innocent and precious.' She smushed Barney's face in her hands and gave him a kiss.

Kitty laughed as Barney squirmed in her arms. 'Then let me buy something.'

Lina laid a gentle hand on Barney's face and he quietened down. 'We do have a full line of all-natural pet care products. Everything from haircare products to toothpaste.' Lina massaged her fingers.

'Where are they?' A blinged-out blonde in glossy red heels came strutting into the salon. She pushed past Kitty and squared up with Lina. 'You're the dog washer?'

Lina stole a glance at Kitty, then nodded to the woman. 'I'm the in-house groomer, yes. Mrs Cornwall?'

The intruder folded her arms across a chest that must have cost a Beverly Hills bundle. Her short, stylish bangs were a blonde that could only have come from a very expensive bottle. 'Where are my dogs?'

The two poodles began yelping and Fred suddenly jumped toward the woman. Lina clapped her hands firmly and all three dogs quieted down.

'Wow, you really have a way with animals,' Kitty said admiringly.

'It's nothing.' Lina shrugged off Kitty's compliment. 'When you've worked with animals as long as I have you develop an understanding.'

'Like Doctor Doolittle.' Kitty smiled. 'I loved those books when I was a girl.'

'Me, too,' Lina said.

'Lovely – you've shared a moment,' snapped the woman. 'Now, where are their leads?'

'Of course,' Lina said with a calmness that Kitty didn't think she could have mustered. 'I'm afraid the dogs did not come with leashes.'

The woman merely glared bug-eyed at her. Lina gulped. She went deep into her office and returned with two nylon ribbon leashes, one blue, one red. 'You can use these if you like, Mrs Cornwall.'

The woman laughed. 'Not for long.' Lina motioned for the poodles to sit. She gently clipped the leashes to the collars. 'All set.'

Mrs Cornwall was frowning. 'What am I going to do with these two?'

Kitty noticed she had the lower lip of a Hapsburg. 'You don't like dogs?'

Victor's widow looked at Kitty as if she'd just now realized she was in the room. 'Who *are* you?' A chill Arctic wind accompanied her words. And though shorter than Kitty by a good two inches, she still managed to look down her nose at her. Quite a trick.

'Kitty Karlyle.' She held out her hand.

'Eliza Cornwall.' The woman's fingers barely brushed over Kitty's hand. 'If you must know, I despise dogs. I loathe animals of any sort.' She tugged at their leashes. The corner of her mouth turned up as she said, 'Unless I'm wearing one around my collar.'

'I don't understand,' said Kitty.

'Mink? Ermine?'

Ewww, thought Kitty. What was next, baby seals?

'Victor, rest his soul, loved his dogs. After my husband became successful financially he got caught up in this whole dog-show competition thing.'

She shook her head as if passing judgment. 'The time he wasted travelling from dog show to dog show, all for the sake of a blue ribbon or a trophy or two. I'll never understand what he saw in the activity.'

'Like the BKA Championship?'

Lina looked up.

'Yes,' said Mrs Cornwall. 'How did you know? He was quite proud of that win.'

'I saw the ring the night we met.'

Mrs Cornwall nodded and shook her head. 'He was always showing off that ring.'

'It meant that much to him?' asked the groomer.

'Winning always meant everything to Victor.' Eliza Cornwall's smile seemed to hold secrets. 'And now he's gone and left me with these two brutes.'

Kitty was stunned. Mercedes and Benz? How could anybody not love those two poodles? OK, so their names were ostentatious. That wasn't their fault. Blame that on Victor Cornwall. The dogs looked absolutely adorable. Certainly not brutish at all. 'What will happen to them now? They're beautiful dogs,' said Kitty, reaching out a hand to pet the nearest one. 'If I didn't already have a dog and cat and one tiny apartment I'd consider adopting them.'

There was a pregnant pause in the air.

'I could take them,' suggested Lina.

Eliza chuckled. 'You couldn't begin to afford them, my dear.' She pulled up the slack on the poodles' leashes and they stood. 'These are quite expensive champion show dogs. I'm not about to let them go for nothing.'

Lina's cheeks reddened.

With those words, Mrs Cornwall marched off with the dogs prancing beside her.

'Wow, a real piece of work, isn't she?'

Lina agreed as she straightened up the salon. 'Yes. I hear she and Victor were married for a dozen years. Of course, he spent ten of those in jail. He'd been out less than a year till now.'

Maybe that had made living with the guy more palatable. 'And now he's dead.'

'Yes, now he's dead.'

A young couple holding hands hovered at the entrance to the salon. A humongous Saint Bernard with a curly pink ribbon atop its head stood between them.

'Mr and Mrs McKee?'

They nodded in unison. It was time for Lina's next appointment. Kitty gathered up Fred and Barney and left her to it. It wasn't long before she caught up with Eliza Cornwall arguing with the resort manager outside the kitchen.

Kitty paused and hovered near a gilt-framed painting depicting Little Switzerland in the nineteen twenties, hoping to eavesdrop. She pretended to admire the heavy-handed painting while craning her ears.

'I don't care. I simply must get in my husband's room,' Mrs Cornwall was insisting.

Ruggiero held his hands together as if in prayer. 'But, the police have said—'

'I don't care what the police said. Victor was my dear, dear husband.' She wiped a nonexistent tear from the corner of her eye.

Kitty moved a squirming Barney up to her shoulder and let go of Fred's leash. He seemed happy standing there. Maybe he admired the painting more than she did.

'I simply must have access to his room. As his widow, it's up to me to see that everything is in order.' She laid her fingers on Rick Ruggiero's upper arm like the spider reaching out to the fly. 'You understand, don't you, Mr Ruggiero?' She batted a pair of thousand-dollar lashes.

He swallowed hard.

'I'm all alone. I have to handle everything now.' She sighed heavily. 'I will need to go through his personal effects.' She sniffled. 'And it is all so very difficult.'

Good grief. Kitty stifled a groan. Were all men such suckers?

'I-I'll see what I can do.'

Eliza Cornwall pecked his cheek, leaving a smear of lipstick that Kitty suspected Ruggiero would wear like a badge of honor for the rest of the day.

Kitty's phone rang and she reached quickly into her purse. Vic's widow turned her way, glaring suspiciously.

Kitty looked at the number on the display, which she didn't recognize and normally wouldn't answer. But in this case, with Eliza eying her, she picked up. Ruggiero, and then Mrs Cornwall, stumped off.

'Hello?'

She almost wished she'd never answered.

TWELVE

Jack was on the line. Kitty was both relieved and delighted to hear her fiancé's voice. But when she heard Elin Nordstrom's laughter in the background her happiness quickly faded. 'Jack, where are you? I've been trying to reach you for hours.'

It felt more like days.

'I'm at the hotel, calling from a phone outside the conference room. I can't talk long. Tell me what's going on. That was a long and twisting message that you left on my voicemail.'

Kitty quickly filled him in, trying to stick to what mattered. Trying not to hear the laughter in the background. What kind of law enforcement conference was this anyway? Shouldn't everyone be all dour and professional? Looking at grim crime-scene photos?

'Look,' Jack was saying, pulling Kitty out of her reverie, 'I wouldn't worry too much. Chief Mulisch seems like a good guy who knows his stuff. And as far as suspecting Fran goes, well, you said it yourself – Victor Cornwall had thousands, maybe millions of potential enemies if you look at all the people whose money he'd taken and lives he'd ruined in his career.' She heard a muffled whisper in the background as Jack continued. 'It'll sort itself out. You and Fran focus on having a good time. Remember, you're on vacation.'

'It's a working vacation.'

He cleared his throat. 'Emphasis on vacation. Focus more on that. You've got an entire crew there to worry about the work part. Let them do their jobs and let the police do theirs.'

Silence hung over the line for a moment as if underscoring the distance between them.

'I suppose so,' Kitty replied finally, though she hardly felt that way. She'd seen how Chief Mulisch had looked at Fran. Did they still lynch people in Little Switzerland? 'When will you be home, Jack?'

'The conference is over on Sunday and we'll be driving back Monday unless we stay over for a meeting in Berkeley that day. You can hang on until then. I've got faith in you. Oops, gotta go.'

Kitty pressed her ear to the phone. Was that Nordstrom she heard calling Jack?

Jack came back on the line. 'Can you believe it? The lieutenant's volunteered us to play a hostage couple in a search-and-rescue training session. What a pain,' he said with a laugh. 'I'll call you later this evening, OK?'

Kitty agreed and rang off. A couple? 'Ooh, that woman.' A passerby glanced her way and she urged Fred to move. This weekend couldn't be over soon enough for her. She never thought she'd miss Hollyweird, but the quicker she and Fran and her pets got back to LA the better she'd feel. Better still when Jack got back from Sacramento.

She ran into Vic's friend coming out of her own suite as she was going in. This was the man who'd been with Vic when they'd all first met. She'd noticed him again that morning in the bistro when she was having coffee with her parents. And he hadn't seemed too upset about his friend's death. In fact, he'd seemed to be having quite an amusing conversation with a man Kitty recognized as being one of the New-Age/New-Pet organizers judging by the smile on his face at that time.

'Excuse me.'

'Hello,' Kitty took a step back, 'Mister—' What on earth was he doing in their room? Was Fran OK? She pulled Barney close. Fred didn't seem bothered by the guy at all. She peered over the man's shoulder, trying to see into her room.

'John Jameson.' He held out a solid hand and Kitty juggled Barney one-handed to keep up with her end of the social contract convention. 'I hope you don't mind. I came to check on you and Fran. After what happened I wanted to be sure you two ladies were OK. Finding Victor like that must have been quite traumatic for you both.'

Kitty said that it was. 'I suppose it's been even harder on you. You and Victor are – were obviously very good friends.'

Jameson laughed. 'You could call it that.'

What did that mean? 'In fact, when I first saw the two of you together I thought you might be brothers.'

'Really?' He appeared genuinely surprised. 'No one's ever said that before.' He laughed again, though this time it degenerated into a cough and he lightly pounded his chest. 'Sorry about that. Old smoker's cough. A nasty habit I've been trying to quit.'

'So you and Vic aren't related?'

'Only in a business sense.'

'Why were you both here at the resort? Was that business?'

'Nah. Vic's really into his dogs now and this whole New-Age thing.'

'But you're not?'

'I'm here, aren't I?'

'Did you and Vic come together?'

'I drove in from Vegas. Vic drove up from Sedona. Like I said, he's taken a fancy to all things New Age and Sedona is like Mecca to that crowd. Why all the questions?'

'Sorry. The police questioned Fran and me into the middle of the night. I guess I'm picking up their bad habits.' She'd been watching his eyes for any signs of deception, not that she knew what she was looking for. The books and movies always made this seem so easy. 'I'll bet they questioned you too. Am I right?'

'What makes you say that?'

'You were the last person to see Vic alive. I mean, you two were together in the lobby when we bumped into you. Not long after that, Victor was dead.'

'He and I split up when the two of you left the lobby. Your friend, Fran,' he jerked his thumb at the door and smiled, 'really wound him up. My room's on the second floor.' He pressed close.

'I was tired of his drinking. The guy had been boozing it up, drinking like a proverbial fish all day.'

'Oh? Was something bothering him?' There were lots of reasons why people drank. Sometimes they had troubles that they were trying to wash away. Or drown.

'Nah.' John waved his hand as if shooing the idea away. 'The man never knew when to stop, that's all. At anything.'

'Maybe that's what got him killed,' Kitty suggested.

John shrugged, glancing meaningfully at his watch. 'I'm off. I've just got time for a quick smoke. I'm on the last panel of the afternoon. Our topic is *Predicting Your New Pet's Personality Based on Their Zodiac*. You and Fran should come.'

'I'd love to but I'm afraid we can't. We have a production meeting.' Thank goodness for Steve and his stupid schedule, thought Kitty. Thanking Steve – wow, that was another first.

'That's what Fran said,' he replied with a grin. 'I guess she wasn't fibbing just to get out of my tedious talk.'

As Vic's friend disappeared around the corner, Kitty raced into the suite, locking the door behind her. Fran was coming out of the bathroom, her hair wrapped in a poufy white towel. 'What was *he* doing here?'

'He who?'

'John Jameson, Vic's friend from yesterday.'

Fran shrugged and rearranged the damp towel. 'He came by to see how we were holding up.' She bit her lower lip. 'I hadn't realized how gorgeous he was. And such a sweetheart.'

'I don't know,' replied Kitty. 'There's something about him that sets off little alarms in my head.'

'There's something about him that sets off a little tingle in my toes,' quipped Fran. 'And,' she added, 'I'm having dinner with him tonight.'

Funny, Kitty still thought Ted Atchison would have been more her type. Then again, Ted seemed so . . . mundane. Fran was not mundane.

'Were you in my suitcase?' Kitty peered at her open bag. Unlike Fran, she was quite fastidious in her packing and several of her shirts looked out of place.

'No, why?'

'Nothing. Were you here in the room the whole time John was?'

'Of course. What kind of question is that?'

'Nothing. Sorry.' She supposed Barney could have jumped on her clothes sometime earlier. It wouldn't have been the first time he'd made a mess of things. When in doubt, blame the cat.

Kitty shook her head. 'I think I'm letting Vic's murder get to me, that's all.'

Fran concurred. 'Let's not let our finding a dead body spoil this trip.'

Kitty sighed. That was pretty much what Jack had said. Her gaze wandered to the window. There was still a little light left in the day and they had a few minutes to themselves before the staff production meeting they'd been required to attend. 'What do you say we take Fred for a walk? Get some fresh air?'

Fran agreed and said to give her a few minutes to get herself together. Kitty pulled the drapes all the way to the far wall. Was that Ted Atchison standing under that poplar with a pair of small birding binoculars dangling from his neck?

A pair of vibrant yellow-chested Western Meadowlarks with distinctive black V-shaped bands sat on a long, gnarly branch above him then flew off to one of the distant roofs as she watched.

Ted turned his head in her direction then marched after them.

THIRTEEN

'**D**o you think I should be worried about Jack spending so much time with Nordstrom?' Kitty was contemplating her features in the dresser mirror as she fine-tuned her makeup.

'Please,' replied Fran. 'Number one, he is not alone with the woman. He's in a hotel full of cops. Number two,' she enumerated with her fingers, 'the man is head over heels. You've got nothing to worry about. Not like me,' Fran added as she examined Kitty's hair with a makeup artist's critical eye and made a few minor tweaks. 'The way that police chief is eying me, I can practically feel those cold steel handcuffs around my wrists already.'

Kitty answered a knock at the door. 'Greg, what are you doing here?' She glanced at the time on the bedside table clock. 'We were just on our way to the meeting.'

Greg pushed through and the show's crew followed. Kitty suddenly felt claustrophobic as the room seemed to visibly shrink.

'Not this again.' Kitty resolutely planted her feet on the carpet.

'I want to get some spontaneous shots for the show. Get your thoughts on how the day has been going, you know?'

Kitty knew she'd like to give him a spontaneous punch in the nose but surrendered to the inevitable. She forced a smile, faced the camera and remarked what a wonderful time they'd been having at the Little Switzerland Resort and Spa. She even gave a shout-out to the manager, mentioning him by name.

While she spoke, she realized she ought to tell some of her clients back in LA about the resort. Particularly Chevy Czinski, a former star of ape-man movies who now lived in near seclusion with a menagerie of exotic animals. He'd love the place. Maybe he could get a group rate. Not that they were likely to accept lions, giraffes and chimps, even if they were paying guests. Well, maybe chimps. After all, they'd accepted and tolerated Victor Cornwall, hadn't they?

Ted Atchison stuck his head in the open door. 'What's all the commotion?'

'Hi, Ted. We're shooting some footage for a little TV show I do.' She waved toward Greg. 'This is my director.'

'A TV show? Cool.'

'Is there something I can do for you, Ted?'

'Not unless you've changed your mind about having dinner with me?'

Kitty blushed. All eyes were suddenly glued to her. 'Sorry.' She held up her left hand. Her ring finger sported a small gold engagement band. 'Taken. But thank you.'

'Wait a second,' said Greg. He tapped his lip a moment and Julie laid a hand on his shoulder. The cameraman kept his camera trained on Kitty. Greg snapped his fingers and said to Julie, 'We've got Kitty scheduled for that dinner and a movie thing with her dog and cat, right?'

Julie nodded.

'Why don't you join us, Mister—'

'Atchison. Ted Atchison,' he replied.

'Right. You're a fan of the show?'

He said yes though Kitty was pretty sure Ted had no idea what show the director was talking about or getting himself into.

'Great. Doors open at seven. Bring your pet.' He rubbed his hands together. 'We'll make this a little Q&A session after the movie with Kitty and fans of *The Pampered Pet*. You could get the ball rolling for us.' He wrapped an arm over Atchison's shoulder. 'Sometimes we get a stiff audience – nobody wants to be the first one to raise a hand and ask the first question, you know?'

Ted nodded, though he seemed unsure of what was happening.

'Don't worry, I'll have Julie write up some questions for you. You won't have to do a thing but memorize a few lines. Try to make them sound unscripted, OK?'

Ted was escorted out the door by Lucy the gofer, looking befuddled and pretty much like a hit-and-run victim.

'That was evil,' said Kitty, shaking her head in judgment at the director.

'Nonsense,' said Greg. 'All's fair in love and TV.'

The placard outside the resort theater room announced that the movie for the evening would be Hotel For Dogs. A little cliché but not surprising. Nothing about the Little Switzerland Resort and Spa surprised her now – not their quirky programs for pets, not their staff with their tranquilizer guns, and no, not even the murder of one of their guests. So why should their choice in movies be any different?

The first person she spotted was the elegantly dressed Eliza Cornwall in the company of Vic's champion poodles. They occupied a semi-detached booth near the door. The theater was posh by any standard and laid out in two sections bisected by the main aisle. Low slung, burgundy-colored leather, half-moon-shaped booths faced the screen. There were plush lambswool-topped pet cushions where tables might otherwise have been.

A red popcorn trolley spitting fresh hot kernels reminded Kitty that the holidays were just around the corner and that she really needed to start exercising more and munching less. Easier said than done but she did manage to make it past the popcorn machine without grabbing a bagful, so two points for her.

Maybe she and Fred could go for a hike while here. There ought to be some great trails in the region. She'd ask the concierge about that when she had some free time. And no matter what Greg or Steve and their schedule said to the contrary, she was going to have some free time.

While Kitty had thought the grieving Widow Cornwall might have preferred spending a quiet night alone with her sorrow, she had to give the woman credit for at least having selected a sleek black outfit with pearls – she appeared to be paying some respect to the recent passing of her husband.

There was no sign of Vic's friend, John Jameson, but then he was supposed to be on a date with Fran right about now.

Kitty smiled in Eliza's direction and received a stiff half-smile in return as the woman whispered into her cell phone. Ted Atchison sat off toward the corner with a long-haired mutt stretched out on the cushion. He waved and she waved back as she made her way toward the front where Steve, Greg and the rest of *The Pampered Pet* crew were waiting for her.

Everyone but Fran, that is. While Kitty had begged Fran to come, Fran had refused, saying that her date with John Jameson took precedence. Kitty called her a traitor. Fran said a girl's got to do what a girl's got to do.

Dr Newhart sat with the group from the show, one hand resting on the bony ribs of a slender greyhound who looked like she hadn't had a decent meal in, well, forever. Maybe Kitty would whip something up for her after the film – a nice juicy steak with all the fat.

'Where's Fran?' Steve said, arms folded across his chest. There was no sign of the Corgis.

'She couldn't make it. Where are your dogs?'

'Roger will be along in a minute.' He stuck his fingers in Kitty's hair then put a finger to her cheek and twisted her head around.

'Hey,' protested Kitty. 'Cut that out!'

'I suppose your hair and makeup will have to do.' He looked around the theater. 'The lights will be low, anyway.'

Kitty fumed.

Greg intervened before she could blow her top. 'Come on, you can have a seat at this booth with Fred and Barney. I'll be at the booth across the aisle with the crew. We'll shoot from there.' Dr Newhart scooched over to make room.

'We've arranged an after-movie Q&A like I said we would.'

Kitty grumbled a few words and sat. At the very least, nobody could bother her during the movie. She expected Fred and Barney would sleep through the whole thing. Maybe she'd join them.

But a third of the way into the movie, she had a better idea.

FOURTEEN

B arney was snoozing against Fred's tummy. Fred's eyes were shut as well and the movie wasn't half over. Kitty bent low and tiptoed across the aisle. 'Ladies' room,' she whispered to Greg while Steve glared at her with his usual mask of annoyance.

Leaving the theater, Kitty approached the front desk and asked if Howie Patterson was on duty.

'Sorry, he's off for the day.' The man behind the desk was tall, with long, dark sideburns that looked like pylons propping up his head.

Kitty's shoulders slumped. 'That's too bad.' She desperately wanted a look in Victor Cornwall's suite and had been counting on the security guard's cooperation to do that. Now what?

'Sorry, miss,' the clerk replied, clearly noting the disappointment on her face. 'Is there a problem?'

'No.' Kitty turned to leave.

'You might find him in his room.'

Kitty turned back around. 'He lives nearby?'

'Right here at the resort,' replied the desk clerk. 'Like a lot of us. Building G toward the southeast corner of the property. That's where a number of the staff live during season.' He explained that the resort employed a lot of temporary staff and that rents were too high in town so the resort put them up on the premises.

'Oh, thank you,' Kitty cried as she hurried off.

'Room 212!'

'You don't know how much this means to me,' Kitty said, laying a hand on Howie's arm as he slid his master keycard across the lock to Vic's suite.

'You don't know how much this means to me if we get caught,' Howie grumbled nervously.

'We won't,' Kitty assured him, though she scanned the hall in both directions for the umpteenth time. The coast was clear.

'I still don't get why you're poking your nose around in this.'

'I told you, Chief Mulisch thinks my best friend may have had something to do with Mr Cornwall's murder. Besides, Fran and I found the body.' That made her feel invested in finding out who had done the deadly deed. 'I'm curious, aren't you?'

Howie rolled his shoulders. 'Not especially.'

Kitty nodded. Howie did not seem like the curious type.

She'd found Howie alone in his room, watching a regional football game on TV and chowing down on a chain-store frozen pizza that he'd nuked in the room's tiny microwave. He was out of uniform for once, in worn blue jeans and a floppy grey NASCAR sweatshirt with a shot of Jimmie Johnson's Number 48 Chevrolet SS on the front. He'd taken a little convincing, a little cajoling and a little damsel in distressing but he'd finally agreed to let her into Victor Cornwall's room.

He pushed open the door. 'I'll stay out here and keep an eye out.'

Kitty nodded and, after a moment's hesitation – the last time she'd been in this room there had been a dead body on the bed – entered. Her hand fumbled with the light switch. The room was laid out just like hers and she found it quickly.

The dogs' lavish beds were gone but Vic's clothes and suitcase were still there. Funny. Kitty figured the police would have confiscated everything.

The checkbook she'd seen on the desk had gone, though. The police must have taken it – either they thought it was evidence or they considered it too valuable to leave lying around in an empty room. Victor Cornwall seemed to have been wealthy despite his lawyer fees, conviction and fines. Someone might be tempted to write him or herself a fat check.

She spent a good ten minutes scouring Vic's room from top to bottom, looking in drawers, under the bed and mattress. She even poked her head behind the dresser.

Nothing.

She'd come up empty-handed.

Howie was waiting for her outside, an expectant look on his face as she stepped back out. 'Anything?'

She shook her head. 'I don't understand it. I was sure there must be some clue as to who killed Mr Cornwall.'

'If there was, I bet the police already found it.'

'He had a ballpoint pen in his hand when we found him.'

'Maybe he was trying to stab whoever it was that was trying to kill him.'

Kitty bit her lip. The security guard could be right.

'Or draft a quick will,' he chuckled.

Howie cracked open the door and took a peek inside Vic's room. 'It looks just like it did when the police finished with it.' He closed the door and then jiggled the knob, making certain it was locked. 'Can't be too careful. Some of these doors don't close all the way automatically. You've got to give them a little pull.'

'Thanks again for doing this for me, Howie.' Even though it had been a wild goose chase. She'd better get back to the movie before it was over, if it wasn't too late already.

'Sure, guess I might as well patrol the grounds while I'm out. We've had a couple of cars broken into. The manager's been hounding me to keep a better lookout.'

Kitty said she hoped her own car would be safe. But then, who'd want to break into an old Volvo estate wagon that already looked like it had been broken into more than once?

She described her vehicle to the security guard and he promised he'd keep an extra eye on it. 'I wouldn't worry about it too much if I was you,' he said. 'No offense but it's mostly high-end stuff. Luxury cars, you know?' Apparently he'd seen Kitty's tired old Volvo. 'In fact, somebody broke into Mr Cornwall's Jag this morning.'

'What?'

'Yep, smashed one of the passenger-side windows right in.'

'The police hadn't impounded it?'

'They have now. They towed it over to the city lot.'

'Was anything taken?'

'Who knows?'

Who knew, indeed? Kitty had lots to think about. She started on her way back to the resort's theater but didn't make it far. Rounding the bend to the corridor that led to her own suite, she spied what clearly looked like the back of Rick Ruggiero's head turning the far corner and quickly disappearing. She noticed that the door to her and Fran's room was ajar.

Her heart jumped into her throat.

FIFTEEN

'**H**owie, come quickly!' She ran around the corner but Howie had disappeared too.

She tiptoed back to her door. This was silly, she told herself. She might have left the door ajar, forgotten to pull it all the way shut like the security guard was cautioning her about. Or maybe Fran had come back early from her date and had forgotten to pull the door shut. That sounded like something Fran would do. It sounded *exactly* like something Fran would do. Kitty was forever having to remind Fran to lock up the apartment behind her.

Kitty nervously licked her upper lip and pushed the door open with the toe of her right foot. 'Oh.'

Ransacked! She sucked in her breath. Clothes were strewn everywhere. The refrigerator door hung open. Drawers were open or askew. Both mattresses lay half-off their bedframes. The intruder had pulled the dresser away from the wall. What had they been looking for? She certainly didn't have any jewelry worth stealing. Except for her engagement ring, and that never left her finger.

She leaned down to pick up the glass coffee urn from the floor. It held the remains of the pot of coffee Fran had brewed that morning. The housekeeper had forgotten to clean and replace it.

'What happened here?'

Kitty screamed, sending a cold shower of coffee all over her legs. Ted Atchison stood in the doorway with Fred, Barney and his own mutt. Cold brew dripped down his arms and hit the floor like dirty rain. Fred barked, Ted's dog cowered behind Ted's legs and Barney went diving under the disassembled bed.

'Sorry,' said Kitty. 'You startled me.'

'So I see.' Ted smiled. 'Too much caffeine?' His eyes seemed to follow the dark drips running down her legs. 'Or did you have a wild party in here?'

'No.' Kitty set the coffee pot down on the tray atop the refrigerator. 'It looks like somebody broke in while we were out.' She shook her fingers, sending coffee rain scattering in all directions. 'Either that or the maid has rage issues.'

'I'll say.'

Kitty frowned. 'I can't believe it.' Especially since she was breaking into another room a few doors down at the time. Ironic, wasn't it? Not that she could find any humor in that at present.

Ted turned serious. 'Are you all right? Was anything taken?'

Kitty shrugged, taking in the room. 'Not that I can see.' She picked through Fran's open suitcase. It didn't look like anything was missing there either, but she'd have Fran check when she got back.

'What are you doing here? And with Barney and Fred?'

Ted shrugged sheepishly. 'The movie was over and you were nowhere to be found.' He scratched behind his ear. 'Man, that guy—' He snapped his fingers a couple of times. 'The smarmy-looking one. What's his name?'

'Steve.'

Ted looked amused. 'Yeah, boy was he mad when he learned you weren't there. You ever see a nest of hornets poked with a stick? Well, that was him.'

Kitty groaned loudly as she looked at her watch. The movie had ended almost half an hour ago. She was supposed to be doing an after-movie meet-and-greet with questions from the audience. Good grief. 'I completely lost track of the time.' She squeezed Ted's upper arm. 'Thanks for bringing the guys home.'

'My pleasure. In case you were wondering, the movie was OK but I was glad to get out of there. I was sitting near some blonde bombshell with a pair of poodles. She spent half the movie whispering into her cell phone.'

'That's Victor Cornwall's widow.'

'No kidding? Maybe he begged somebody to kill him.' Ted slowly circled the room. He stopped at the sliding glass door and pulled on the handle. 'This door's locked. Nobody got in or out this way. Any idea what they might have been looking for?' He toed a chair cushion that had been knocked to the floor.

'None at all.' Kitty tried coaxing Barney out from under the bed and failed. Maybe he was better off where he was. 'It could have been random.'

'Maybe,' Ted agreed. 'I'll help you straighten up.' His hands went to the sideways dresser.

'I don't think we should touch anything until we've notified the authorities,' Kitty said.

Ted nodded. 'We'd better call the front desk. And the police.'

'Definitely.' She wiped her dripping hands down the sides of her ruined blue dress. 'Give me a minute to wash this coffee off first. It might sound vain but I don't want to get caught looking like this.'

'I think you look great,' Ted said. 'But you go ahead. I'll hold down the fort.'

She came out several minutes later after rinsing her legs in the tub and throwing on a fresh pair of jeans and a heavy flannel shirt that belonged to Jack. 'Who was that on the phone?' She'd heard the suite phone ring while she was under the shower.

Ted rose from the edge of the bed that wasn't hanging out into space. 'Some cop.'

'So the police are on their way?'

'No, I don't think so. I mean, I haven't called them yet. I was waiting for you, like you said. This guy was calling from Sacramento.'

Jack. 'What did he say?' She'd have to call him right back. After she'd called and reported that her room had been broken into.

'Not much. He asked for you. I told him you were in the shower and he hung up.'

Kitty groaned.

He handed the receiver to Kitty. 'If you don't mind, I think

I'll rinse off a bit myself while you let the hotel know what's happened.'

Ted disappeared into the bathroom. Kitty dialed the front desk to report the break-in and the clerk at the desk said he'd let the police know right away.

Ted's dog was scratching away at the bathroom door. The mixed-breed definitely had a fair amount of terrier in him. A white patch ran from his chest to his chin. His slender body was tan with tufts of thick hair sticking up every which way. Kitty pulled him gently away by the collar. 'Come here, you.' She was afraid the dog would mark it up so badly that she'd get hit with a bill from the resort for the charges for repairing and refinishing it.

On the front side the stainless-steel tag gave a four-digit number and identified the animal as Chloe. The back side read Little Switzerland Pet Shelter and gave a telephone number. Kitty held Chloe's face in her hands a moment and looked the long-haired mutt over. Yep, definitely a Chloe. Hadn't Ted said the dog was a male? Kitty straightened. Chloe ran off to play with Fred who bounced into action. She could hear water running in the sink in the bathroom. Atchison was whistling. 'Are you from around here, Ted?'

'What's that?' She heard the water shut off.

'I asked if you were local.'

He opened the door then wiped his hands on a white towel. 'No. I'm from San Juan Capistrano. How about you? Did you call the police? Are they coming?'

'I live in Los Angeles.' A cold chill ran up her fingers. She suddenly hoped that the police were coming.

And soon.

SIXTEEN

The sharp knock of knuckles on the door sent a wave of relief coursing through her. Kitty didn't think she'd breathed even once between the time Ted came out of the bathroom and then. She opened the door quickly. Chief Mulisch and another officer stood in the hallway. The second man looked like a younger, taller and thinner version of the chief, albeit with a quickly receding hairline that belied his obvious youth. His eyes were the same color as the chief's.

'Hello, Chief Mulisch. Thank you for coming so quickly. I was expecting Deputy Nickels.'

'Deputy Nickels is working at the pharmacy this evening.' He explained that the LSPD was a small group. 'Only four full-timers and three part-timers. Nickels works at the pharmacy downtown.'

The chief twisted his jaw and strode to the center of the room, one hand on his weapon. 'What are you doing here, Atchison?' He squinted at Ted.

Ted cleared his throat and held out his hand. 'Ted Atchison, yes. I'm a friend of Miss Karlyle's.'

'Ted was kind enough to bring Fred and Barney back to my room for me.'

'Fred and Barney?' Chief Mulisch's brow went up as he frowned. 'You should've asked them to stick around,' he said. 'I might have had a few questions for them.'

'Go ahead and ask them,' Kitty replied, waving toward Fred and Ted's dog, Chloe, who were lying side by side under the small table by the sliding door.

'That's Fred and Barney?' asked the younger officer.

'The Lab is Fred. Barney's under the bed somewhere.' Why couldn't that nice Deputy Nickels have come? He'd interrogated both Fran and Kitty after the murder. Though the questions had been serious, he hadn't seemed like such a bad sort.

The two officers shared a look. 'You trying to poke fun at me, Miss Karlyle?' Chief Mulisch asked sternly.

Kitty reddened and her heart skipped a quick beat. One more second of her life she'd never get back. 'No, sir.' She shook her head. 'Not at all. I guess I'm just jittery – what with the murder and now this break-in.' She flashed a wan smile.

The younger officer was stooped over inspecting the door and frame. 'No signs of any damage.' He ran a hand along the door jamb. 'Technically not a break-in.'

'Good catch, son.'

'Son?'

Chief Mulisch smiled. 'This is my son, Peter.' He clapped the young man on the shoulder. 'He's only a deputy now but, believe me, this boy's going places. Probably have my job one day,' laughed the chief.

As if encouraged by his father's words, the deputy asked Kitty and Ted if they had any idea who might have wanted to do this to her suite and what they might have been looking for.

Kitty hesitated.

'Spit it out,' ordered Chief Mulisch.

'Well.' She sat at the edge of the bed and Ted quickly sat beside her and patted her leg. She scooshed over. 'I did see Mr Ruggiero turning the corner that way.' She pointed to where the corridor went outside.

Peter Mulisch's eyes lit up. 'You think Rick Ruggiero busted into your room?' He slapped his belt. 'That's a hoot.' He leaned over Kitty. 'You do realize that Rick is the manager of this resort, don't you?'

'Hey—' Ted interrupted. 'If Kitty says she saw the manager then that's who she saw.'

Kitty gulped and nodded. 'It's OK, Ted. The police are only doing their job. I know Mr Ruggiero is the manager but I'm sure that's who I saw.' As manager, he would have a master key to her room. To all the rooms. That would explain why there were no physical signs of a break-in. She said what she was thinking.

'No offense to your dog, Miss Karlyle,' said Chief Mulisch, 'but I think you are barking up the wrong tree.'

Deputy Mulisch laughed. 'Good one, Dad.' He pulled out a black leather-bound pad and pen. 'Was anything taken? Did you have any valuables in the room?'

Kitty shook her head. 'Not that I can tell – taken, that is. I didn't have any jewelry or money or anything like that, at least nothing worth stealing.' She pointed. 'And what jewelry I did bring is there on the dresser.' A small pile of inexpensive bracelets and earrings lay spread across the corner of the dresser. She rose, unable to sit any longer, her nerves singing. 'What happens next? Are you going to be taking fingerprints?'

Chief Mulisch said no. 'With all the guests going in and out of these rooms, plus the housekeeping and maintenance staff, I'd be surprised if there was anyone's prints that I didn't find.' He strode to the door and motioned for his son to follow. 'You let us know if you discover anything missing. Otherwise, try to put this all behind you. It could have been a random occurrence. These things happen, even in a nice little town like Little Switzerland.'

'Like Mr Cornwall's murder and then his car getting broken into the very next day?' Kitty said pointedly.

The chief stretched his neck. 'So you heard about that, did you?'

Kitty nodded. 'Was anything taken from the vehicle?'

'Well, now, if you were a member of the Little Switzerland Police Department you might be entitled to know that.'

Kitty wanted to scream but kept her cool, at least on the exterior. 'What about the murder? Have you found the killer? Identified any suspects?'

'Oh, yeah. You're sharing a room with her.'

'Fran Earhart never hurt anybody. I'd stake my life on it.'

'Sleeping in the same room with her, I'd say that's exactly what you are doing. Good night, Miss Karlyle.' His finger toyed with the safety latch. 'And remember to keep your doors locked.'

'Wow, quite a piece of work, isn't he?' Ted stood beside Kitty. 'Can I help you clean up now?'

'I'm really tired, Ted. Thank you, but I think I'd like to rest now.'

Ted said he understood and called his dog. As he stood in the open door, Kitty said, 'Ted, how did Chief Mulisch know your name?'

'What?' He smiled. 'I introduced myself, remember?'

'No.' Kitty shook her head. 'Before that, he asked what you were doing here. He called you by your name.'

Ted hesitated only a second but Kitty caught it. 'You're right. I guess he remembered me from earlier today. I popped in the police station when I was walking around town. I thought somebody there might be able to recommend a good place for lunch.' He smiled. 'That's how I met you.'

'That's exactly what I told Fran.'

'Pardon?'

Kitty explained how Fran had recognized him leaving the police station as she was being escorted in.

'That explains it.' He said goodnight and Kitty watched him growing smaller and then disappear around the bend.

That was what she'd told Fran and that did explain it. But was it the truth? Or was Ted Atchison a criminal of some sort? Maybe even an unnamed suspect in Victor Cornwall's murder? That would also explain what he was doing down at the police station.

There was a lot about Ted Atchison that Kitty didn't know. And a lot she wanted to find out.

SEVENTEEN

She grabbed the phone book out of the night table drawer, scooped up the phone and looked up the number to the Little Switzerland Pet Shelter. She quickly dialed, repeating the ID number she'd seen on the dog collar over and over in her head so she wouldn't forget. Maybe she could learn something about Ted's dog, Chloe.

All she got was a voice recording telling her that the shelter was closed, reeling off the hours of operation and wishing her a good day. She'd ring back in the morning. She wanted to call Fran to tell her what had happened but didn't want to interrupt her date. Fran didn't like anybody messing with her dating life. Not that that ever stopped Fran from sticking her nose in and voicing endless opinions about Kitty's own love life. She pushed her bed back into place as best she could and flopped down on top, anxiously waiting for Fran to return.

The next thing she knew, someone was shaking her by the shoulders. Kitty woke with a start and cried out before realizing she wasn't being murdered, 'Oh, it's you!'

'Yeah, it's me,' Fran said, pulling back. She was wearing her Bob Marley T-shirt and a pair of gray drawstring pants. 'Who were you expecting? The party police? Because it looks like you had some fun here last night. What happened, anyway?' She indicated the mess that had not been miraculously put back together by kind lederhosen-clad elves in the night.

Kitty sat up on her elbows and explained.

'Wow,' Fran said over and over again as her friend filled her in.

'What about you?' Kitty asked, fluffing her pillow and stroking Fred's chin. He sat on the bed beside her. 'The date went well, I take it?'

Fran shook her head. 'Not exactly. I mean, it started out OK.' She walked to her suitcase and pulled out a fresh skirt and shirt. 'John invited me to Yappy Hour. We were going to go out to dinner afterward.' She accepted the skirt and rejected the blouse, going back for another.

'Yappy Hour? Seriously?' quipped Kitty, her eyes rolling up into the back of their sockets like a pair of cheap blinds.

'There's a sign in the bar if you don't believe me.'

Kitty could just picture Fred coming back with a buzz on. It wasn't a pretty picture.

'You should have been there,' exclaimed Fran. 'They held the most darling pet fashion show in the lounge. There were local designers showing off their fashions for pooches and even some fall knitwear for cats. Very fashion forward.'

'Sorry I missed it,' replied Kitty. Not.

Fran grabbed Kitty's hand. 'They had the cutest little tuxedo. I thought of Fred the minute I saw it. He'd look adorable in a formal outfit.'

'Fran,' said Kitty, pulling away, 'even if he were going to the puppy prom, I don't think Fred would like to be caught dead in a tuxedo. What's next? Bridal gowns for the pooch in puppy love?'

Fran's eyes dilated. 'Say, you just might have something there.' She rubbed her thumb and index finger together quickly enough to start a fire – if only she'd been a Girl Scout. The closest she got was being a woman scouting for men. 'We could start up a business.'

Kitty clapped her hands together against her cheeks excitedly. 'We could call it Say Woof To The Dress!'

Fran hugged her. 'So you're in?'

'Sure,' answered Kitty. 'When poodles fly.' Fran let go. 'And are allowed to take off and land from LAX.' If Kitty had been dripping sarcasm any more fiercely she'd have needed a towel to wipe herself off.

'You are such a buzz kill, Kitty Karlyle.'

'Never mind that,' Kitty answered with a laugh. 'Tell me what happened on your date.'

'Like I said, not much. John got a call about a half hour after we met.'

Kitty wondered if John had subjected Fran to the famous ploy of having a friend call and bail you out of a bad date routine. She kept these thoughts to herself.

'We'd barely finished our first round of drinks here in the Alpine Grotto when he got a call and suddenly had to leave.' She lifted her shoulders. 'Business, he said.'

The Alpine Grotto was the lounge attached to the main restaurant. 'I don't understand. What did you do then? Where did you go?' Fran hadn't come back to the room.

Fran grabbed a fresh pack of nylons and headed toward the bathroom with her clothes, a skirt and blouse folded atop one another. 'I went for a walk into town. I guess I was feeling sorry for myself. I had a drink or two.' She grinned broadly. 'Maybe three.' She held up three fingers. 'In fact, I ran into that wacko Colonel Mustard and some woman coming out of some shop. I thought the two of them were a couple but then he had the nerve to ask me to have a drink with him right in front of her.'

Fran yawned then continued, 'Turns out she was a workout partner.'

'Muscle shop? You mean a gym?' Fran nodded and Kitty grinned. Fran was talking about Chef Moutarde, no doubt. Hard to imagine the Mussels from Brussels in a muscles shop. 'How many margaritas did you let him buy you?'

'They weren't margaritas.' Fran chuckled. 'They were mojitos. Henri complained the whole time that the drinks weren't nearly as tasty as the ones he gets when he's in Havana. Says it's because the bartender wasn't using *yerba buena*, whatever that is.'

'Cuban mint.' Kitty was familiar with the herb.

'As for how many,' Fran said, batting her eyelashes, 'a lady never tells.' She ignored Kitty's snort. 'Anyway, then I came back here and found this mess and you knocked out on top your bed. Since you were still breathing and there were no signs of strangulation, I decided to let you sleep.' Fran turned the corner. 'Now, if you don't mind, I'm going hit the shower,' she called.

'Then it'll be your turn.' Her head poked back around. 'And I'd be quick if I was you, because we have an episode of *The Pampered Pet* to film in less than an hour.'

Now that Kitty thought about it, Chef Moutarde was certainly strong enough to have strangled Victor Cornwall. Probably one-handedly. And he worked for the resort. She wouldn't put it past him to have found a way to have a master keycard. He could probably get in and out of anywhere with no one the wiser.

She'd have a few questions for the *bon chef* when she saw him at the taping this morning.

Kitty rushed to feed Fred and Barney then showered and dressed. They dropped the pets off at the resort's country club across the broad grass courtyard. Barney was scheduled for a morning session in The Treehouse Room.

Not knowing what to expect, Kitty was impressed. The Treehouse Room turned out to be an enormous two-story, glass-walled space with an expansive carpeted tree planted in its center. The carpet colors mimicked the colors of a tree – darker brown for the trunk and limbs, with some green shapes mimicking leaves that were actually ledges. There were nooks, crannies and caves aplenty. Robotic birds of a multitude of species chirped like the real deal. The birds were so realistic Kitty imagined they might have come from Disney's shop.

'Unfreaking believable,' Fran said, her mouth agog. 'If I die and go to kitty heaven this is what I want it to be like.'

Kitty placed Barney on the floor. While tentative at first in his new surroundings, once settled he quickly flew up the tree and out of sight. How on earth would she ever get him back down if he didn't want to come?

The man in charge of the treehouse, dressed in an off-white safari suit and pith helmet, told her not to worry. A human-sized ladder ran up the middle of the trunk. 'There hasn't been a cat yet that I ain't been able to coax or cajole out of this tree when the time has come to rejoin his or her owner,' he claimed in a charming south Texas drawl.

Kitty hoped so. She didn't savor the idea of having to go climbing up the carpet-covered trunk trying to snatch Barney up like a ripe California orange.

Fred was slated for a round of golf. Doggie Disc Golf to be exact, according to the information poster taped to the wall outside the Canine Clubhouse designed to look like a stereotypical doghouse, only on steroids. Kitty thought it was kind of cute; Fran thought it was kind of weird. 'I feel like I've walked into a scene from *Honey, We Shrunk Ourselves*,' Fran quipped, walking through the arched entry.

They found a dozen or more dogs and owners sitting in the clubhouse dining room and joined them. The pro was going over the instructions for the game. He paused when Kitty made her late entrance, cleared his throat then continued.

No humans were allowed in the game, a thirty-six-hole round, except for what the pro labelled the resort's officially sanctioned 'catties' – the resort seemed to love its little puns – who would carry the assorted size and weight golf discs for each dog contestant. He held several up in his hands. These discs, he explained, had been designed especially for dogs. They had the resort's logo blazoned on their top sides. 'And they'll be vying for this,' the man said, proudly hoisting a gold dog bone mounted vertically on a plate-sized wooden base. 'The Top Dog Trophy.'

Murmurs of excitement rippled through the crowd. The dogs themselves seemed unimpressed with the trophy and more interested in sniffing each other.

'Good luck, Fred.' Kitty patted his side.

'Take no prisoners,' added Fran. 'That trophy will look great over the fireplace.'

'Too bad we don't have one.'

They watched Fred lumber off with the other canines making up his foursome – two Springer spaniels and a border collie. He was in good hands and looked happy enough. It was show time and she was due back in the banquet hall where they'd filmed the cooking demonstration the day before.

Her mom and dad were in the audience. Despite Steve's protest, she stopped to say hi and told Fran she'd be up in a minute.

'Good morning, Kitten,' her father said, releasing her from his hug. 'How are you holding up?'

Kitty said OK and explained how their room had been ransacked the night before.

Mrs Karlyle was shocked and said so. Her hands flew to her face. 'It's no wonder we haven't heard from you. I left several messages.'

'Sorry, Mom. It's been crazy around here. Not much of a relaxing getaway, to tell you the truth. I'm sorry I haven't had more time to spend with you both. Let's get together this afternoon, OK?'

'That's all right, dear. It's perfectly understandable,' replied her mother. 'All the more reason why your father and I have decided to drive home.'

'What?' Kitty's jaw fell.

'That's right, Kitten. Mom and I are heading home after your show.'

'But why? You just got here.'

Mrs Karlyle smiled warmly and took her daughter's hand in hers. 'We can see how very busy you are, sweetheart. And all this murder business – well, I don't mind telling you that it makes me a little uneasy.' She glanced at her husband and he nodded agreement. 'Frankly, we wish you'd go back home, too.'

'I wish I could,' Kitty said. 'But it's not that easy.'

Her mother commiserated. 'We'll see you soon. Come down next weekend, perhaps, when this is all over. Bring Jack with you.'

Kitty promised she would. If there was a Jack when this was all over. The last time he'd called her room some strange man had answered and said she was in the shower. And she'd never called Jack back to explain. What must he be thinking?

There was barely time for a quick run-through of the morning's script. While Greg was busy getting his crew into place, Steve sent Kitty to the kitchen to meet up with Chef Moutarde and complete the pre-show food prepping.

'Hello, again, Chef.' Kitty buttoned up her pink chef's coat. The studio had hers custom-made with her name stitched on one side and *The Pampered Pet* stitched on the other all with darker, contrasting pink thread.

'Miss Karlyle.' Henri was dressed immaculately – crisp white necktie, toque and a double-breasted jacket. The kitchen was a flurry of activity, both for the show and the resorts regular guests. The chef was deboning a salmon.

No chef appellation for her. Kitty resigned herself to the fact that Chef Moutarde was not a fan. She grabbed a knife and began dicing beef into one-inch cubes. 'Terrible about Victor Cornwall's murder, isn't it?'

He threw the floppy fish down on a hot, oiled aluminum pan where it started sizzling madly. It was like something out of a Mel Brooks movie. The poor salmon flopped like it was being resurrected in some mad doctor's lab experiment.

'Victor Cornwall didn't know his Bolognese from boloney,' Chef Moutarde exclaimed, his thick Walloon accent coming through as loud and clear as his sentiments. 'The man was always complaining about the food that I served him. And his pets . . .' He pushed the fish around in the pan as if he enjoyed hearing it hiss. 'Nothing was good enough for his dogs.' He picked up a cleaver and slammed it down across the midsection of another poor salmon. 'Forgive me if I do not shed a tear for such a man.'

Kitty took a step back. The chef was a bit wild and loose with the knives for her taste. 'I hear a lot of people lost a lot of money over the years because of Victor's schemes.' Had Henri Moutarde ever invested any money based on one of them?

Chef Moutarde stopped and looked at her. 'Do we not have a cooking show to prepare for?'

Kitty blushed. 'I was merely wondering if you or anyone you might be close to might have invested with Mr Cornwall.'

His eyes turned to ice. Not an easy thing to do in a hot kitchen. 'I have agreed to play your sous chef for the day. I have not agreed to answer all your petty questions.'

Henri tossed his blade in the sink to the sound of a loud metallic clatter, then stormed off and cornered Greg's assistant, Julie, who stood reviewing her notes near the walk-in fridge. Kitty could only imagine what he was doing now. Probably bad mouthing her. Oh, well. It wasn't like Julie could fire her.

And she'd never even had a chance to ask the chef how his sort-of date went with Fran.

EIGHTEEN

'Wow,' said Fran, munching on a leftover carrot as she helped Kitty pack up after the taping. 'Henri looked more like he'd rather stick your head in his oven than work as your assistant this morning.'

'Was it that obvious?' Kitty rinsed her hands in the big kitchen sink. She was relieved that the show was done. Greg, Steve and the crew had gone off to review the footage. Chef Moutarde had left, no doubt to harangue his staff. That left her free for what seemed like the first time in ages. Maybe she could start to relax after all. It also left her free to investigate Victor Cornwall's death. And though she couldn't put a finger on it, something was driving her to dig deeper into finding out who had murdered the man – as distasteful as he was.

'Oh, yeah. I worried for your life every time you turned your back. I thought he might just plunge a knife into it.'

Kitty shivered. 'Must you?' The image of a knife in the back was an image she had seen once before and would rather not relive.

'So spill. What did you do to get him so angry?'

'In the first place, the guy is always angry.'

Fran nodded. 'You've got me there,' she agreed.

'In the second place, all I did was ask him before the show about Victor Cornwall.'

'And?'

'And the chef was not one of his fans.'

Fran practically spat, sending munched carrot bits flying. Spittle-covered bits of carrot attached themselves like veggie ticks to Kitty's apron front. 'Sorry.' Fran wiped the carrot away. A kitchen worker gave her the ugly eye but she continued anyway. 'But nobody was a fan of Victor Cornwall's.'

It was Kitty's turn to nod. It seemed like Victor Cornwall had made nothing but enemies. Had his poodles even liked him?

'Do you think Henri disliked him enough to murder him?'

Kitty explained how Chef Moutarde said that Victor was always complaining about the food. 'But he didn't admit to ever having invested in one of Victor's schemes.' She dried her hands on her apron. 'I wish there was some way to find out for sure.' She turned to Fran and rested her hand on her friend's shoulder. 'Maybe you could ask him?'

Fran stepped back. 'Me? Forget it,' she said, waving her hand in the air. 'No way.'

'Why not? After last night, the two of you—'

Fran cut her off before she could finish the sentence. 'Whoa, hold your horses, girl. There is no two of us. There's just me. I only let the man buy me a few drinks. We are not a couple.'

She wriggled her eyebrows. 'Now, John. That's another matter.'

'Oh? I thought things hadn't gone so well?'

'They went fine until he got that phone call,' Fran corrected. She smiled coyly. 'And I learned a thing or two that you might be interested in.' She tapped Kitty playfully on the bridge of her nose.

'Such as?' Kitty pulled off her apron, dug a tube from her purse and reapplied her lip gloss.

Fran lifted herself up onto the stainless-steel kitchen counter and made herself comfortable. 'Such as how John and Victor were college roommates.'

So that was how the two men knew one another.

'After that, they became business partners on a few real-estate deals.'

'What kind of deals?'

Fran shrugged. 'I don't know. Boring stuff. Buying and renovating properties then renting them out and flipping them when the market was right.'

'Were they partners in Vic's infomercials?'

Fran shook her head. 'No. John says Vic changed. Got greedy. According to John, Victor cheated him on some big deal the two of them had been putting together for months. At the last minute, Victor cut him out. John admitted he was furious.'

'I'll bet.' But was he furious enough to kill? If so, why wait so long? Did revenge take time to simmer, like a good stew?

'That's what led to the two of them going their separate ways.' Fran leaned against the back counter, a fat grin on her face.

'What is it?' Fran was holding something back, though Kitty knew Fran well enough to know it wouldn't be for long. 'Go ahead, spill.' What did Fran know that she didn't?

'Victor Cornwall got greedy in more than one way.' Fran leaned in. 'You see, it wasn't just more money he was after.'

Kitty was puzzled. 'What else would a man like Victor Cornwall want?'

'He wanted John's wife.'

Kitty gasped.

'And he got her.'

Of course, thought Kitty. She should have known. That was exactly the sort of thing a man like Victor would want. 'That's incredible! Why, John must have hated Victor. I can't believe they came here acting like good friends and—' Kitty stopped dead in her tracks. 'Wait a minute,' she said, grabbing Fran's arm. 'Are you telling me—'

Fran smirked. 'Eliza Cornwall is the former Eliza Jameson.'

Kitty listened in stunned silence as Fran went into the details of how Victor had stolen John's college sweetheart and wife nearly fifteen years ago. Could John have carried a grudge all these years? Why had they come here acting as friends? Could John really have forgiven Victor for such a heinous thing?

Had John Jameson finally snapped and strangled Victor? John could easily have killed him. They were together only minutes before. Maybe John hadn't gone back to his room like he said – maybe he'd gone with Victor to his room. The two men argued and John finally lost it. All that pent-up anger over losing his wife and his money. John Jameson quickly shot to the top of Kitty's list of suspects and she said so.

Fran disagreed. 'No way. John says he forgave Vic and Eliza a long time ago.'

'What makes you think he's telling you the truth?' It wouldn't be the first time a man had lied to Fran.

Fran leapt off the counter. 'Because I'm having lunch with the man and I can't afford to think otherwise.'

'Lunch? Fran, you can't. He could be a cold-blooded killer.'

But there was no talking Fran out of her date. Fran went off in search of coffee and Kitty went to her room to grab her coat.

It was time to check out the animal shelter in town and find out some more about the mysterious Ted Atchison.

The Little Switzerland Pet Shelter was on Lausanne Avenue, a quiet side street off Basel, the town's second largest street. A tattered canvas awning out front bore the letters LSPS. Kitty pressed her nose against the dirty plate-glass window on the street and peered inside. A small woman in purple with her back to the glass was playing with a beautiful silver-gray and white Husky with pale blue eyes.

Kitty pulled open the door to the sound of a tinkling bell and the woman turned. 'Welcome to the LSPS,' the woman greeted them. She wore a flouncy, high-collared purple sweater and purple slacks that were both covered in dog and cat hair. Her face was lightly lined with wrinkles and her eyes twinkled like tiny blue stars.

Kitty slipped in a pool of dog piddle near the door and slid into the skid-marked wall. She hadn't been the first victim of the doggie danger. Judging by the scuff marks on the wall this was a common occurrence. The woman came running with a fat roll of paper towels. Kitty held onto the wall with one hand as the lady quickly and efficiently wiped her shoe and then the floor, muttering her apologies the whole time. Yep, thought Kitty, the woman had definitely done this before. She had it down like a finely honed Vaudeville routine.

'I am so sorry. It's impossible to keep up with these guys.'

'It's OK, really.' Kitty laughed. It wouldn't be the first time or the last that she'd land in some piddle. The woman wiped her shoe and the floor once more for good measure and tossed the dirty towels in a nearby plastic bin.

Kitty took an immediate liking to the woman. Her first impression was that she was looking at a relic of the psychedelic sixties. Did Janis Joplin really die or had she simply quietly retired to run a volunteer animal shelter in the hills of Little Switzerland?

Several dogs roamed loose and one extremely well-fed calico cat sat sunning himself on a tattered cat perch near the door. A curtain divided the small front room from the back, from which emanated the sounds of many more dogs and the lone voice of another woman talking to them in a high-pitched tone while she apparently worked.

The room smelled like dog but Kitty didn't mind that one bit. In fact, it made the tiny storefront seem rather homey.

Kitty introduced herself to the woman and the Husky.

'I'm Sheila Shepherd,' said the woman, running a hand up under her sweater and scratching. 'That's Jane.' Her cuffs were worn thin. This was a woman who was obviously comfortable in her own skin and didn't seem to care what anybody else thought. A refreshing change of pace from the cast of Hollyweird.

Kitty ran a hand along the Husky's thick double coat. 'She's beautiful.'

'Are you interested in adopting?'

The woman's face turned hopeful and Kitty hated to disappoint her. 'Sorry, I live in a small apartment and I already have a dog and a cat. A black Lab and a tuxedo cat.' Kitty explained how she'd adopted Fred from a shelter and how Barney had followed her home.

Sheila nodded appreciatively. 'It sounds like he basically adopted you.' She grinned and tossed Jane a small treat that she'd pulled from her pants pocket. 'Nice. Cats have good instincts, you know.'

Sheila rubbed the tummy of the fat cat on the perch. The animal barely managed to partially lift one eyelid before falling back into his snooze. 'If your Barney likes you then I like you, too.'

The woman in back called Sheila's name. 'Time to give Starr her eye drops!'

'I'll be right back,' said Sheila, dusting off her hands. 'Starr suffers from a touch of conjunctivitis and always puts up a fuss when it's time for her eye drops. Doesn't know what's good for her.'

Kitty nodded sympathetically. Fred had had pink eye once and had suffered plenty. 'Do any of us?'

'Make yourself at home,' Sheila said with a wink as she pushed aside the curtain and retreated to the backroom.

Kitty waited until Sheila disappeared and then approached the small counter near the back wall. There was a dented four-drawer metal file cabinet in the corner with a messy stack of papers atop it. An open bag of dog food for seniors spilled small bits of kibble across the countertop.

Kitty took a quick look at the doorway to the backroom from which the sounds of one struggling dog and two struggling women emanated. She didn't have much time. With Jane shadowing her, she cautiously stepped behind the short counter. The top drawer of the file cabinet stuck for a moment then popped free with a mousy squeak that Kitty feared would draw attention. She froze. No one appeared in the doorway.

A couple holding hands passed by out front and glanced in the window and smiled. Kitty smiled back, hoping she didn't look guilty. She certainly felt guilty. Sheila Shepherd was such a kind woman, she felt bad snooping around her animal shelter like some sort of spy or thief. Not that feeling bad was going to stop her. Kitty riffled through the thick rows of manila folders. Most contained info on the various pets who'd been in and out of the shelter, including their histories, both personal and medical.

Unfortunately, they had been filed by the name of the animal, not the person who had adopted them. That wasn't going to help her at all, especially since she hadn't yet come across a file for Ted's dog, Chloe.

But it was drawer number two that held the real surprise.

NINETEEN

Wedged between a rumpled brown paper bag, which Kitty peeked inside and discovered contained a cheese sandwich on white bread, a green apple and a stack of old receipts, sat a large and slightly wrinkled white envelope with the Little Switzerland Resort and Spa address and logo in its upper left-hand corner.

Inside the envelope were more bills than Kitty could count. And these bills all had Ben Franklin's picture on them. Nice-looking guy, that Ben.

What was that all about?

'Thanks, Sheila.'

Kitty quickly shut the drawer and swung around. Sheila stood in the doorway, wiping her left hand on her slacks. Her right hand held a lined piece of paper. Starr's name was written in red at the top. Probably the dog's medical chart.

Kitty couldn't swear to it but she thought she saw the woman's eyes go to the file cabinet before turning their attention back to her. 'Still here, eh? What can I do for you? See anything you like?'

Kitty stepped back around the counter. She definitely liked all the Benjamins. She cleared her throat. 'I was looking at the photos on your wall.' Kitty gestured to an old pockmarked corkboard on the wall behind the counter. The board was covered with recent shots that looked like they'd come off a computer printer mixed in with a lot of yellowing Polaroids.

Sheila smiled. 'Those are just some of the lucky pets we've found homes for over the years.'

'That's sweet,' said Kitty. 'It's a wonderful thing that you're doing. Have you been doing it long?'

'Nearly twenty years,' Sheila said proudly. She plopped herself down on a plain pine stool, setting Starr's medical chart on the countertop. 'I got tired of working in a cubicle. I wanted to do something more useful, less confining.'

'I bet it hasn't been easy.'

Sheila slapped her knees. 'No, young lady, it hasn't. Not everybody wants to adopt a pet these days. Too many folks only want a pet with a pedigree, like they do when they buy a fancy car or some such silliness. And sometimes those that do adopt a pet get to feeling like it's too much trouble and then return them.'

'That's awful.'

Sheila nodded.

'My friend, Ted Atchison?' Kitty began, casting her web with caution. 'He picked out a dog here.'

Sheila's ears perked up. 'Oh,' she beamed, 'Mr Atchison. Such a nice young man.'

'You remember him?'

'Of course I remember him. I might look old but I'm not so old as to be addlebrained.'

Kitty swiftly apologized. 'I didn't mean anything by it, Sheila. I'm sorry. I didn't expect you to remember.'

'Well,' Sheila rose with a groan and petted a skittish sheep dog that had risen to her feet for the first time since Kitty had come in, 'I remember. He came in only yesterday afternoon, just as I was closing for the day.'

Kitty tugged at her ear. 'Yesterday?' Ted had said he'd had the dog for over a year. And that he and the dog had come up from San Juan Capistrano. Hadn't he?

Kitty realized right then and there that if she was going to keep snooping into things then she might want to invest in a notebook.

'Yes. He wanted desperately to get a pet, he said.' Sheila smiled. 'Usually I like folks to take a couple of days, you know, and think it over. Make sure they're certain that they can handle the responsibility.'

She pulled a pair of glasses from her slacks pocket and studied the sheep dog's face close up. She turned to Kitty. 'I wouldn't want him returning her in a couple of days.' She turned back to the dog and bit her lip as she held the dog by the snout. 'Eyes are looking a bit inflamed. I'm going to have to keep an eye on you,' she said, giving the dog's snout a wiggle.

Sheila turned back to Kitty and wiped her hands on her legs. 'But Mr Atchison was quite insistent. And like I said, he did seem very nice. How could I say no? Pets are what I live for. He picked out Chloe, an affectionate mixed-breed that I've had for over five months. I was happy to see her go to a good home. The two of them seemed to really hit it off, too.'

Kitty muttered something about how nice that was but inside her brain was in turmoil. Something was so not right about Ted Atchison. And she'd been alone in her room with the man.

'We found homes for three dogs and two cats since Monday.' Sheila pointed to several recent shots on the corkboard. There was a close-up of Ted and Chloe taken right there in front of the counter. Kitty hadn't noticed it earlier. That was definitely the dog that Ted was calling his own.

'Yep, it's been a good week,' Sheila was saying, 'especially after that anonymous donation we received yesterday. That's huge. There's so much good I can do for these guys with that kind of money. One thing we've always struggled with around here is funds. Enough funds to keep the doors open, keep the animals fed and healthy . . .' Her voice trailed off.

Kitty's eyebrows had risen and hadn't come back to earth yet. A huge donation. That could explain the envelope full of money that she'd just seen. Had the hotel made the donation? It would make sense. Sheila ran an animal shelter and adoption – the resort catered to pets. 'That big, huh?'

Sheila gestured her closer with an arthritic finger. 'Fifty thousand dollars? You bet that's big.'

Kitty straightened. 'Fifty thousand dollars?'

'Yep, found it in an envelope stuffed in my mailbox.' She jabbed a finger toward the banged-up mail slot in the door. 'It was there when I came in yesterday morning. Amazing, isn't it? A gift from above, that's what Mr Atchison said.'

'You told Mr Atchison about it?'

'Sure, why not? I'm telling the world.' Sheila ruffled her hair. 'Well, maybe not the taxman,' she said with a chuckle.

'I'll never tell,' replied Kitty, happy to be the woman's co-conspirator. Kitty figured it wouldn't hurt to keep on Sheila's good side.

'He seemed as excited as I was.'

'Mr Atchison?'

Sheila nodded. 'Such a nice young man,' she said again. 'Are you two a couple?'

Kitty shook her head no. 'Just friends.'

'You might want to think about making it something more than that.' She grabbed onto Kitty's arm. 'You don't want to let a man like that get away.'

No, thought Kitty, you sure don't. 'Do you think the resort might have given you the money?'

'You mean the Little Switzerland Resort and Spa?'

Kitty nodded.

'I don't think so. Don't get me wrong, they've given us a few thousand dollars a year, plus supported us with extra food and other supplies over the years. But nothing this big. Besides,' Sheila added then paused for a moment as she went to the file cabinet with Starr's medical sheet in her hand. No doubt she was about to place that paper in one of the folders. 'Why keep it a secret?'

Fresh, cool air struck Kitty's face as she held the front door open with one hand. Why indeed?

'Wait just a minute,' hollered Sheila. She stood beside the open file cabinet, hands on her hips.

Kitty froze, one soggy foot out the door. Had Sheila suddenly realized that Kitty had been snooping? 'Y-yes?'

'You never did say why you'd come in.' Sheila had a big grin on her face.

Kitty breathed a sigh of relief. 'Oh, silly me.' She reached into her purse and pulled out her checkbook. 'I wanted to make a donation. After hearing my friend Ted talk about the wonderful work you're doing here I just knew I had to contribute something.'

'Well, aren't you sweet, child.'

Kitty quickly scratched out a check for five hundred dollars then raced back to the resort.

TWENTY

Kitty spotted John Jameson loping through the lobby in a red flannel shirt and jeans. He was clutching a small navy bag, like the kind you'd carry to the gym. He was alone and heading in the direction of the pool and exercise room. If he was going for a workout, he would have to wait. She had a few more questions for him. Like how did he feel about Victor Cornwall stealing his wife? And had Victor swindled him as well?

She made a beeline past the fountain and headed after her quarry. He was moving quickly with long strides. She had to move fast because if he made it to the men's locker room before she got to him she'd lose her chance. There were some boundaries even she was loath to cross.

Kitty almost lost him when she passed by an open room full of women spread out on mats across the floor. They were all on their hands and knees. A white leotard-dressed instructor hovered over one skinny woman, clutching her ribcage. OK, she must be the yogini. But what had stopped Kitty wasn't the sight of all these women doing some form of yoga with their master. Oh, no. What had brought Kitty to a skidding stop was the absurd image of the dogs that were perched atop each woman's back.

A small placard outside the room announced this was the Downward Dog Duet Class. Hmmm. Kitty chewed her lip as she watched. None of the dogs looked happy or comfortable. She couldn't for the life of her imagine putting Fred on her back like that. And she was positive that neither she nor her Lab would enjoy it if she did.

Kitty forced herself to look away from the bizarre scene, realizing her quarry might be getting away. She spotted a flash of red flannel and angled toward it. Sure enough, it was John Jameson. She was less than twenty yards from him when he turned to the left. He passed the spa, the indoor pool and the exercise room. Where was he heading?

Her question was quickly answered as Jameson stopped unexpectedly outside the grooming salon. The door was closed and there was no light coming through the big plate-glass windows on either side. Kitty ducked behind the corner. As she watched, he pulled out what looked like the same pair of driving gloves she'd seen stuffed in his back pocket the other day. He slipped them on.

What on earth? She held her breath.

Jameson tried the handle. The door opened and he squeezed inside, closing the door behind him. Moments later, shadowy light spilled out from within.

This was very interesting. Was Miss Dolofino inside? She might have been in the inner office. Did he have an appointment with her? He didn't have a pet with him. Who goes to a pet groomer without a pet? Come to think of it, she'd never even seen the man with a pet. Did he even have one?

Were he and Lina having a tryst? That would be embarrassing to barge in on.

Maybe Jameson was as big a player as Victor. Kitty was going to have to warn Fran about that. Kitty moved to the salon door and slowly turned the knob, hoping not to make a sound. Whatever was going on inside and whoever was doing it, she wanted to catch them unawares. The front room was empty. The light was coming from the lamp on Lina Dolofino's desk, which Jameson stood over, his hands shuffling through some papers. His back was turned slightly away from her. Several drawers hung open as if he'd searched them. There was a half-smoked cigarette between his lips.

'You're not supposed to be doing that.' Kitty turned up her nose at the acrid odor of tobacco smoke.

Jameson jumped and his pupils dilated. 'Oh, it's you.' The stub of his cigarette danced between his lips.

'There's no smoking allowed in the resort.'

He snatched the remains of his cigarette from his mouth and squashed it in a Little Switzerland ceramic mug on the desktop. John apologized. 'Sorry. Like I said, I'm trying to quit.' He smiled. 'Promise not to tell?' His gym bag was on the floor beside the waste bin.

'What are you doing here?'

He came toward the door and for a minute Kitty worried for her safety. Should she really have come into this empty office alone and confronted a possible killer? He already looked at the very least like a burglar.

She held her breath as Jameson came toward her and only let it out again as he passed by into the front room. 'I was looking for the groomer. I wanted to check on my appointment.'

Kitty glanced at the desk quickly then turned her attention to John. She didn't like the idea of having her back to the guy no matter how smitten with him Fran might be.

'You know, I've never seen you with your pet. What sort of animal do you have, Mr Jameson?'

'A pit bull.' He must have seen the look on Kitty's face because he asked, 'What's wrong?'

'Pit bulls can be quite dangerous.'

'Yes, they can.' His eyes locked onto hers for a moment. 'But not Hugo. He'd never hurt anyone.' His hands played over the edge of the grooming table. 'Unless he thought that someone was trying to hurt me.'

Kitty nodded. 'Like Victor Cornwall hurt you?'

His brow shot up. 'Whatever do you mean, Kitty?'

'I hear Eliza used to be your wife.' Why was his smile so scary? Did he practice that face in front of a mirror?

He shrugged and stuffed his gloved hands in his pockets. 'It's no secret. As you must know, I told Fran all about it. And she told you. That is who told you, right?'

Kitty nodded.

'So, you see, it's all ancient history. Victor and I may have had our ups and downs but we were friends. I would never kill the man.' He arched an eyebrow as he said, 'Isn't that what you're thinking? You think I killed Victor?'

'I don't know what to think.' Something about this guy made her feel like she was attempting to balance her legs on constantly shifting sands. 'You were the last one to see him alive.'

Jameson pulled another cigarette from the pack in his shirt pocket and held it inches from his lips. His other hand brought out a slender gold lighter. 'Except for the real killer.' He lowered the unlit cigarette. 'You'll excuse me now.' Jameson bowed his head slightly and left quickly.

Kitty exhaled with a whoosh of air. She waited until John turned the corner then went back into Miss Dolofino's office for a closer look around. Whatever Jameson was looking for, he hadn't appeared to have found it before Kitty had arrived. But what had he been looking for? That was the million-dollar question.

She poked around. There was not much on the desk or in the drawers of any significance – a package of butterscotch candies, some hotel stationary, the usual assorted papers and an appointment book, a bottle of hand lotion. Kitty ran her finger down the handwritten list of names. John Jameson's name did not appear on the list of appointments for that day or any day looking forward.

Funny, that.

Her eyes fell on Jameson's gym bag. He'd left it behind. She squatted and slowly unzipped it. A new pair of sneakers rested atop a baggy pair of shorts, a rolled-up pair of socks and a polyester Nike T-shirt. All completely ordinary.

Kitty put everything back in the bag and zipped it shut. She looked at her watch. She still had a little time to herself. If she could track down Lina Dolofino maybe she could come up with an explanation for what John Jameson was doing alone in her salon.

At the very least, the groomer should be made aware of his clandestine activities.

TWENTY-ONE

Kitty rapped on Lina Dolofino's door. She had been told by the spa director that she might find the groomer in her room. She lived in one of the outbuildings, like Howie, the security guard. 'Lina?'

'Hello, Miss Karlyle.' The groomer stood in the doorway, barefoot, looking comfy in a baggy pink sweatsuit. Kitty had seen the exact set of sweats in the gift shop. 'What brings you here?' Her hair was pulled up in a loose knot atop her head.

'Call me Kitty. Everybody does.' Maybe she'd pick up the navy-blue men's set of sweats for Jack as a souvenir of her stay. What better than a Little Switzerland Resort and Spa-branded pair of sweat pants and matching sweatshirt?

'Are Fred and Barney all right? They didn't have a reaction to any of my grooming products, did they? We use only the finest organic and hypoallergenic shampoos and conditioners.'

The woman had gone on the defensive. 'No, it's nothing like that,' promised Kitty, waving her hands. 'Fred and Barney are doing great.' She took a breath and plunged ahead. 'Do you have a minute? Can we talk?'

The groomer seemed to hesitate for a moment then pushed the door open for Kitty. 'Sure, I suppose so. I'm not busy. It's just me and Olivier.'

Kitty craned her neck, trying to see over Lina's shoulder. 'I'm sorry. You have company? I could come back later.' Not that she wanted to.

Lina lightly laughed. 'He's out on the patio. Would you care to meet him?'

Kitty followed Lina out onto the small first-floor patio facing the hotel tennis courts. A couple of mismatched wrought-iron outdoor chairs and a banged-up table, all of which looked like they had seen better days, took center stage. Hotel management had probably retired the castoffs from the paying rooms and recycled them by giving them to their staff.

A pint-sized kiddie pool stood against the far wall with an artificial grass-covered plank leading up and into it. The top half of a cat litter box occupied the corner of the concrete pad.

Lina scratched her head a moment then bent under the table. 'There you are.' When she popped up again she had a beautiful turtle between her hands.

'A turtle.'

Lina grinned. 'Yes, this is Olivier. You thought I was talking about a gentleman, weren't you?'

Kitty nodded.

'Sorry, Olivier here is more my speed these days.' She held his face up to her nose. Olivier didn't seem to mind a bit.

Kitty reached out and stroked its carapace. 'A cooter, isn't it?' The creature was nearly a foot long with a dark mahogany shell, alternately patterned scutes – like turtle-sized plates of armor – and pale pink plastron.

Lina nodded. 'A Northern red-bellied cooter, to be precise.'

'What's wrong with his eye?' The turtle's right eye was misshapen and appeared permanently shut.

'I found Olivier by the side of the road. He'd been struck by a car.'

Kitty's heart went out to the little guy and she said so.

'I took him to a vet who had to stitch up the eye socket. I bartered with him. In exchange for giving Olivier here some medical attention I provided some dog grooming services to his patients' pets for a time.' Lina ran her pinkie gently along the underside of Olivier's neck. 'I'm not sure he could survive on his own in the wild again.' She set Olivier on the ground. 'So I've been taking care of him ever since.'

'That's very sweet of you. He's lucky you rescued him.' Kitty watched the turtle scoot along the ground and head up the ramp. He got around pretty quickly for a one-eyed turtle. Olivier landed in the pool with a splash, swam over to a squat water-soaked log and clawed his way up to sun himself. 'How can you be certain it is a he?'

Kitty didn't know much about turtle anatomy and there wasn't much to see.

'They say that the female's plastron – that's the underside of the shell – is more of a true red.' Lina shrugged. 'Honestly, I simply have no idea. But he hasn't complained about his name yet.' Lina went inside and Kitty followed. 'You wanted to talk to me?' She sat on the edge of her bed and motioned for Kitty to take the chair in the corner.

Kitty admired how well kept Lina's room was. Howie's room was a pigsty in comparison. She folded her hands on her lap. 'How well do you know John Jameson?'

Lina's high forehead furrowed up like a freshly turned fallow field. 'Who?'

'John Jameson – tall, athletic, brown hair. He looks very much like Victor Cornwall, in fact.'

Lina's eyes danced. 'The dead man?'

'That's the one.' Kitty explained how Vic and John had arranged to meet here as friends, how she and Fran had literally bumped into them and then just as unfortunately had literally stumbled on Vic's dead body.

'That's terrible,' said Lina, shaking her head the whole time. She pulled her feet up under her in some yoga pose that Kitty didn't think she could have managed even if her legs had been composed of raw pretzel dough. 'What does this have to do with me? Why do you ask about this Mr Jameson?'

'I saw him in your salon earlier.' Kitty told Lina how she'd been trying to catch up with Jameson to ask him some questions about his relationship with Victor Cornwall. 'Before I could catch him he opened the door to the salon. It didn't appear to have been locked—'

'It never is.'

'—and disappeared inside.'

Lina's back stiffened. 'My salon?'

Kitty nodded. 'I wasn't sure what to do. And for all I knew, you might have been in there.'

'When was this?'

'Right before coming here to see you.'

Lina shook her head. 'I've been here for a couple of hours. I don't have any appointments until mid-afternoon.' Her face looked troubled. 'Is he there now?'

It was Kitty's turn to shake her head. 'No. I waited a few moments then crept inside to see what he was up to. Believe me, if I'd seen that he was there meeting you I would have left immediately.'

'Of course,' Lina said, dismissing Kitty's apology. 'What was he doing?'

'He told me he was checking the appointment book for his pit bull's session with you,' Kitty replied.

'I don't believe I have a Jameson on the schedule for today, nor a pit bull.'

Kitty didn't add that Lina didn't have a Jameson on the schedule for at least the next week. If she'd told the groomer that she'd know she'd been snooping as well.

'That makes sense. When I was secretly watching him he was riffling through the papers on your desk. It looked like he'd been poking around your office, nosing around in your drawers.'

'Why?' Lina unlocked her legs and her feet hit the ground.

Kitty had no answer.

'We must go.' Lina jumped off the bed. She hurried to the front, where she slipped on a pair of sandals, pulled open the door and beckoned for Kitty to follow.

Arriving at the salon, Lina flipped on the lights. All was quiet and there was no sign of John Jameson. Kitty wondered if he might have come back after Kitty left. She may have caught him before he was finished doing whatever it was that he was meaning to do.

'Everything looks in place out here,' Lina said, walking slowly around the grooming station.

'Do you have any idea what he might have been looking for? Is there anything here worth stealing?'

Lina laughed. 'See for yourself. Nothing but hotel towels and supplies. We don't even have a lock on the door.' She showed Kitty, running her hand over the smooth doorknob. 'I can't imagine any of our guests being so hard up as to need to steal the shampoos and soaps.'

Kitty had to agree. It just didn't make sense.

Lina's hand strolled down the pages of her appointment book. 'As I said, there is no appointment for a John Jameson or a pit bull.'

Kitty snapped her fingers. 'The dogs!'

Lina's eyes shot up.

'Don't you see?' said Kitty. 'It's the dogs.'

'I don't understand,' Lina answered, straightening her desk and firmly shutting all the drawers. 'What dogs?'

'Victor's dogs,' Kitty said. 'The two poodles that you were keeping an eye on until his wife, Eliza Cornwall, showed up to claim them.'

Lina pursed her lips. 'I still don't quite understand.'

Kitty took Lina's hands. 'Not only did you have the dogs, you had their things. Their beds, their toys . . .' Kitty's eyes lit up. 'The dog collars.' She'd remembered seeing a fat diamond-studded collar on each poodle. 'Do you have them?' Kitty's heart sank. 'No, wait. Mrs Cornwall has the dogs now. And the collars.'

'No.' Lina hurried out to the front room. There was a granite counter with cabinets above, doors below and a deep sink in the middle. To the left and right of the cabinets were shelves stocked with hotel-branded products – shampoos, conditioners, ointments, nail polish, mouthwash, powders, potions and lotions. All of it for pets.

Lina pulled open the door under the sink, slid out a yellow bin, reached in and lifted up a plastic bag.

'The collars.' Kitty's fingers touched the stones through the plastic.

Lina nodded. 'The police had confiscated the collars. I guess they were looking for fingerprints or bloodstains, or DNA or something. Like you see on TV.' She handed the bag to Kitty for inspection. 'When they were finished, they brought them to me. The police thought I still had Mr Cornwall's dogs but his wife had already come to get them. There was no answer when I phoned her but I left a message for her that she could come and fetch the collars anytime.'

Kitty fondled the collars. 'Do you suppose they're real?' She looked up at Lina. 'The stones, I mean?' Rows of small, glittering diamonds were held together on a band of white gold. If the gold and diamonds were all real – and knowing Victor Cornwall as well as she suspected she did, she figured they would be – then these dog collars would be worth big bucks. Enough money to kill somebody over.

'I'm afraid I have no idea,' Lina answered. 'I think it's time these went to Mrs Cornwall. I don't want to keep them here any longer. Not that I relish having to see that woman again.'

Kitty agreed with both statements. 'She's not a very pleasant woman, is she?'

Lina laughed. 'Not very.'

'What about her husband, Mr Cornwall?'

Lina shut the cabinet door and dropped the bag with the collars onto the grooming table. 'He brought Mercedes and Benz in every day. He was meticulous in taking care of those poodles. They were very much prized possessions.'

Kitty didn't doubt that for a minute. Men like Victor Cornwall were notoriously into their prized possessions, whether it was dogs, horses, yachts, cars or even women.

Like the former Mrs Cornwall. Had she been nothing more than a prized possession that Victor had stolen from John? A man doesn't like it when another man steals his possessions. John might not have come to Little Switzerland intending to murder Victor Cornwall but something inside the man might have snapped. Had John found himself unable to endure seeing Victor Cornwall with his ex-wife?

'Did you ever invest in one of Mr Cornwall's financial schemes?'

Lina's exotic laugh filled the room. 'I've never made enough money to risk losing in a late-night TV scam.'

'I'm sorry.' Kitty blushed. 'I didn't mean to offend you.'

'No offense taken. I didn't become a pet groomer for the money.'

Kitty understood completely. When she'd started her gourmet pet chef business she had known that the odds of getting rich were astronomically against her. The odds of merely keeping food on her own table were almost as astronomical. She had to thank her lucky stars that the cooking show had come along when it did. 'I could take those collars to Eliza for you.' It would give Kitty the perfect excuse to speak with the former Mrs Cornwall again.

Lina handed Kitty the baggy. 'Sure, why not?'

Kitty stuffed it in her purse before the groomer could change her mind. She had a million questions running around in her head. And every time she asked one of her suspects a question, another million questions sprung up like nasty leaks.

It was time to track down Eliza Cornwall and see if she could finally come up with some answers for a change. As she stepped out into the hall she realized the one thing she had not seen in the salon: John Jameson's gym bag.

It had gone.

TWENTY-TWO

'Miss Karlyle.' Eliza Cornwall stood in the entry to her suite, holding the door open with one icy hand. The slinky black knee-length number holding her hourglass figure together looked more like man-eating than mourning wear. 'We were all expecting to hear from you after the movie.'

'Sorry about that. My room had been burgled.'

'How dreadful. Was anything taken?'

'Not that I could tell,' Kitty replied. Steve and Greg had both threatened to scalp her over missing the Q&A but so far she still had all her hair. 'May I speak with you a moment, Eliza?'

Eliza's lower lip turned upward. 'I'm rather busy. I was getting ready to go out.' Nonetheless, she beckoned Kitty inside. 'What is this about?' She went to the bathroom and Kitty reluctantly followed. Eliza was gazing at her reflection in the wall-to-wall mirror. Mrs Cornwall's reflection looked at Kitty and said, 'You wouldn't be interested in purchasing Mercedes and Benz, would you?'

It took Kitty a second to realize the woman was talking about the poodles and not the luxury cars, not that she was sure which would have set her back more money. 'No. I'm afraid I couldn't. I have my own pets and not a lot of extra space.'

Eliza shrugged, reached into her black satin makeup bag and pulled out a small vial of perfume.

Kitty unclasped her purse and pulled out the Ziploc bag. 'I brought the dogs' collars for them. Where are they?' She'd spotted their beds but not the poodles.

'Dog-sitter,' Eliza replied. 'Like I said, I'm meeting someone. Why do you have their collars?'

'The police returned them to the hotel staff after checking them for fingerprints or something, I guess.' Kitty held out the bag. 'The groomer had them and I offered to bring them over. I thought you'd be anxious to have them back.'

Eliza's eyes went briefly to the bag. 'Toss them on the bed on your way out, would you, dear?'

Toss them on the bed? Diamond-encrusted gold collars? Just like that? Maybe they weren't so valuable after all. Mrs Cornwall certainly didn't seem relieved or particularly happy to have gotten the collars back. Kitty held onto the plastic bag. 'They are beautiful.' Even in the bathroom light the diamonds flashed brilliantly.

Eliza shrugged and twisted the tiny silver cap off the crystal perfume bottle. 'I suppose.' She laid her pinkie over the open top and tipped the bottle briefly, just enough to wet her fingertip. 'If there's nothing else' – she turned to Kitty, seemingly forcing herself to take her eyes off her own reflection – 'I am running late.'

Who was Eliza meeting? Could it be her former husband, John? Were they accomplices in Victor Cornwall's murder? 'Eliza, do you have any idea who might have wanted to harm your husband?'

She laughed. 'You're joking, right?'

Kitty wasn't and said so.

'Vic had a list of enemies the proverbial mile long. If you don't believe me, ask the police – or Vic's former office assistant. She kept a record of every anger-driven wacko that sent him a threatening letter or email.' She paused for a beat. 'Like your friend, Fran Earhart. The police asked me about her.' She shook her head. 'Like it was Vic's fault her family and the rest of them lost all their money.'

'Wasn't it?'

'They were all grown men and women. Vic sold them something to believe in.' She turned back to her reflection. 'If they couldn't make it work that was their problem. Not Vic's, not mine.' OK, so Eliza Cornwall was not the most sympathetic creature walking the face of the earth.

Eliza looked at her finger. Most of the perfume seemed to have evaporated. She picked up the bottle and repeated the process, ending up with a drop on her pinkie once again. 'Vic paid for it with a stint in prison and millions of dollars in forced restitution. If anyone had a right to be angry it was Vic and me. We lost nearly everything. Those people cost us millions.'

Kitty tried to show some sympathy but it wasn't easy and she wasn't sure if she was succeeding or even wanted to.

'We have to live in a gated community with twenty-four-hour armed security to keep some distance between ourselves and those people. Do you know how expensive that is?'

Wow, thought Kitty, talk about a rough life. Not.

Eliza lifted her right pinkie and rubbed it behind her right ear. She then quickly repeated the process for the left.

'What about Mr Jameson?'

'John?' She looked doubly amused now. 'Do you think John might have murdered Vic?'

'He did have reason to hate him.'

Eliza laughed. 'Because of me, you mean.' She'd said it as a statement of fact, not a question. 'John had his chance.' She fastened a pair of platinum earrings then suddenly paled and braced her hands against the bathroom counter.

'What's wrong?' Kitty was suddenly alarmed. Eliza did not look well at all. 'Are you all right?'

Eliza began wheezing and her eyes looked imploringly toward Kitty before rolling up inside her eyelids and disappearing from view.

Mrs Cornwall collapsed in a heap to the floor. Kitty knelt down beside her and felt her wrist. There was a pulse but it was weak. 'Eliza!'

Kitty cradled Mrs Cornwall's head in her lap and dialed 911.

TWENTY-THREE

'Let me get this straight, Karlyle,' Chief Mulisch began. He paced side to side in the small visitors' lounge, occasionally pausing to stop and hitch up his belt. 'You went to Mrs Cornwall's hotel suite?'

'To return Mercedes' and Benz's collars.'

'Right, to return those dog collars.' The collars in question sat on the table beside Kitty. She hadn't felt comfortable leaving them lying around Eliza's room with no one there to keep an eye on them. At the very least she felt they ought to be locked in the hotel safe.

But there had been no time for that. The ambulance had arrived and Eliza Cornwall had been whisked to the Little Switzerland Medical Center, a surprising non-Alpine themed brick facility on the opposite end of town. Kitty had followed in her own car.

It hadn't taken Chief Mulisch long to show up at the medical center with Deputy Nickels in tow and start quizzing her. Unfortunately Kitty had very few answers and this was only making the chief angrier.

'Why you and not the groomer?' The chief didn't give her time to answer. 'Why always you? Everywhere I turn?'

'We've been over this and over this. I've told you everything I know.' She wished Deputy Nickels was asking the questions. He was so much nicer; maybe he'd acquired better people skills due to his day job as a pharmacist. But Chief Mulisch had sent him to the nurses' station to get some data for the police report.

Chief Mulisch scowled. 'I don't like it, is all. First Mr Cornwall gets himself killed in my town.' He turned his gaze toward the ER doors. 'And now his wife is in the ICU and you're in the thick of it. Again. Something stinks and it ain't Swiss cheese.'

A doctor came out of the ICU and approached the chief. He whispered something that Kitty couldn't catch but he was definitely talking about Eliza. She'd heard that much.

Chief Mulisch nodded and the doctor retreated.

Kitty stood. 'Is Mrs Cornwall going to be all right?'

Chief Mulisch appeared to be considering whether or not he wanted to share. Had he been that way on the playground as a child, too? Kitty held his gaze. Finally he said, 'She's got some sort of acute peanut allergy. Went into anafractal—' He fumbled for words.

'Anaphylactic shock?' Kitty finished for him.

'Yeah,' he said with a raised eyebrow. 'That's it. How'd you know?'

'I know a thing or two about food.' Did he think she'd been responsible for Eliza's condition just because she knew what it was called? 'As a chef,' Kitty explained, 'I need to know such things. A severe peanut allergy can be deadly.'

Chief Mulisch wrapped his arms around his chest. 'Can it now?'

He was eying her with a renewed interest that was making Kitty uncomfortable. She found herself taking a small step backward – out of the possible reach of handcuffs and Taser guns. 'The perfume!'

'Pardon?' said Mulisch.

'Eliza was applying perfume,' Kitty explained, 'first to her finger, then behind her ears. Like this.' Kitty went through the motions, dabbing her finger behind each ear.

'Where's this bottle now?'

Kitty shrugged. 'Still in her room, I suppose. I didn't touch it.'

'I'll send a man over to pick it up. That bottle could be evidence. It might even have some fingerprints on it. And if any of those prints aren't Mrs Cornwall's they might lead us to a suspect. Nickels!' He called the deputy over and explained the situation. 'I want you to get over to the resort and bag that bottle of perfume.'

'Will do.' Deputy Nickels stood between Chief Mulisch and Kitty. He held a small top-folding notebook in his right hand. 'Peanut allergy, eh?' His head bobbed up and down. 'Nasty business, that. I expect she'll recover with no serious side effects.'

'You really think so?' Kitty asked.

'Oh, sure. With the proper treatment she'll be good as new.'

'That is what the doc told me,' Chief Mulisch acceded.

'What about Victor Cornwall?' asked Kitty. Maybe she could find out something new about who or what killed the man. After all, they were in such a touchy-feely-sharing moment. It was a real lovefest. 'Any news on the case?'

Deputy Nickels snorted. 'Does anybody even care? He'll be in the ground in a couple of days and I expect that most of the people who show up to see him go in the ground will be there to make sure that he not only goes in but stays in.'

Kitty was shocked. Where had *that* come from? Deputy Nickels had seemed so calm and collected the other night, practically Buddha-like. Why the change?

'Now, Jerry Lee, that's no way to talk about the dead,' Chief Mulisch said. 'Even if you did lose a few dollars in one of the man's schemes.'

'A few dollars?' Deputy Nickels said. 'You call Jennie and me losing our condo *a few dollars*?'

'Where's your friend, Ms Earhart?' Chief Mulisch asked Kitty.

'Why, you don't think Fran had anything to do with what happened to Mrs Cornwall, do you?'

He shrugged noncommittally. 'She's got a temper. I found that out when I interviewed the lady.'

Kitty couldn't argue with that. Fran could be volatile at times. But Fran was no killer and Kitty said so. 'This could have been an accident.'

'Maybe,' agreed the chief. 'But I'm not buying it. Ms Earhart had plenty of reasons to hate the deceased and his wife,' Chief Mulisch shot back. 'And she was seen outside the victim's door only minutes before you discovered the body. Pretty convenient, don't you think? Maybe she wanted to give herself the perfect alibi by being there to discover the body with you.'

Kitty wasn't believing that for a minute. 'If we're going to suspect everybody that ever gave money to Victor Cornwall by investing in one of his phony business deals, your jail will never hold them all. I'll bet this county couldn't hold them all.'

She turned to Deputy Nickels. 'It sounds to me like even your own Deputy Nickels here had a pretty good motive to murder Vic. You seem pretty knowledgeable about peanut allergies.'

Deputy Nickel blushed and spluttered, 'Hey, I didn't kill anybody.' He turned to the chief. 'Honest, Chief. You know me.'

'Besides,' said Kitty. She felt a little bad throwing the deputy to the wolves – he seemed like a decent sort – but she had to protect Fran first. 'Victor Cornwall was strong and obviously in top shape. I would imagine it would take a man to have overpowered and strangled him. Not a smaller, lighter woman like Fran.' Her eyes ran up and down the deputy. He certainly looked more Victor's size.

The chief appeared to be doing the same thing as he looked his deputy over. Deputy Nickels looked at them and he appeared nervous. 'Who says he was strangled, anyway?' he sputtered. 'We don't know that.'

'Oh?' Kitty was surprised. 'I just assumed.'

'Yeah, well, there are—'

Chief Mulisch ordered Deputy Nickels to keep quiet. 'We

don't know for certain what killed Victor Cornwall yet. The body's at county. We have not had the results of the full autopsy. Could be another day or two. We do know that his blood alcohol level was through the roof. How much fight does a drunk man have in him? Besides, he was so high he might not even have realized he was being strangled.'

Kitty gave this information some thought. What the chief said was certainly possible. But maybe Victor wasn't drunk. Could Victor Cornwall have been poisoned too? 'Did Victor Cornwall have a peanut allergy?'

The chief rubbed the side of his neck. 'I couldn't tell you that.' His eyes were cold. 'Even if I knew,' he admonished the deputy, 'we are not in the habit of sharing our investigations with cooks.'

'I'm a gourmet pet chef.' Kitty pulled herself up to her full height. Kitty was a stickler about what people labeled her job. Cooks simply threw things together in pans or, worse still, microwave ovens. She prepared meals crafted with love and care and years of experience.

'Well, I've got a Golden Retriever whose quite happy every time I open a can of Alpo,' said the chief. 'Comes running likes he's just won the dog lotto.'

Deputy Nickels laughed. Kitty's face turned the color of an eggplant that had just bounced down two flights of stairs. 'Good night, Chief.'

She turned the corner and stormed out. She'd come back tomorrow during visiting hours to see how Eliza was doing. Maybe Eliza would know who might be trying to bump her off next. Were there any next of kin to consider? Who would inherit the Cornwall's money if both Vic and Eliza were deceased?

As she headed for the door, she heard Deputy Nickels say to Chief Mulisch, 'Yeah. You should've heard what that Chef Moutarde back at the resort had to say about that little girl. He said he'd rather serve his guests' pets Spam than the uninspired meals Ms Karlyle came up with.'

Their crude laughter echoed off the linoleum floor, stinging Kitty's ears. She squeezed her hands together so hard her knuckles turned white as icebergs. Had that bonky Belgian cook really called her food uninspiring? Who did he think he was? And who did Deputy Nickels think he was calling her a *little girl*?

She was going to show them all. She'd solve this case and rub it in their noses like a plate of uninspired *moules frites* – Belgian mussels and fries.

TWENTY-FOUR

Kitty's hand was shaking as she pushed open the door to Eliza Cornwall's hotel suite. It was a nice room – even nicer than hers, with a great view of the mountains. Mercedes and Benz were nowhere in sight. Apparently the dog-sitter was keeping them. Or maybe Lina. She'd done it before. Then again, maybe they were out playing a round of eighteen-hole night-time doggie golf with Audi and BMW filling out the foursome. Anything seemed to be possible at the Little Switzerland Resort and Spa.

Kitty hadn't had much trouble talking Howie into getting her a keycard to Eliza's room. He'd seen the ambulance and heard how Kitty had been with the woman when she'd collapsed. The news had spread quickly among the entire staff. Getting him to believe that the hospitalized woman wanted Kitty to pick up a few things for her from her room had been a piece of cake.

Eliza's bathroom smelled like someone had dropped a flower bomb in it. The small, fancy bottle of perfume lay on its side, its contents spilled out. Kitty bent down and took a sniff. It certainly smelled OK. She knew better than to touch the bottle. The police would be testing it for prints and she didn't want them to find hers. Kitty drew the curtains shut to keep out prying eyes, then examined the room more closely. She'd have to move quickly. Deputy Nickels could show up at any time to collect the potential evidence. How would she explain her presence?

She couldn't.

There was nothing interesting in Eliza's luggage – at least nothing incriminating. There were plenty of outfits that Kitty would have killed to own but nothing that pointed to Eliza being a killer.

Kitty carefully refolded a stunning red maxi-dress with a gold-plate round the neckline when it struck her. These were not grieving widow clothes, these were *I'm on a vacation and I want to look hot clothes.* As evidence, the suitcase contained two bathing suits and a tennis outfit. Apparently Victor's widow was not of the very grieving variety.

Kitty crossed to the king-sized bed where Eliza's black handbag sat on the corner atop the comforter. A lady knows you never look in another woman's purse. It's an unwritten rule. But when you're tracking down a killer you can't always go by the rules.

The purse was a large black leather shopper – you could fit a small dog or a couple of cats inside. Kitty unpeeled the zipper and pulled the sides apart. Wallet, comb, brush, makeup, a few receipts, a plastic bag from a local store that held two unopened pairs of nylons, a ballpoint pen, sunscreen.

Kitty was about to zip the bag shut when her eyes fell on a printed sheet of paper that had been folded over several times. She grabbed it between her fingers and unfolded it carefully. 'A speeding ticket,' she said aloud. There was nothing unusual about that. Except that this ticket was dated three days ago and it had been issued in Santa Barbara. Victor and Eliza lived in Sedona. Eliza said she'd come up *after* receiving the news of her husband's death.

She was lying. But why? What was she hiding?

The suite door rattled as a fist pounded outside. 'Anybody here?'

Kitty gasped then covered her mouth before her heart could escape. It was Deputy Nickels. She could not let him discover her in Eliza's room. She stuffed the speeding ticket in her pocket and dived under the bed. But the bed was having none of it. It had been built on a platform. Kitty cursed. The door was swinging open even as she raced behind the chair in the corner near the drapes.

'Hello?' Kitty could hear the detective as he stepped into the center of the room. She swallowed hard. Please, please, please, she pleaded, do not search the room.

She heard the deputy as he accidently hit the switch for the bathroom fan then turned on the bathroom light. She could see its subtle glow from her hiding place as it washed over the ceiling.

'I don't think the lab's going to find anything on this but what the chief wants, the chief gets.'

There were tiny noises and Deputy Nickels was whistling. Then the soft padding of footsteps in her direction. Kitty froze, willing her heart to stop beating so loudly. To her ears it sounded like a marching band was parading across her tight chest.

'Karma can be a real killer,' Nickels chuckled, 'can't it?' The footsteps stopped nearby, though the whistling continued. Nickels could not have been more than five feet from her. 'Well, well, what have we here?'

Kitty bit her lip and prepared for the worst. He'd found her! 'Mrs Cornwall might want this.'

Kitty watched the purse float upward. A minute later, he was gone. Kitty breathed a long sigh of relief as she heard the satisfying click of the door closing. She gripped the back of the chair and lifted herself up. That had been close – too close. Her legs trembled as she crossed the carpeted floor. Eliza's purse was now gone. So was the bottle of perfume.

Kitty turned her head slowly and looked at the glowing numbers of the clock face. It was nearly one a.m. Chef Henri Moutarde was one of her top suspects – and with that nasty disposition of his, she could only hope he did prove to be the killer. She needed to get a look at the kitchen. There may be some incriminating evidence there. After what had happened earlier, nearly getting caught poking around in Eliza's room, she decided it would be better to wait until the resort was asleep.

She twisted and looked at Fran. Kitty had heard her finally tiptoe in around eleven-thirty and she appeared to be sound asleep now. Fred and Barney were asleep on the sofa. Kitty pulled back the covers and slipped into her shoes, having worn her clothes to bed – a black turtleneck sweater and jeans. Fred lifted his head for a moment as Kitty opened the door but then settled back down. Fred was a Lab, not a night owl.

Sure enough, the halls were deserted but for the occasional TV sounds coming from behind closed doors. A lone clerk manned the registration desk. She waited until his back was turned then crossed the broad lobby to the wing of the hotel that held the main restaurant and other amenities, like the salon and pool.

Kitty knew that the main banquet room, the one they'd been using to film her show, opened in the rear directly into the back of the kitchen. That's where she was heading. If someone was about and saw her enter the restaurant past the hostess station they might get suspicious and report her. She couldn't take that chance.

She pushed open the door. A lone light bulb shone from outside the door to the walk-in fridge. While kitchens normally gave Kitty a warm and fuzzy feeling, this one – maybe it was just because it was the middle of the night – was giving her the creeps. Kitty knew her way around reasonably well. They'd been using this kitchen extensively as a prep area for the show. She crept along in the direction that she was pretty sure she would find the pantry.

Turning the corner and passing a pallet of dry goods waiting to be stored, Kitty noticed a light spilling from an open doorway. She crept to the edge of the door and slowly braved a peek.

Moutarde. What was he doing here at this hour? Three hours after closing?

The chef sat behind a massive oak desk, his chef's coat unbuttoned to the waist, a goblet of a dark liqueur close to hand. His eyes scrolled pages of documents and he had an ugly look on his face. Then again, didn't he always?

Kitty really wanted to get a look in that pantry. If it contained peanut oil, and she suspected it would, then that would give Chef Moutarde the means. All she needed now was a motive. And opportunity. Speaking of opportunity, Kitty could use one now herself. There was no way she could cross in front of Moutarde's open door unseen. She needed a diversion.

Kitty crept back the way she'd come. At the opposite end of the kitchen she knew they kept the dishwashing equipment, like the sinks, glass washer and the twelve-rack pot-and-pan washer. The stainless-steel beauty was just the ticket. It had been a while since she'd handled a commercial pot scrubber but she had little trouble setting the controls by the light of her cell phone. She set the timer to begin a rinse cycle in three minutes, then crept back to a hiding spot behind a pair of large carbon dioxide tanks against the wall near Moutarde's office.

Kitty waited and waited what seemed like an eternity. Finally, the sound of pressurized water moving around inside the dishwasher echoed through the empty kitchen. Moutarde cursed.

At least, she figured it was a curse. It sounded like one. She didn't speak French but the tone seemed clear. She heard the sound of him pushing back his chair. A moment later he came out, looked this way and that and headed toward the sound.

Kitty waited until he was out of sight in the darkness then pushed forward. She had meant to check the pantry first but couldn't resist the open invitation to find out what the chef was doing at his desk at such a late hour.

Financial records lay scattered about. Kitty wasn't good with finances and couldn't make heads nor tails of the numbers. There were several cooking certificates in frames on the wall and behind the desk a framed copy of *Boston Magazine* showed the surly Belgian on its cover. A small photo in a gilt frame on the corner of his desk showed a restaurant called Chez Moutarde. So the chef had once had a restaurant of his own. What was he doing here in Little Switzerland then? Had he been a victim of the economic downturn like so many others and forced to close his doors?

On impulse, she took a picture of the desktop with her phone then, checking to make sure the coast was still clear, headed for the pantry. Once again using the light available to her from the phone's screen, Kitty scanned the rows of products. There had to be peanut oil somewhere, she just knew it.

Then a terrible thought struck her.

How was she going to get out of the kitchen?

Chef Moutarde was not going to stay gone forever. He'd turn off the pot-and-pan washer, maybe poke around a little to be certain nothing else was amiss. Then he'd return to his desk.

She could be stuck here for hours.

The pantry light exploded overhead, bathing the largish room in white light.

'What are you doing here?' Chef Moutarde held a nasty meat cleaver in his right hand. It was the ProChef X15. Sweet blade. Kitty had seen the man chop through pork bone with that cleaver so she knew the damage the chef could do to her with such a weapon.

It didn't look like she was going to need to worry about getting out of the kitchen after all. It was getting out *alive* that might be the problem. She backed into the shelf behind her. A plastic jug teetered on the edge and she caught it in her hands.

Peanut oil, of course . . .

She held the plastic jug between herself and the chef as he stepped closer, the cleaver waving dangerously in front of her nose. Was he about to murder her? Like he had Victor Cornwall?

The chef growled something French at her, his face locked in outrage.

Kitty was certain of it.

This was the end.

TWENTY-FIVE

'Freeze!' Chief Mulisch hollered. His gun was drawn and its black muzzle seemed to fill the pantry.

'Chief!' shouted Kitty. 'Thank goodness you're here. This man was about to kill me.' She jabbed the jug to indicate Chef Moutarde. 'I think he murdered Victor Cornwall, too.'

'Miss Karlyle,' Chief Mulisch said, evenly, 'put down the . . .' He frowned. 'Weapon?' He blinked and lowered his pistol.

Kitty looked at the jug of oil. 'This?' She kept one eye on the armed and dangerous policeman while balancing the oil back on the wire shelf. Chef Moutarde had lowered the cleaver. His arm hung loosely at his side. He bounced the nasty-looking blade up and down in his hand. She didn't know how the chief had gotten here so fast or what he was doing here in the first place, but he was a godsend.

Kitty looked from the chief to Deputy Mulisch, his son, who had accompanied him. 'What are you waiting for?' She looked at both officers. 'Aren't you going to arrest this man?'

Deputy Mulisch looked like he was about to bust out a laugh. One look from his dad seemed to quell the impulse. Chief Mulisch scratched his jaw with the barrel of his weapon. 'Arrest him? Chef Moutarde here is the one who called us. He said someone had broken into the kitchen, causing criminal mischief, ransacking his office—'

'Ransacking his office! All I did was shuffle a few—' Kitty snapped her mouth shut. Of course, this was several seconds too late. Ransacking his office. Please. All she'd done was move a couple of papers around on his desk. She had to give the guy credit for having even noticed. The self-proclaimed Mussels from Brussels had a good eye. Not a great palette, though. Kitty had tasted enough of his food to know that the man relied too much on his fats. And his roux, well, don't even get her started. Roux was the foundation of practically all the major French sauces. His roux was runny and tasted like he substituted recycled newsprint for wheat flour.

Kitty shot Moutarde a dirty look. She needed to do some quick thinking. 'It's not what you think, Chief.' Kitty pleaded with her hands. 'I was . . . I was hungry.' Yeah, that sounded good. 'I was looking for something to eat.'

Chief Mulisch holstered his gun. 'You can tell me all about it down at the station.'

Kitty blanched. 'Y-you're arresting me?' This was so not good. What would Fran think? What about *The Pampered Pet* crew? Steve was going to go supernova. And the brass at CuisineTV. Her nascent TV career could be chopped off as quickly as it had begun. And what about her mom and dad?

Kitty groaned.

What was Jack going to think? Fiancée of a Los Angeles police detective – arrested! It would probably make the front page of the *Little Switzerland Gazette*.

Deputy Mulisch unclipped his handcuffs and stepped forward. The chief put out a hand to stop him. 'Now, now. That won't be necessary, Deputy. Will it, Ms Karlyle?'

Kitty gulped and shook her head no.

'We'll get this all sorted out downtown.' He turned to the chef. 'You'd better come too.'

'*Avec plaisir*,' replied Moutarde.

The police station wasn't so bad. Once you got past the fact that you were under arrest, thought Kitty. The interrogation room was downright cozy. She studied her palms. So why was she sweating?

'Let me get this straight,' Chief Mulisch said, smothering a yawn. His hand reached to his mouth. There were bags under his eyes. Apparently the man did not sleep in his uniform, having tossed on a rumpled flannel shirt and khakis that looked like they'd been spending more time at the bottom of the laundry basket than they had on clothes hangers. A lightweight navy LSPD jacket and black loafers completed the ensemble. 'You went to the pantry at one o'clock in the morning looking for something to eat.' His fingers drummed the tabletop. 'You couldn't, perhaps, have considered checking your minibar?'

Kitty sat across from him at the long wood veneer table. 'Minibar,' she said, forcing a smile. 'Now why didn't I think of that?' Deputy Mulisch was leaning against the front counter on one elbow while conversing with Moutarde. The chef's gestures were animated and he flashed Kitty an angry look now and then. He did it again and she cringed. 'Look, I think that man could be responsible for Victor Cornwall's death *and* Eliza Cornwall's near death,' Kitty whispered, leaning in toward the chief.

'Ms Karlyle.' Chief Mulisch shook his head, the weariness practically dragging his face to the ground. 'We've been over this and over this.' His hands beat the table. 'What possible reason could Chef Moutarde have for killing Victor Cornwall?'

'I don't know yet,' Kitty admitted. 'But I'm going to find out.'

'What's that supposed to mean?' He stood over her. 'You need to leave policing to the police, Ms Karlyle.'

'I'm trying to find a killer for you. And save my friend.' Kitty stared him down. 'I'll do whatever it takes.'

'Maybe a night behind bars will convince you otherwise.' His brow went up two notches.

Ouch. The man was good. 'But the peanut oil,' began Kitty. 'You saw it. Eliza is allergic to peanuts.'

'What I saw was you pilfering the resort pantry in the middle of the night.'

'I told you, I was—'

Their argument came to a halt as a commotion arose outside the door. Both turned. Rick Ruggiero, the resort's manager, was in the lobby. He spoke to Deputy Mulisch then jabbed his finger several times in Chef Moutarde's direction. The chef didn't look happy. But again, that was par for the course. Ruggiero spun on his heel and yanked open the door to the interrogation room without knocking or asking permission to enter. 'Harry, what the devil is going on here?'

Chief Mulisch strode over and rested a hand on the manager's shoulder. 'Calm down, Rick. Everything is under control.'

Ruggiero had an orange-striped pajama top tucked into a pair of relaxed-fit jeans and was wearing a baggy black overcoat. What little hair he had couldn't settle on a direction or a style. 'My night duty clerk called and informed me that Ms Karlyle has been taken into custody! Have you all lost your minds?' He looked accusingly at all three men.

'Now, Harry. Your chef called in a nine-one-one to report somebody skulking around in the kitchen. We found Ms Karlyle in the pantry.' His lip twisted up at the corner in a wry smile. 'She says she was hungry.'

'So?' The manager looked flabbergasted. 'Give her some food, for goodness' sake!' He glanced at Kitty and she dutifully gave him her best innocent and hungry look.

Chief Mulisch shuffled side to side as if balancing on quicksand.

'But she broke into your kitchen, sir,' Deputy Mulisch said. He was in full uniform. Kitty wondered if he had been on duty when the call came in or just liked to play dress up even after hours.

'Broke into?' snorted Ruggiero. 'We don't even keep the kitchen locked up.' He glared at his chef. 'What's to break into?'

'I suppose if the chef doesn't want to press charges . . .' Chief Mulisch looked to the chef.

Ruggiero was looking at the chef too and not very happily. He threw a backhanded wave at Moutarde. 'Of course he doesn't want to press charges. Furthermore,' the manager said, drawing himself up to his full height, 'the Little Switzerland Resort and Spa does not wish to press charges. Ms Karlyle and the crew of *The Pampered Pet* are our special guests. Our *very* special guests.'

Ruggiero turned to Kitty and pressed his hand in hers. 'I apologize sincerely for any inconvenience or embarrassment,' he said, shooting a quick look at the chief, 'this incident may have caused you, Ms Karlyle. If there is anything at all I or my staff can do for you, please do not hesitate to ask.'

Kitty smiled. 'That is very kind of you, Rick, but I'm sure we can put this all behind us.'

'I'm sure the chef is equally sorry for this – this,' he waved his hands in the air, 'misunderstanding. Isn't that right, Moutarde?'

Chef Moutarde muttered something in French then made his reluctant apologies to Kitty.

'Count your lucky stars that Ms Karlyle has such a kind heart, Moutarde. And think twice before calling the police to have one of our guests arrested, would you?'

Moutarde's face heated dark red. 'Of course,' he said with a smile, but there was no hiding his rage – at least not from Kitty.

TWENTY-SIX

K itty slipped off her shoes inside the door. Sleep, all she needed now was sleep. Assuming her rattled nerves would let her get any rest. Her body and soul had been raked over the coals. First Henri Moutarde practically pounces on her with a meat cleaver, then the police drag her down to the police station. That was it. In the next life, if there was one, she was coming back as a tuxedo cat. Preferably one with a Beverly Hills or Bel Air zip code.

Fran's bedside light shot to life. 'Where have you been, young lady?' Fran's arms were folded across her chest and her hair was tucked into a hairnet. She wore a Jamaica Reggae Festival 2003 T-shirt.

'Are you crazy, scaring me like that?' Fred loped over and rubbed against Kitty leg. She nuzzled his nose absently. It helped to calm her nerves.

'Tell me about it.' Fran sounded insulted and more than a little put out. 'I wake up in the middle of the night and you're nowhere to be found. What on earth were you up to?'

Kitty slumped into the side chair near Fran's bed. 'I decided to do a little snooping.'

'Without me?' Fran huffed and pulled off her hairnet.

Kitty shrugged. 'You were sound asleep.' She grinned. 'You came in pretty late yourself. I didn't want to disturb you.'

'Yeah, well, I had dinner with John.'

'Oh, Fran . . .'

'He's a good guy. I can tell.'

Kitty couldn't agree less. Fran was a terrible judge of men. But there was no telling the woman that. It would only make her angrier and more stubborn. Kitty crossed to the sink and poured herself a glass of water, partly out of thirst and partly to keep her friend from seeing the look of disapproval on her face. Her throat was parched and scratchy from all the fast talking she'd had to do.

'So, did you discover anything?'

Kitty poured some water into the pets' bowls while she was at it, then returned to the chair. 'I discovered that the police around here have no sense of humor.' Kitty told Fran how she'd gone to the resort's kitchen in an attempt to look around the pantry and been caught by Chef Moutarde.

Fran listened in wide-eyed disbelief and hooted when Kitty described Henri catching her in his pantry and then Chief Mulisch showing up with his gun drawn.

'It really wasn't all that funny,' Kitty said, holding up her head with her hands. She'd been afraid for her life. Then her freedom.

'I can't believe you went snooping around without me. You know you can count on me. Besides,' she said with a grin, 'I love snooping. Just ask any of my ex-boyfriends.' Fran pushed back the covers. 'Do you really think Henri might have had something to do with Vic's murder?'

'I don't know,' Kitty said through another yawn. 'He's got a temper – we know that. And he admitted that he didn't think much of Victor because he always complained about the food. But is that enough to kill a man over?' The Belgian was certainly hot-headed enough. 'I saw handfuls of financial papers on the chef's desk.' Kitty showed her the picture she'd taken with her phone. Fran couldn't make heads nor tails of the numbers either.

'It does seem a little weird that he'd be hanging around the restaurant in the middle of the night.'

'What are you doing?'

'Let's Google him.' Fran had crossed to the desk and woke her computer tablet. Kitty flicked on the desk lamp. Fran entered the chef's name in the search engine and hundreds of entries appeared. Many were dead ends but there were more than a dozen legitimate hits and Fran scanned each one.

'Here's something,' said Fran. Her fingers paused over the screen, enlarging the news item. 'Henri had a restaurant some years ago in Boston.'

'I know.' She told Fran how she'd seen the cover of *Boston Magazine* in the chef's office and a picture of Chez Moutarde.

'OK,' Fran said, 'but did you know that, according to this article in the *Herald*, he lost that restaurant?'

'Oh?' Kitty leaned in for a closer look, holding her palm up to her mouth to catch a yawn. 'Let me see.'

She scanned the online news article. It seemed that Chef Henri Moutarde had been forced to close his successful eatery due to having used its equity as leverage in a downtown development deal. When the deal went bust, the bank foreclosed on his restaurant. Ouch.

'This article was written when a news writer discovered Henri working as a sous chef at the Omni Parker House Hotel.' Fran tapped the screen, calling up an image of the hotel.

Restaurant owner to hotel sous chef. That was quite a big fall.

'Interesting,' Fran said, tapping a sharp nail against her teeth.

'What?' Kitty asked. Was there something about Victor maybe?

'The Omni Parker House is supposed to be the home of the Parker House roll *and* Boston cream pie.'

'Oh.' Kitty fell to the edge of the bed, exhausted. She reached out and rubbed her aching feet. A glance at the bedside clock informed her that it was now three-fifty in the morning. 'We may as well get to bed – try to get at least a couple hours rest in before this *vacation* continues.'

'Here's something else.' Fran's hand traced the screen.

Kitty raised an eyebrow. 'Yes?'

'It says here that Ho Chi Minh was a baker at the Parker House and Malcom X was a busboy.'

Kitty shook her head. 'OK, now you're just making things up. Please, turn that thing off and get some sleep.'

'I'm not making anything up.' Fran thrust the tablet under Kitty's nose, forcing her to look. 'JFK had his bachelor party there.' Fran jiggled an eyebrow. 'Wish I could have been there to see that.'

Kitty's eyes scanned back and forth. Interesting, but it wasn't going to help her solve Victor Cornwall's murder. Not unless Victor Cornwall's murder was somehow tied into the JFK conspiracy. She rather doubted it.

The next morning, groggy despite two cups of strong in-room coffee courtesy of Wolfgang Puck, Kitty sat back down at the desk. She pulled a pad of resort stationary from the drawer and a pen.

Fran came out of the shower, bundled in a frothy white robe, her hair wrapped in a white towel. 'What are you up to?'

Kitty ran the tip of the pen over her lower lip. 'I'm making a list of suspects and possible motives.'

Fran sat down on Kitty's unmade bed and crossed her legs. 'Who've you got so far?' She pulled a bottle of the resort's free lotion from the pocket of the robe and began rubbing her legs down, first the right, then the left.

'Besides you, you mean?' Kitty's face broadened into a wicked smile.

'Very funny.' Fran pulled a face. 'You should be a comedian rather than a gourmet pet chef,' she said, putting air quotes around gourmet pet chef.

'I'm putting Colonel Mustard at the top of my list.' Kitty diligently wrote out the chef's name.

'You're just mad because the guy went after you with a meat cleaver.'

'Gee, you think?' cracked Kitty. 'He had the means and the motive. All we need now is opportunity.' She turned to Fran. 'Who's next?'

Fran thought a moment, tossing the empty lotion bottle in the trash bin. 'John Jameson, I suppose.' She frowned. 'I don't believe it for a second, though.'

Kitty jotted down his name. 'He had the motive and his ex was Vic's current wife, not to mention he'd lost a bundle of money because of Vic. That's a double motive in my book.'

'I don't know,' quipped Fran. 'You've seen Eliza Cornwall.

You've talked to her. The man might have been happy to see her go. That woman is a piece of work.'

Kitty pouted. Fran had a point. But still. 'Speaking of Eliza . . .' She dug into her purse and handed a slip to Fran.

Fran unfolded it. 'What's this?'

'It's a speeding ticket that Eliza received.'

Fran looked only mildly interested.

'She received that ticket,' said Kitty, tapping the back of the paper with her finger, 'two days before her husband was murdered.'

'So?'

'Read where she got the ticket.'

'Santa Barbara.' Fran shrugged. 'Yeah?'

Kitty waited.

'Oh, Santa Barbara.'

Kitty nodded. 'Eliza told us she'd been in Sedona when she'd gotten the call that her husband had been killed and that she'd drove out west afterward. But,' said Kitty, clasping her knees, 'Santa Barbara's not more than an hour's drive from here. If Eliza was already in the area she had plenty of opportunity to kill her husband. She could have been waiting for him back in his suite.'

'And when he showed up,' said Fran, picking up the thread of the conversation, 'she strangles him or bops him on the head or something.'

'Exactly,' concluded Kitty.

Fran agreed that it was very interesting indeed. Then her face fell.

'What's wrong?'

'You forgot one thing. The police telephoned Vic's wife to break the news to her about her husband.' Fran bit her cheek. 'She would have to have been home in Arizona then to receive that call. It looks like she has an alibi after all. You can't be in two places at once.'

Kitty was shaking her head. She rummaged in her purse and pulled out her cell phone.

Fran smiled. 'Of course.' Eliza could have said she was in Sedona, Arizona. But she could have been in or near Little Switzerland, California the entire time. 'That makes three –

Jameson, Moutarde and the ex-Mrs Cornwall. Who else have you got?'

Kitty tapped her teeth with the pen. 'You're going to laugh but hear me out.'

Fran's brow dug up furrows.

'Jerry Lee Nickels.'

'Deputy Nickels?' Fran asked dubiously. 'LSPD Deputy Nickels?'

Kitty explained her reasoning and Fran agreed that she might be onto something. 'You should have heard the man,' Kitty said. 'He has a lot of pent-up anger at Victor Cornwall.'

'Him and me both,' admitted Fran. She pointed to the paper. 'Put Nickels' name down.'

As Kitty dutifully wrote the deputy's name next on her list and added a few notes, Fran went to answer the knock at the door.

TWENTY-SEVEN

'Can I come in?'

Kitty swiveled the desk chair around as Ted Atchison strode into the room. Fran had left the door open. He was carrying a small tray holding several cups of coffee and scones wrapped in paper. It all smelled heavenly. 'Sure – I never say no to a man bearing gifts. Especially when those gifts include fresh hot coffee and pastry.'

Fran, walking behind Ted and carrying an ice bucket, shrugged for Kitty's benefit then cinched the belt of her robe tighter around her waist.

'Good morning, Ted.' Kitty maintained a poker face. She glanced at the list on the desk. She'd forgotten to add the mysterious Mr Atchison to her list. 'Those are for us, right?'

He held out the tray. 'Of course. Treats for the sweets,' he said with a smile. He wore denim jeans, hiking boots and a loose-fitting Dodgers sweatshirt.

'Thank you.' Kitty grabbed a cup of coffee and popped the lid, letting the steam rise to her nose and tickle her senses with the scent of dark roasted beans. 'What's the occasion?'

'No occasion. Have a scone,' offered Ted.

Kitty carefully selected an orange-cranberry creation, while Fran chose the blueberry.

'I heard what happened last night,' Ted explained. He helped himself to the last scone – cinnamon crunch. 'I figured you must be exhausted.' He flashed his most alluring smile. Kitty had to admit, the man could turn on the charm. Not like Jack, but not bad. Not bad at all.

Nonetheless, Kitty was alarmed. Had the little incident last night made the news? Who had blabbed? How much trouble was she in with the crew and the network? She was surprised Steve Barnhard hadn't already been down here banging on her door to be let in so he could admonish her.

'I ran into the guy working the front desk last night. He mentioned it. He told me how the police had been called and the next thing he knew you and Henri Moutarde were heading down to the police station with Chief Mulisch and his deputy.' Ted took a slow sip of his coffee and smacked his lips. 'What happened?'

Kitty breathed a sigh of relief. The news hadn't spread far. Hopefully Rick Ruggiero would keep it from going any further. Maybe she would have to have a word with him about that. She could ask him to keep his staff in check. She didn't want the little episode to become general knowledge. 'Nothing, really. It was all a misunderstanding.'

Fran signaled Kitty.

'What is it, Fran?'

'Can you help me get these curlers out of my hair?' She patted the towel on her head.

Kitty's nose wrinkled up but she followed Fran to the bathroom. Fran closed the door behind them. 'Curlers? What curlers?'

Fran placed her hand over Kitty's mouth. 'Shh. Keep your voice down.'

Kitty lowered her voice. 'What's going on?'

'I don't want Ted to hear.'

'Hear what?' Kitty was growing exasperated and her coffee was out there growing cold.

'I don't think you should be telling Ted anything,' Fran said. 'What's he doing here anyway?'

'You heard him. He said he learned what happened and brought us some coffee. And scones. They're delicious, by the way. I'm going to have to meet the resort's baker. Do you think they'll share the recipe? Mine always turn out so flat by comparison.'

'I don't trust him.' Fran pulled out her mascara and fiddled with the cap.

'Now that you mention it . . .' said Kitty, her voice trailing off.

Fran spun around. 'What is it? Spill it, girl.'

Kitty explained her trip into town, how she'd gone to the dog shelter and learned that Ted Atchison had only adopted his dog Chloe the other day.

Fran was smirking. 'I knew it,' she whispered. 'He's up to something. Ted Atchison could be our murderer.' She glanced at the closed door. Kitty followed suit.

'But why?' asked Kitty. 'What would his motive be?'

Both women thought in silence. 'Face it,' said Kitty, 'sometimes coffee is simply coffee.'

'Everything all right in there?' called Ted.

'One sec—' Kitty called.

The women returned. Fran's hair was still wrapped in the towel. 'False alarm,' she said, patting the towel atop her head then biting down into her blueberry scone.

'As I was saying,' began Kitty, 'it was all a misunderstanding. I was out for a stroll. I couldn't sleep. You know how it is and I, we, the chef and I, thought we heard a burglar.'

'A burglar, eh?' Ted's brow went up. 'Where? What do you suppose they were after?'

'I don't know. I mean, nothing.' Kitty pulled a piece off her scone and tossed it in her mouth. 'Like I said,' she swallowed, 'it was all a misunderstanding.'

'Got it.' Ted had polished off his scone. 'Well, gotta go,' he said, glancing at his watch. 'I'll see you two later. Are you coming to the carnival?'

'Carnival?'

'Hadn't you noticed? It's part of the New-Age/New-Pet Conference. They've set up a small carnival on the other side of the resort. I hear there will be rides for pets, mostly designed for the man's best friend variety, I'm sure.'

'I'm sure,' replied Kitty. 'Speaking of which, how's your dog?'

'Great, great.' Ted laced his fingers through his hair.

'The two of you seem to have such a close bond. I guess it comes from being together so long.'

'You bet.' A slight redness came to the sides of his face, highlighting his nose by its pasty and prominent comparison. Ted cleared his throat. 'Well, like I said, gotta run.'

'Thanks for the scone,' Fran said, crumbs falling from the corners of her mouth as she spoke.

Kitty drummed her fingers on the desk.

'Well, that was weird,' Fran said after Ted Atchison had gone.

'Weirder than you think,' Kitty replied.

'What do you mean?'

Kitty turned and waved for Fran to look at the desktop. A blank-sheeted notepad looked back. 'All my notes are gone.'

Both women looked at the closed door, while Kitty wondered what Ted had wanted with her notes and list of suspects.

TWENTY-EIGHT

The ladies took Fred and Barney to a late breakfast. The scones had been delicious but not enough to fill either woman's appetite that morning. Kitty ate poorly, however, because she couldn't stop looking around to see if Chef Moutarde was creeping up behind her with a meat cleaver in his hand.

'Is your baker in the kitchen?' Kitty asked.

'I'm afraid he's left for the day,' replied their waiter.

'Too bad. I wanted to convey my compliments on his baking skills. The scones we had this morning were the best I've ever had.'

'I'll tell him you said so. I'm sure he'll be very pleased.'

'Tell me,' Kitty added, 'is Chef Moutarde in this morning?'

The waiter said he had not seen the chef and didn't seem too happy to hear the Belgian's name.

'Tough man to work for?' Kitty asked with a smile.

'Almost as tough as the rib-eye he serves up,' quipped the young waiter.

'That bad, huh?' Fran said between sips of black coffee.

The waiter shrugged and looked to the side. 'Maybe I shouldn't say anything. I've worked for worse.'

Kitty followed the young man's gaze. Rick had come into the dining room and was speaking with the hostess, his hand resting lightly on her shoulder. 'Has the chef worked here long?'

'Longer than me, and I've been here two years. He and the manager go way back.'

'Really?' Kitty was surprised. The way Rick was laying into the chef last night sure hadn't given her the impression that the two were friends. Of course, just because they had a history together didn't mean it was a friendly one. But still . . .

The manager glanced over at their table and waved. The waiter suddenly appeared antsy. 'Is there anything else I can get you?' He dropped a dog biscuit in front of Fred, a tuna treat down for Barney and set a small chocolate mint next to each woman's plate.

When Kitty said no, he quickly totaled up their bill and departed. 'Did you see that?' She unpeeled her mint and popped it in her mouth.

'You mean the way the kid clammed up when the manager showed up?' Fran pushed the bill toward Kitty. 'No, I didn't see a thing.'

'Very funny.'

'Maybe he's afraid that the manager will think he's slacking off?'

'You're right. It could be perfectly normal. But I forgot to put the manager on our list of suspects.' The list that Ted Atchison had stolen.

How could she have forgotten her suspicions about the manager? 'Remember,' she said, 'I saw Rick near our room right before I discovered it had been ransacked.'

Fran nodded. 'You also made a good point,' she said, jabbing her fork in the manager's direction, 'when you said that Ruggiero's got a master key to this whole place.'

Their eyes clung to Rick as he left through a side entrance. Now that Kitty had time to think, he had seemed awfully anxious to keep Kitty out of the clutches of the police last night. Was he simply being kind to a guest? Or did he have some ulterior motives of his own? Were he and Henri Moutarde hiding something? Were the two men afraid that Kitty was getting too close?

'Maybe they were stealing from the resort and Victor Cornwall stumbled onto them as they were hauling caviar out the back door or something,' suggested Kitty.

'Stranger things had been known to happen,' agreed Fran. 'They could be skimming. Selling food supplies out the back door or buying them cheaper than what the books show.'

Did they suspect that Kitty might know something, whether she knew what the something was or not? Did they fear she might inadvertently say something to the police that would lead back to them?

Kitty signed for the check and stood. Sitting here wasn't going to solve anything. Kitty and Fran split up in the lobby, agreeing to meet later for lunch in town. It was an off day for the show so she could do as she pleased.

Almost.

Fran said she was going to do some sightseeing, which mostly meant shopping. Kitty had a session with Dr Newhart scheduled and she knew that if she bailed on it that Steve would rake her over the coals. She would be seeing him this evening because he'd made her promise to make up for missing the last post-movie Q&A session with the public by attending tonight's movie.

Not only had she agreed to speak afterward, she'd agreed, with some arm twisting, to make treats for the pets attending the showing. Chef Moutarde would be preparing the snacks for the people in attendance. She wondered what he would do. Certainly not something as mundane as popcorn. Too pedestrian for the likes of the Belgian chef. Whatever he served, she was determined that what she made for the pets would be better. And definitely, absolutely, it was going to be more *inspired* than whatever he dished out.

Kitty was not looking forward to seeing the chef again but she was looking forward to the movie, *Lady and the Tramp*. She had made Jack watch it – twice – and liked to think that if they were cartoon dogs, that's the two they would be.

She ran into Steve and Roger coming out of Dr Newhart's suite as she was going in. Their two Corgis were with them, dancing between their feet. 'What are you doing here? Checking up on me?'

It was Roger who answered. 'When Steve told me about your sessions with Doctor Newhart,' he laid a hand on Steve's arm, 'I told him that I thought it would be great for us, too.'

They departed and Kitty flopped down on the sofa.

'Tired?' asked Dr Newhart. The poor man was wearing a coat and tie again. Didn't he ever let go?

Kitty nodded. 'It's all this murder and mayhem. Victor Cornwall gets himself killed, his wife gets poisoned and my room gets ransacked.'

Dr Newhart took a seat across from her and folded his hands on his lap. 'It is difficult, yes. But it is important that you try to put all of these troubles out of your mind.' He gestured toward Kitty's animals. 'Be more like Fred and Barney. Free yourself.'

Kitty eyed her pets. Fred was already stretched out on the warm rug, his paws under his jowls. Barney was in some weird yoga pose licking his tail. Life should be so easy.

Dr Newhart fished in his jacket pocket. 'I wanted to give you this.' He held out a folded sheet of lined yellow paper.

Kitty reached out and took it. 'What is it?'

'I have another referral for you.'

Kitty unfolded the paper. 'Bobby Bridges and Traci Nelson?'

He nodded.

'*The* Bobby Bridges and Traci Nelson?' Bobby was a member of a famous Hollywood acting family with a long line of stars. Traci was a television star on a popular comedy.

'That's right. They're here at the resort with their dogs, a pair of brother and sister Irish setters. They attended the taping of your show which they enjoyed very much. They would like you to cook for them.' He paused for a beat. 'If you're interested? I know how busy you are with the show—'

'No, no, of course I'm interested,' Kitty replied quickly. 'The show only tapes one or two days a week. Besides, who knows how long *The Pampered Pet* will last? This is show business – things get cancelled all the time.' She had lived in Hollywood's shadow long enough to know the truth of that. It was a ruthless business. She stuffed the paper in her pocket. 'I hadn't even noticed Traci and Bobby in the audience.'

'They were in disguise.'

Kitty could understand that perfectly. The little bit of celebrity she had recently acquired due to the TV show was already wearing thin. 'But why did they ask you to give me their contact info?'

Dr Newhart tugged at his collar. 'They – their dogs, I should say – are clients of mine. I suppose Bobby and Traci wanted to check with me first. Of course, I was happy to recommend you.'

'Thank you,' said Kitty. 'I really appreciate this. You say they have two Irish setters?'

He offered Kitty a cup of tea and she declined. He poured himself a cup as he replied. 'Yes. Beautiful animals. You'll adore them.' He returned to his seat.

'I'm sure I will.'

'So, Kitty,' the doctor said, squeezing a thin slice of lemon over his cup and stirring, 'tell me about your relationship with Fred and Barney? Is it amicable?'

'Amicable?' Kitty looked from Dr Newhart to her pets and back again. 'Sure, I mean, they're a cat and a dog.' She smiled. 'A lot easier to get along with than people, right?'

Dr Newhart cocked his head. 'Oh?'

Realizing she'd said the wrong thing, Kitty cleared her throat and tried again. This time she'd go on the offensive. She glanced out the window then looked him in the eye. 'Doctor Newhart, I was wondering . . .'

'Yes?'

'Did you ever invest in one of Victor Cornwall's schemes?'

Dr Newhart laughed, his perfect white teeth flashing. That was the first time Kitty had ever seen that. She didn't think he had it in him. Even Barney was looking at him now. 'I never met the man. I'd seen his infomercials,' the doctor said, 'and his books in the stores, but I've never subscribed to succeeding through schemes.

'Besides,' he added between sips of tea, 'eight years of school took me ten years to pay off my student loans from UCLA. I don't buy anything that I can't afford to pay for.'

More good advice. Kitty rose. 'Doctor Newhart, would you mind if we cut our session short?'

He raised an eyebrow.

Kitty looked out the window. Sunshine spilled in, casting a warm, yellow glow over them. 'I'd like to get out and take Fred for a hike. I hear there are some great trails around the resort and I'd like to try one.'

'I think that's a splendid idea,' Dr Newhart replied. 'Seize the day.'

Kitty grinned. That was exactly what she had in mind.

TWENTY-NINE

K itty dropped Barney off in the room, making sure he had plenty of food and water. Cats weren't big hikers. She changed into a comfortable pair of jeans and a lightweight gray sweater. Though it was fall and they were in the mountains, the weather report for today promised the temperature would be mild. She laced up her sneakers, wishing she'd brought hiking boots, and hitched Fred up to his lead. He pranced excitedly and tugged at the leash to pull her along as if he knew exactly where they were going and couldn't wait to get there.

Kitty waved to Howie who was sauntering along the curved drive then cut across the grounds. Steam rose off the water of the Olympic-sized and dog bone-shaped pool. Loungers and tables sat scattered generously about the patio. Bright blue and green striped umbrellas jutted out from the center of the tabletops like lollipops. Two waiters skittered around serving food and drinks.

Rick Ruggiero pulled up in a golf cart alongside Kitty as she rounded the corner past the half-dozen tennis courts. 'How are you today, Miss Karlyle?' Before she could answer, he added: 'I want to apologize again for last night. Perhaps it's best if you avoid the kitchen, especially after dark.'

Fred sniffed the manager's feet. Kitty gently pulled him back before he left slobber all over the squeaky clean black shoes. 'I confess I'm a little tired, but otherwise none the worse for wear. How about you? I'm sorry you had to get dragged down to the police station in the middle of the night.'

'Don't worry about me,' the manager replied, rubbing his hands along the cart's black steering wheel. 'All part of the job of running a place like this.' He waved his arm, indicating the resort grounds.

'I can't imagine what Chef Moutarde was doing there at that hour . . .' She left her words dangling there. Would Rick take the bait?

Rick seemed to shrug off any idea of there having been something unusual about the chef's behavior. 'Henri told me he was trying to catch up on the quarterly inventory reports.' He smiled. 'I have to confess that I've been hounding him about keeping better track of food costs.' His hands drummed the wheel. 'So,' he said, abruptly changing the subject, 'where are you off to? Can I give you a lift?' He waved to the cart's empty seats.

Kitty declined, explaining that she and Fred were going to try one of the hiking trails she'd heard so much about.

'Good idea. You've got the perfect day for it.' Rick put the cart in gear and turned around on the narrow sidewalk. 'I'd suggest the Matterhorn Trail.' He pointed up the path. 'If you follow this walkway another fifty yards or so you'll see a large wooden sign that traces the paths of three of our trails: the Schilthorn, the Wendenhorn and the Matterhorn. We've named them after three peaks in Switzerland.'

'Looks like we've got plenty of choices, eh, Fred?' She patted the Lab's side.

'The Schilthorn is the shortest, not much more than a half mile out and a half mile back,' explained Rick. 'The Wendenhorn is an easy walk and goes around the lake. Personally, I like the Matterhorn.'

That figured. 'The Matterhorn, you say?'

Ruggiero nodded. 'If you're looking for a bit of a challenge and some great scenery, that's the one I'd choose.' He disappeared, the little cart buzzing down the walk.

Kitty followed Rick's advice. She found the large brown sign marking the trails in yellow as they snaked through the countryside. Rustically carved text provided descriptions, an indication of each trail's distance and difficulty level. The Matterhorn wound in a five-mile loop through the mountains, coming back down on the other side of the resort. It was rated moderate. How hard could it be?

'You up for it, Fred?' Why was she even asking? Fred was always up for anything. He was a dog after all, and dogs were born ready.

The hike began easily enough, rising slowly uphill. The path was reasonably wide and consisted mostly of packed earth with the occasional log or small boulder thrown in the mix. After tripping a couple of times, Kitty realized she was going to have to keep one eye on the ground to keep from breaking a leg or landing on her face. Fred, of course, being fleet of foot and possessing whatever innate ability it was that every dog possesses, was having no troubles at all.

There were few hikers on the trails. Many, like her, had brought their pets. Though did that guy with the Dachshund really think his dog was enjoying the strenuous walk? With those cute but stubby legs? She didn't think so.

Others hiked solo or in small groups. Kitty watched jealously as one couple hiked past her holding hands. That should be her and Jack. A couple of ridiculously fit-looking men and women came along pedaling madly on mountain bikes, grunting as they whizzed past. Kitty couldn't begin to imagine how they managed the steep incline. Some folks were cut out for the Iron Man competition; she feared she wouldn't even be competitive in the Marshmallow Man competition.

About two miles in, with the sun beating down and her unexercised muscles and limbs squawking, Kitty paused, leaning against a large Douglas fir for support, taking in deep, rasping breaths. Fred, on the other hand, seemed perfectly content. She regretted she hadn't brought snacks and water for both of them. The air was cool and dry. Her throat was parched and the sneakers she had on were designed more for long shopping trips to the mall than hiking up the sides of mountains.

Kitty's phone vibrated in her pocket. She'd turned off the ringer for her meeting with Dr Newhart. 'Yes?' It was Jack. Her heart jumped. 'How are you?' His voice was distant and crackly.

'Hi, sweetie. Can you hear me?'

'Just barely. Fred, don't go too far.'

'What was that?'

'I was telling Fred not to wander away.' Kitty explained that she was on one of the hiking trails near the resort. The land actually belonged to the California Department of Parks and Recreation. She'd spotted their sign along the trail a ways back. 'Jack? Jack?'

She glanced at her phone. Zero bars. She'd lost him. Kitty
punched in his number from her directory and it went straight
to voicemail. She hung up and tried again. Still nothing. As she
debated whether or not to try a third time, her phone rang and
she answered. 'Jack?'

'Sorry about that,' he said. 'I guess we've got lousy reception.'

Sure, she had to be out in the boonies now of all times. 'I miss
you,' Kitty said quickly, fearing they'd be disconnected once more.

'I miss you, too, Kitty. I wish you could have come with me
instead of having to be there.'

He was so sweet. 'How did your demonstration with the lieutenant go?'

Jack groaned. 'Terrible. Don't get me started. You know I hate
being in front of crowds.'

She knew. Jack was fairly reserved – except when he was in
detective mode. He told her what a bad time he'd had and how
boring the conference had turned out to be.

'What about you?' Jack inquired. 'Who was that guy that
answered the phone in your room the other night?' He laughed.
'Should I be jealous?'

Jack was not the jealous type and he'd been in love with Kitty
practically from the moment he'd laid eyes on her. What he saw
in her, she didn't know, but whatever it was, she was sure glad
he saw it.

'That was Ted. He's a guest here. Greg, that's the director,
roped him into participating in a spot for the show.'

'I see. Maybe next time you can let him rope me. I can't cook,
but—'

'Hello? Grrrr . . .' Kitty squeezed the phone in her hand.
They'd been disconnected again. Kitty wouldn't mind being tied
up with a rope to Jack right now. Not to mention it beat being
out in the wilderness with no food or drink. And no cell phone
coverage. She growled again. A clear sign that she'd been
spending too much time with dogs lately.

She moved to the edge of the trail that swept up severely on
her left and even more severely down on the right. She held
up her phone and scanned the trees looking for a clear spot where
she might get better reception. If she had to, she'd climb to the
top of one of the big firs. Just as she saw the hint of a second

bar rise up on her cell-phone screen, a hard blow to the back of Kitty's right shoulder sent her spinning around then tumbling down the mountainside. The cell phone flew from her grip and, as she twisted her head and threw out her arms, she saw a brown hiking boot hit the ground.

All she heard after that was the sound of her own body as she fell willy-nilly through the brambles and over the rocks. She covered her head with her hands as best she could and prayed that she would come to a stop soon.

THIRTY

She must have passed out momentarily. When she came to her senses Fred was standing there licking her cheek. She reached out to pet him. 'Fred,' she said, extending her fingers painfully. At least he appeared to be OK. 'Oooh.' She groaned and fell back, her head banging against a small rock. She saw more stars in that moment than a cosmonaut on the International Space Station saw in a week.

What had happened?

What kind of idiot had run into her? A jogger? Some nut on a mountain bike?

Why hadn't they, stopped to help? Had she been intentionally pushed?

Her blood froze as she heard the sound of a herd of feet shuffling down the embankment toward her and gasped. Did feet come in herds? Was she hallucinating? Delirious? Fred woofed a couple of times but his tail was wagging. She took that for a good sign.

Besides, she was in no position to run away.

'You OK there?' It was Sheila Shepherd, the lady from the pet shelter. She had four dogs with her on separate leashes. She wore khakis, a multicolored tie-dyed peace sign T-shirt, hiking boots and a yellow bandana that held back her hair. With all the dogs and leashes fanning out in front of her in all directions she looked like a weird hippie-dog hybrid. Was she on her way to Woofstock?

OK. With thoughts like that, Kitty was sure she was delirious. She nodded. 'I-I think so.'

Sheila dropped the leashes and the dogs, free to wander, danced around her and made quick friends with Fred. 'Can you stand?' She held out a free hand.

Kitty reached out, stifling a moan, then hesitated. Sheila was wearing hiking boots. Had Sheila pushed her off the cliff and now returned to the scene of the crime? Possibly to see what harm she'd done? Maybe even to finish her off?

It could even be a ruse to give herself an alibi.

Sheila looked concerned. 'Are you OK?'

Kitty gulped. She let Sheila take her hand and pull her to her feet. She didn't have a lot of options. Every bone in her body screamed but she could barely hear them because every muscle, every tissue, every organ was screaming all the louder.

'Anything broken?'

Kitty looked herself over, slowly, carefully. 'I don't think so. Only some scrapes and bruises.' Her jeans were ripped in a dozen places. She could probably get top dollar for them now on Rodeo Drive.

Sheila shook her head. 'You gotta be careful out here.' She wagged her finger. 'A young girl like you shouldn't be out hiking alone in these woods. You could get hurt. Attacked, even.'

Kitty examined her torn hands. Her broken fingernails. That ship had sailed. 'You seem to be alone,' Kitty said. 'What are you doing here?'

Sheila plucked a twig from Kitty's shirt. 'I come out this way all the time. No one's going to bother me. Not when I've got these guys with me.' She indicated the dogs. 'I like to take a few of them out at a time. It's not healthy for the dogs to always be cooped up inside the shelter.'

That made sense. Besides, what possible reason could the pet-shelter operator have for wanting to push her down a cliff anyway?

'What's going on there?' A male voice sounding oddly familiar shouted from above.

'Down here,' called Sheila. 'Give us a hand, would you. My friend fell.'

'Be right there!' called a second voice.

Moments later Steve and Roger appeared with the Corgis. 'Good grief, Kitty,' said Steve. 'What did you do?'

Kitty cocked her head to one side. Did he really just say that? Her hand instinctively reached for a rock. Oh, not a big one. A small one would do.

'You three know one another?' Sheila scratched her jowl.

Kitty explained that she worked for Steve and that Roger was a friend of his.

'Let's get her up on the trail and to the medical center,' Sheila commanded.

'No, that won't be necessary,' argued Kitty. 'It's OK, really. I'm fine.' She dusted herself off, biting her tongue to keep from shrieking in agony. 'I can walk, see.' She tottered a few unsteady limping steps by way of demonstration.

'That's it, boys,' ordered Sheila. 'I'll mind the dogs.' She put two fingers to her lips and whistled sharply. The dogs came running. Even Fred shot to attention. 'You two grab hold of that girl and let's get her to the ER.'

'Is that really necessary?' Steve asked rather cattily.

'We've got to make sure no bones have been broken.' She poked a finger in Kitty's face and pushed up each eyelid. 'She may even have a concussion.'

Kitty frowned and massaged her freshly bruised eyeballs. Up until the moment that Sheila had thrust her fingers in her face, her eyeballs had been just about the only part of her that didn't hurt. Now they hurt like the dickens.

Kitty put up a fuss as Roger and Steve carried her awkwardly back up the steep embankment. Neither man was cut out for action. Kitty figured Sheila could have done a better job of it all by herself. Despite her deceptively diminutive size, the older woman could probably toss her over one shoulder and hike straight up the mountain without so much as pausing to catch a breath. Kitty kept her rambling thoughts to herself. No point hurting anyone's feelings. The guys were only trying to help.

After what seemed like hours of poking and prodding by the same doctor who'd been attending to Eliza Cornwall the night of her admission, Kitty was pronounced reasonably whole. Dr Peter and an army of nurses now knew her better than she knew herself and seen parts she couldn't hope to see with a good dental mirror and the flexibility of a carnival contortionist.

'Nothing's broken,' pronounced Dr Peter, the emergency department physician. He was an affable young man who must have been in his mid-thirties, with a thick black moustache that covered most of his upper lip.

'That's good to know,' replied Kitty.

His eyes twinkled as he said, 'It was touch and go there for a while, but—'

'I'll live,' Kitty said.

He patted her arm. 'Yes. The nurse will be in to have you sign some papers and I've written a prescription for a pain medication. Then you will be free to go. Just don't go hiking again anytime soon.' He pulled out his prescription pad and looked at Kitty over the edge of his thick brown glasses. 'You're not allergic or intolerant to aspirin, are you?'

Kitty shook her head no.

'Good, then I'll prescribe Percodan.'

'That's all right, doctor. I don't think I'll be needing anything like that.' And she had no intention of hitting the trails, at least not for a very long time.

He smiled a doctor's all-knowing smile. 'Miss Karlyle, you may not think you are going to need any medication.' He arched a brow sagely. 'But wait until tomorrow; you may wake up wishing you were dead.'

'Huh?'

'It would not surprise me if every muscle and bone in your body was singing in pain.' He patted her hand again. 'Take the prescription. Have it filled,' Dr Peter suggested, 'just in case.' He tore off the prescription and handed it to her.

She scanned the paper, trying to make sense of his chicken scratch. Maybe you had to be a pharmacist to read the language. Pharmacists probably had to pass at least Chicken Scratch 302 in college to graduate. 'How is Mrs Cornwall doing, Doctor?'

'Very well. Very well indeed. We're keeping her one more day. Her body has had quite a shock to the system but she's young and healthy. I'm confident she will make a full recovery.' He jotted some notes on his PDA then thrust the device back in his white doctor's coat. 'She was very lucky.'

'You mean she could have died?'

'It's rare, but it does happen.'

Fran was waiting for her in the lounge outside the nurses' station. 'Girl, are you OK?' Fran jumped up to greet her. A nurse had wheeled her out in a wheelchair. Hospital policy, she'd been told.

'I'm fine, really. I'm sure it looks worse than it is.'

'No, you look good,' Fran said.

'That's a bald-faced lie and you know it.'

They both laughed. 'OK, busted,' admitted Fran. 'You look like, well, like you fell down the side of a mountain.'

'What are you doing here? How did you find out where I was?'

'Steve called and filled me in. I raced right over.'

'Thanks.' They were alone in the small lounge but for two nurses, one male and the other female, eating yogurts at a small table looking out on a compact, plant-filled atrium with a small koi pond.

'I brought you some clothes.'

'Good. I was afraid I was going to have to leave dressed like this.' Kitty tugged at the paper weight pale blue hospital gown she'd been dressed in. She hadn't been looking forward to being seen in public in it. 'Is there someplace I can get dressed?' Kitty asked the nurse.

The nurse told her she could change in one of the small admitting rooms off the ER. Fran offered to steer. 'That woman from the animal shelter took Fred back to the resort for you.'

'You mean Sheila?'

'Yeah, that's her. Steve and Roger hung around the waiting room until I got here then took off. I told him he should stay. Steve said he had a coast-to-coast conference call scheduled with the network that was life or death.' Fran helped Kitty into a loose-fitting skirt and blouse. 'What a weasel. Couldn't even stick around long enough to be sure you were OK.'

Kitty told Fran not to be too hard on her producer. After all, he may not have saved her life but he and Roger had carried her up the mountain and then a good mile or so down the trail without complaint until the medics with the stretcher had shown up to take over.

The two medics had lugged her the rest of the way down on the folding stretcher to the trail head where an ambulance had been waiting to meet them and lead them to civilization and the Little Switzerland Medical Center – a place Kitty was now getting very familiar with.

Fran pulled back the curtain and headed down the hall. 'Hey,' said Kitty, 'why don't we go see how Eliza's doing?' If she was awake and alert, maybe Kitty could get some answers from her. About who might have wanted to poison her and why she lied about only arriving in town after her husband's murder.

As they swung around the corner, Kitty had a straight view into Eliza's open door. 'Stop,' whispered Kitty. Eliza was sitting up in bed, the pink bed sheets cinched up around her waist. Her hair and makeup were immaculate and she looked absolutely gorgeous. A smoky-taupe silk pajama top with wide lapels clung to her skin, exposing a narrow but deep V of perfect skin. How did she manage to look so sexy lying in a hospital bed?

The woman had been poisoned the day before and looked like she was ready for the red carpet. She either had good genes or a good witch doctor. Whichever it was, Kitty wanted it. A quick thought passed through Kitty's mind. Could Eliza have been faking it? No, she'd been there. Eliza wasn't that good an actress. Besides, no way she could have fooled the doctor and his medical staff.

And why would she want to connive her way into the Little Switzerland Medical Center?

John wore cuffed charcoal trousers with a silver gray turtleneck sweater. He was handing her a bouquet of flowers – yellow and red roses interlaced with delicate white baby's breath, all wrapped in green tissue.

Eliza took the flowers with both hands, smiled and placed them on the tray beside her. Kitty had read somewhere that in some cultures it was offensive to accept a gift with one hand; accepting with two hands showed that you appreciated the gift and respected the giver. Did Eliza know this?

John leaned in and kissed his ex-wife on the lips.

'The rat,' muttered Fran.

'Quick,' whispered Kitty, her hands gripping the wheelchair's armrests, 'wheel us into that room across the hall.'

Fran nodded and pushed Kitty across to the open door at a diagonal to Eliza's. The rubber tires of the wheelchair rolled silently over the linoleum. There were two beds in the room, both empty.

'Turn me around,' Kitty insisted, twisting this way and that. 'I can't see anything.'

'Sorry.' Fran turned the wheelchair on a dime; she was like a pro with the thing. Kitty was going to have to ask her if she'd ever driven one before. But right now she had better things to do.

They watched in silence as John and Eliza canoodled. Kitty patted Fran's hand. Her friend had to be hurting. Not that she'd expected anything serious to come of Fran's vacation romance with John Jameson, but it still had to hurt to see him in the arms of another woman, especially when that woman was his ex.

What were they talking about in there?

Had they plotted Victor's death together? It was looking more and more like they might have. Were they a couple again? Did John want his ex-wife back? Maybe Eliza and John had been having an affair behind Victor's back. Talk about irony.

Jameson handed his wife a glass of water he'd poured from the plastic pitcher on the nightstand. As she drank, he glanced at his watch then gently ruffled Eliza's hair.

Uh-oh, it looked like he was getting ready to leave. Kitty motioned for Fran to shut the door. Fran peered out the door's small rectangular glass window, careful to keep her face far enough away that John wouldn't spot her. 'I'd like to strangle that guy.'

'Be careful what you say, Fran. That's what got you into the trouble you're in now.'

Fran nodded. 'Right.' She turned to Kitty. 'You can forget I said that.'

'Forgotten. Keep your eye on those two,' Kitty admonished. 'I want to know what's happening.'

'Relax,' Fran replied. 'What's happening is that John has gone.'

'Are you sure?'

Fran made a face. 'Trust me – the scum has left the building.'

Kitty chewed her bottom lip a moment. 'Let's give it a minute and then go pay the grieving widow a visit.'

Fran smiled. 'I like the way you think. I'd like to have a word with her myself.'

After waiting a minute or two, Kitty had Fran wheel her across the hall. 'Better let me do the talking,' Kitty said under her breath as Fran pushed her through the open doorway. The last thing she needed was for Fran to get Eliza's hackles up. If the ex-Mrs Jameson and widowed Mrs Cornwall became defensive, she'd zip her cosmetically enhanced lips and tell them nothing.

They discovered Eliza sitting up in bed leafing through a copy of *Glamour*. 'Kitty.' Eliza lowered her magazine to her lap. 'What happened to you?'

Kitty almost forgot her own injuries and the fact that she was being tooled around in a wheelchair. A girl could get used to this limousine service. 'Slight mishap on the trail.'

Eliza frowned but quickly let it go. The woman no doubt had a primal fear of frown lines. 'What room are you staying in?'

Was Eliza afraid she might be gaining a roommate? That might not be a bad idea – infiltrate the enemy, get close to her. Learn who she saw and when. Would Dr Peter admit her? Not bloody likely. Unless she was willing to fake a worse injury than she'd sustained, and the likelihood of her pulling that off seemed infeasible. 'I'm good to go,' answered Kitty. 'The doctor's given me a clean bill of health. A few cuts and bruises. Nothing to keep me.'

Eliza pouted. 'I wish I could say the same. The doctor tells me I have to stay another night in this awful place.'

Kitty looked around the private room with its high thread-count sheets and elegant mauve draperies, private bath, the flat-screen TV mounted in the corner. The around-the-clock service. Yeah, awful, wasn't it?

'Was that Mr Jameson I saw leaving?' Did Kitty detect a slight flush wash over Eliza's face?

'Oh.' Eliza pushed two fingers through her hair. 'Did you see him?'

'I thought I noticed him down the hall.'

Eliza nodded toward the flowers. 'He brought me flowers. He's such a dear.'

Was he now?

'So what's the deal with you two? John's your ex, right? Are the two of you getting back together again?'

'Excuse me?' If Eliza had been covered in feathers rather than unblemished skin, every feather would have been ruffled about now.

'Fran,' Kitty said through gritted teeth. Leave it to Fran to rattle the suspect. Here Kitty was trying to butter the woman up and Fran had to go and rile her. If Fran wanted honey she'd probably go beat it out of the hive rather than try to coax it out of the bees.

'Who is this woman?'

'This is Fran Earhart. She works with me.' Kitty shot Fran a look that might have knocked a lesser woman to her knees and wheeled closer to the bedside. Time to change the subject. 'So, flowers, huh?' She sniffed the bouquet. 'Very nice.'

Eliza plucked at the flowers. 'Yellow and red roses. John knows my weaknesses.'

I'll bet he does, thought Kitty. 'Does that mean your ex-husband might stand a chance with you?' Kitty held her breath, expecting an angry explosion.

Instead, Eliza bent her head back and laughed. 'Don't be silly. John's a sweetheart but I was married to him once.' She folded her arms. 'And once was enough.'

'So you aren't having an affair with him?'

'Of course not.' Eliza pushed the buzzer beside her bed. 'I think the two of you should leave.'

Uh-oh. 'What about the speeding ticket?' Kitty said quickly.

'What are you talking about?' Eliza huffed.

'The speeding ticket you got only a few days ago in Santa Barbara.'

A stout no-nonsense-looking nurse with a pageboy haircut blocked the doorway. 'Everything OK in here, Mrs Cornwall?'

'No, I would like to get some rest.' She glared at Fran and Kitty. 'But it's quite impossible under the circumstances.'

The nurse cleared her throat and stepped to the side. 'I'm afraid you two ladies will have to leave now.'

Fran turned Kitty's wheelchair around and lunged for the door. 'I know you were just an hour or two away from here in Santa Barbara when you got that ticket,' Kitty hollered, twisting back to face Eliza. 'You could easily have driven to Little Switzerland and murdered your husband.' The nurse slammed the hospital room door behind them and stayed with them the rest of the way. Kitty fumed. That hadn't gone as well as she would have liked. She never did get any answers from Eliza.

Now she had more questions than ever. She toyed with the idea of going back and confronting Eliza once more, but the nurse looked like she could have played left tackle in high-school football and didn't seem the type to tolerate any nonsense.

With the nurse keeping an eye on them, Kitty signed out at the desk then Fran wheeled her out under the portico and told her to sit tight. 'I'll pull the car around.' Fran explained how the manager had loaned her one of the resort's courtesy vans.

When Fran arrived with the van, the left-tackle nurse made sure she got in.

THIRTY-ONE

F ran pulled up to the curb outside the Little Switzerland Market and Pharmacy.

'Ouch!' Kitty groaned and rubbed her shoulder. Did she say 'pulled up'? She meant bounced up. Kitty's shoulder did some bouncing of its own, off the van door. If she let Fran drive her around much longer she was going to need that pain medication.

'Sorry,' said Fran. 'I'm not used to driving something so big. Sure is nice though.' She ran a hand along the dash. 'You ought to think about trading in that old Volvo of yours. A vehicle like this would be great for you.' She pushed a recessed button on the key to lock up. 'It even comes with an MP3 connection.'

'Does it come with its own ATM?' Jack had recently had to replace his Jeep and the last thing Kitty wanted was for them to have another car payment. Fran told her she worried too much. That was OK, because the way Kitty figured it, Fran worried too little. Between the two of them, hopefully they got it just about right.

With a tiled roof as red as the Swiss flag, the market was sandwiched between the Yodel Inn on one side and the Alpine Mountain Cheese Shoppe on the other. The Alpine 4U Card and Gift Shoppe sat directly across the street. Kitty had noted the name of the store on the gift tag that had come attached with Eliza Cornwall's flowers.

Inside the market, they discovered a small but well-stocked grocery with two checkout lanes located near the automatic entrance.

'Hey, there's Bobby Bridges and Traci Nelson.' Fran pointed to a weekly gossip rag on the rack by the cash register. 'Did you know they're staying at the resort?'

'Doctor Newhart told me.' The photographer had caught a shot of Bobby and Traci holding hands at the beach. 'Wow, what big news. Couple holds hands at beach. Stop the presses.'

'I haven't caught a glimpse of them yet,' she said, pulling on her lower lip and ignoring Kitty's baiting sarcasm. 'I'd love to see them. Maybe get Bobby's autograph.' She dropped a hand on Kitty's shoulder. 'I heard that Bobby took a swing at Vic a few days ago.'

Kitty was about to tell Fran to get back on point, but this got her attention. 'He what?'

'Took a poke at Vic.' She faked a punch. 'Got him pretty good too.'

Kitty gave this some thought. 'That might explain that light bruising under his eye.'

'Yeah, I suppose it could.'

Kitty lowered her voice. 'Don't you see? Bobby could be the killer.'

'I don't think so,' Fran replied with a quick shake of her head. 'Look at those dreamy eyes. Bobby would never harm anyone. I mean, in the movies, yeah, maybe.' She folded her arms across her chest. 'But not in real life.'

'I'm still putting him on the list.'

'What list?'

'The suspect list.' The list Ted had stolen from her. 'Now let's move on.' Kitty swatted Fran's hand as she reached for the magazine and urged her forward.

Two cheaply framed photos adhered to the wall below a stack

of small green shopping baskets. The first was a shot of the store manager; the second was an equally amateurish-looking shot of Deputy Jerry Lee Nickels. It identified Nickels as the store's pharmacist. Well, well, well, thought Kitty. 'I wonder—'

'Wonder what?' Fran said.

'Follow me.' Kitty strode carefully up and down each aisle. As she wandered up the baking aisle, she slowed. 'Bingo,' she said pointing toward a low shelf.

'What am I looking at?'

'Peanut oil,' Kitty said, picking up a plastic bottle and turning it around in her hand. She placed it back on the shelf. The pharmacy counter was located in the back of the store. Nickels was there at the register speaking to a man who had his back turned to them. He looked familiar, though.

The man turned his face to the right. Kitty recognized that profile.

'Isn't that—'

'Yeah,' said Kitty. She lowered her voice and beckoned for Fran to follow. She wanted a vantage point from which they could see but not be seen.

'Ted Atchison. What's he doing here?' He was dressed as he'd been that morning, in baggy cargo pants and a blue chambray shirt. His hiking boots were dusty. Had he been responsible for her tumble? Ted had been the one to tell her about the trails. Had he been planting the seed? Luring her out to the mountains where he could kill her?

Seeing him again, he did look rather devious. Those twitching eyes, that sharp nose. Maybe Fran's sense about him had been right all along. Ted Atchison was clutching a small white bag, the kind that pharmacists stapled drugs in – or payoff money.

'What do you suppose the two of them are talking about?' Fran whispered.

Kitty shook her head side to side. 'They do seem to be talking a long time. I wonder if they know each other.'

'How could that be?' Fran asked. 'Nickels is local. Ted said he was from San Juan Capistrano.'

'Yeah, but remember,' said Kitty, 'his dog, Chloe, came from the local animal shelter. Maybe Ted's local, too.'

Fran scrunched up her face. 'Why would he lie about a thing like that?'

'Let's ask him.' She was also going to ask him why he'd stolen the list of suspects she'd written up.

'Look out!' Fran said.

Kitty turned in time to see a blowzy elderly man with thick-rimmed glasses turn the corner of the aisle a little too quickly. His cart went up on two side wheels then slammed into her hip. Kitty went down and the cart fell across her legs. Fortunately, the guy hadn't done much shopping yet – some toilet paper and a bottle of gin. She pushed down her skirt.

The old man scooped up the gin in both hands while Kitty massaged her thigh. 'You OK?' He squinted at her, his bug-eyed milky cataract brown eyes blinking.

'Yes,' Kitty managed to say. Fran lifted the cart up on its wheels and tossed the toilet paper inside. 'I'm fine. Thanks.' What was one more bruise when she already had a couple dozen?

'OK,' he said quickly. He set the liquor in the baby seat, grabbed the handle of the cart with both hands and sped off around the next corner.

'That guy could do some real damage,' quipped Fran.

Kitty was still rubbing her hip. 'I think he just did.'

Fran's look of bemusement turned to one of concern. 'You sure you're OK?'

Kitty said she was sure. 'Let's go tackle Ted.' She headed toward the back of the market. 'When we're through with him, we'll tackle Deputy Nickels. He lost a bundle to Victor Cornwall, too. He and his wife lost their condo.'

'That would put a murderous thought in a person's head.'

Kitty concurred. But when they got to the back of the store, Atchison was gone.

A young woman with fluffy blonde hair stood at the pharmacy register now. Nickels was dispensing pills into a small plastic vile behind her but stepped forward as he watched Kitty and Fran approach. 'I'll take this, Sally.'

The young woman moved away. 'What are you doing here?' Nickels asked. He was in pharmacist rather than deputy mode today, dressed in charcoal slacks and a navy-blue lab coat.

'I came to fill a prescription.'

'I see you brought suspect *numero uno* with you.'

Fran opened her mouth but a look from Kitty shut it again.

Kitty didn't need Fran stirring up any more trouble, especially with the police. Fran was in enough of a jam as things stood. Particularly since she was the last one to have seen Victor alive – excluding the real killer, of course.

Nickels looked rather dubious but held out his hand. Kitty reached into her purse and drew out the prescription that Dr Peter had given her.

He looked it over. 'You'll have to give me a few minutes.'

'Was that Ted Atchison I saw leaving a minute ago?' asked Kitty.

'Could've been. Why?' He leaned over the counter, towering over Kitty like an impending storm cloud. 'You're not nosing around in Victor Cornwall's murder investigation, are you?' He glared across the counter at her. 'The chief told you to stay out of this, Ms Karlyle.'

'Why?' demanded Kitty. 'What are you afraid of? Afraid I might find something the police missed? Or,' she said, fueling his fire, 'are you afraid I might find something you'd rather I didn't?'

His eyes turned to steel. 'What are you trying to say?'

'I'm wondering what it is that you and Ted Atchison might have to hide.'

Nickels cursed. His young assistant glanced at him then turned away when she caught the look he gave her. Kitty flushed.

'Me and Atchison hiding something?' He forced a laugh. 'That's rich.' He was practically gloating. 'I don't even know the man.'

'You don't?' said Fran.

'No, I don't,' Nickels said forcefully. 'He came in to fill his allergy prescription.' He shook his head. 'I'll tell you one thing, that guy sure is a talker.' He pointed a crooked finger at Kitty. 'Almost as bad as you.'

'What do you mean?'

'Asking a million questions. Wanting to know about Victor Cornwall's murder, what the autopsy might have shown, if we had any leads.' Nickels snorted. 'Like it's any of his business.' He leaned toward Kitty once more. 'Like it isn't any business of yours.'

Kitty tried another tack. 'I notice you carry peanut oil.'

'So?' His eyebrows folded up as one.

Kitty said nothing, watching his face to see what he might give away.

'Oh,' he said finally, drawing the word out. 'You mean Eliza Cornwall.' He rolled his eyes. 'If I wanted to poison somebody I've got my choice of a lot better stuff than peanut oil.' He waved his arms in the direction of the stacked bins of prescription medications behind him.

He had a point. She imagined the pharmacist had a near infinite supply of poisons at hand. What was to say that he hadn't poisoned Victor Cornwall with one of them before strangling him for good measure? The police never had released the results of Victor's autopsy. 'Were there any traces of poison in Eliza's husband's body?'

Nickels snatched Kitty's prescription off the counter and spun around. 'It won't be ready for twenty minutes!'

'But I—'

'Thirty if you keep bugging me!'

'Come on, Fran,' Kitty said, pulling her friend away. They obviously weren't going to get any further with Deputy Nickels at the moment. 'I want to see a man about some flowers.'

'Huh?'

'Never mind. Follow me.'

They dodged traffic and pushed into the Alpine 4U Card and Gift Shoppe. A tiny bronze bell attached to the inside of the door handle announced their entrance.

'Welcome to Alpine 4U.' A svelte forty-something woman in a flowing dress ablaze with cerise and cream peonies greeted them. She stood behind a small glass counter. Her right hand held a tape dispenser. An unwrapped package, a pair of scissors and a roll of wrapping paper lay to one side. A similarly aged man in rumpled jeans and a red and black checked flannel shirt sat in a wood rocking chair behind the counter, his nose in a book. 'Can I help you with something?'

'Just browsing,' said Fran. She spun a rack of postcards near the entrance.

'Let me know if I can help.' The woman pulled out a length of silver paper, picked up her red-handled scissors and carefully cut. Her dirty blonde hair was swept up atop her head, bound together with a black silk ribbon.

'Actually . . .' said Kitty, approaching the counter.

'Yes?' The woman smoothed the gift wrap with the side of her palm and looked up.

'A friend of mine bought some flowers from you today. A Mr Jameson?' Kitty raised an eyebrow.

'I remember him.' The woman smiled at her husband. 'He ordered the roses. He said he had a friend in the hospital.'

'That's right.' Kitty laid her hands on the counter. 'They were beautiful. Your whole shop is wonderful.' Kitty sighed. 'I love flowers.'

The woman grinned some more. 'Glad to hear it.'

'Care to buy some?' muttered the man in the rocker.

'Oscar.' She rolled her eyes. 'Don't mind my husband. 'He's not much of a people person. But he's great with his hands.'

'I understand,' said Kitty. 'I was thinking of ordering some flowers also. For the same friend.'

'Did you have something particular in mind?' The woman came out from behind the counter.

Kitty scanned the flower and gift shop. She studied the vases in the refrigerated glass box along the wall and pointed. 'Those look nice.'

The woman slid open the glass door and held her hand in front of a vase. 'These?'

Kitty nodded.

Fran slithered up beside her and muttered, 'What are you doing, girl?'

Kitty told her to shush. 'I'll take them.'

The shopkeeper slid the arrangement out and closed the door. 'A very nice choice.' Her hands picked lovingly at the flowers. 'Orange Asiatic lilies, fuchsia carnations, red Peruvian lilies, lavender chrysanthemums and lush greens.' The woman took Kitty's selection to the counter. 'Will you be delivering them yourself?'

Kitty leaned forward and sniffed. The flowers were arranged in a clear glass bubble vase and smelled divine. She had no doubt that Eliza would like them. She also had no doubt that Eliza would not be happy to see her and Fran show up again anytime soon. 'Do you deliver?'

'Of course. Since they're going to the same person as Mr Jameson's order, I have all the info I need.' She pushed a small tray of cards and envelopes toward Kitty. 'All you have to do is fill out a card.'

Kitty picked up the proffered pen and hesitated over a simple Get Well Soon message card. 'Actually, I'd hate to give the same card that my friend John gave.'

The woman smiled and tapped another card a couple rows over. 'He picked that one, if I remember correctly.' She tapped the side of her skull. 'And I always do.'

Jameson had selected a card whose cover bore a teddy bear clutching a red heart. 'Cute,' said Kitty. She hesitated with the pen yet again. 'It's always so difficult knowing what to say.'

'I suppose,' the woman said. 'Say what comes natural.'

'What did Mr Jameson, I mean, John, write?'

The shopkeeper looked taken aback. 'I wouldn't know. He filled it in himself.' She folded her arms across her chest. 'My husband and I aren't in the habit of reading people's private notes to their recipients.'

Uh-oh. Kitty could see she was losing the woman. 'I didn't mean anything like that.' She scribbled quickly. 'I'll tell her I hope she gets better soon.' She turned the pen toward Fran. 'Did you want to add something, Fran?'

Fran snorted. 'I can think of a word or two.'

Kitty took that for a no. She glanced up at the woman then stuffed the message in the tiny envelope she'd been given. The florist took the envelope and placed it carefully within the bouquet.

Kitty concealed her shock as the woman rung up her purchase. This little detour into Alpine 4U had turned out to be a dead end. A very expensive dead end. Her credit card was going to be as bruised as her tailbone.

The door tinkled.

'Hello, Harry.'

'Hello, Mindy. Hi, Oscar.' The man reading a book waved though his eyes never left the page.

Kitty turned. Fran was looking miserable.

Beside her stood Chief Mulisch.

THIRTY-TWO

'I've been looking for you two.'

'What happened?' said Fran, putting a low display of gardening tools between herself and the chief. 'Did Deputy Nickels call you? Did he go crying to you about us being in his pharmacy?'

Chief Mulisch appeared puzzled. 'I've been looking for you,' he said, turning to Kitty, 'because I heard about your little mishap out on the Matterhorn Trail. I was hoping to catch you at the medical center. I specifically asked the doctor to keep you until I'd had a chance to speak with you and take your statement.'

The chief explained how he'd just come from the Little Switzerland Medical Center. 'They told me you'd left in the resort's van.' He jabbed his thumb at the window. 'That's it, right there. In front of that fire hydrant,' he added rather pointedly.

Kitty's breath caught in her throat. Fran shut her eyes and muttered something unintelligible under her breath.

'I'd move it soon if I were you.'

Fran promised she would.

Kitty and Fran threw emergency signals at one another, all useless. Wasn't there some sort of Morse code-like class that one could take, learn how to do dots and dashes with one's eyelids? How great would that be? She'd sign herself and Fran up for that course.

'Doctor Peter did mention you would want to speak with me.' The doctor had asked Kitty to stick around until the chief showed up but she had really wanted to leave. Besides, if the police wanted to find her, they knew where she was staying. 'I know I should have waited. It's not the doctor's fault I didn't, it's mine,' explained Kitty. 'I'm not a fan of hospitals. Besides, I wanted to get my prescription filled.' She shoved her credit card back in her wallet. 'That's why we went to the pharmacy.'

'Hmmm.' Chief Mulisch seemed to be mulling her words over.

'So you weren't over there trying to worm information about an ongoing murder investigation from one of my deputies?'

'Of course not,' Kitty said quickly. Too quickly. It didn't help that she was blushing. 'Merely filling a prescription.' She made a point of looking at her watch. 'As a matter of fact, it should be ready about now. If you'll excuse us—'

Chief Mulisch stuck his arm out. 'Not so fast.'

Kitty and Fran looked at one another. There was little else they could do. Already, here was a perfect example of how that Morse code eyelash batting class could have come in handy. 'Yes?' Kitty said after a moment's hesitation.

'I'm going to need that statement.'

'But my prescription—' Kitty began.

'Your prescription can wait a couple of minutes. Come on.' He held open the door. *Tinkle tinkle.* 'There's a coffee shop two doors down.'

They followed the chief to the Petit Suisse Bakery Café. He ordered three large coffees from the girl behind the counter who looked like she belonged on the side of a jar of Swiss cocoa. 'You want anything else?'

Kitty's stomach was screaming. She ordered a raspberry-filled cruller. Fran never said no to pastry. She ordered an éclair. The chief fished a fat leather wallet out of his back pocket and paid. Neither woman argued the matter.

Kitty slid into the green booth at the window and Fran joined her. Chief Mulisch sat across the table, his hands playing some unfamiliar tune on the tabletop. The coffee came in thick orange ceramic mugs. Kitty laced her fingers around her cup, soaking in the warmth. She could feel herself beginning to slip away. It hadn't been a long day but it had been an arduous one.

A man and woman with a small child in a highchair were the only others present. The man wore one of those green felt Tyrolean hats Kitty had seen in several of the shop windows. It looked brand new. More Austrian than Swiss, Kitty believed, but the tourists didn't seem to know the difference. A yellow-and-black feather stuck out the back of its corded hatband.

The woman's matching hat rested atop her purse on the table. The toddler's tot-sized version was covered in pink cupcake frosting, which the woman was vigorously trying to scrub out by repeatedly dipping her paper napkin into her water glass, wiping then starting the process over again.

Kitty winked at the toddler as she broke her cruller in two. Raspberry filling oozed out slowly onto her plate and she licked it up with her finger. Yummy, not too sweet and just the right amount of tartness. The crust was golden and flaky. She took a big bite. No point being dainty. Who was she trying to impress? No one at this table.

'If this is so important why didn't you come down to the medical center?' Fran began. 'Kitty could have been killed out there. Or don't you care?'

Kitty held her breath. Chief Mulisch raised his cup to his lips, blew across the surface of his coffee then set it down. He hadn't ordered any pastry but he had added four sugar packets to his coffee. That would give him a pretty good sugar buzz all on its own.

'I was out of town, if you must know, Ms Earhart. Investigating leads into the murder of Victor Cornwall.' He turned the full weight of his gaze on Fran. 'You do remember Mr Cornwall, don't you, Ms Earhart? After all, you were the last person to see him alive.'

'I didn't kill anybody. You know yourself that there are lots of people who might have wanted to see Victor Cornwall dead – people he bilked, the man whose wife he stole . . . and who knows who else?'

'Yeah, but like I said,' Chief Mulisch picked up a stainless-steel spoon and rubbed the bowl with his thumb, 'you were the last person to see him alive.'

Fran fidgeted in her seat and took a big hunk out of her éclair. Her jaws worked up and down as she chewed hard. She swallowed and gulped down her coffee.

'Purportedly,' Kitty added in Fran's defense. 'What about Bobby Bridges?'

The chief laughed. 'What about him? You want me to see if I can get you his autograph?'

'No,' said Kitty. 'I heard he got into an altercation with Victor Cornwall several days before Victor was murdered.'

'Oh,' drawled Chief Mulisch, waving his hand at her. 'That was nothing. I mean, he clocked him pretty good.' He chuckled.

'But Victor didn't want to press charges. Bobby's a bit of a hothead. He told me all about it. It seems Cornwall conned him and his wife, Traci, out of a few million bucks in a phony real-estate deal down in Costa Rica.' Chief Mulisch stopped and raised his cup to his lips. He licked his lips then continued, 'When Bobby ran into Victor here, the discussion turned heated. Bobby admits he punched him.'

'You say Victor conned Bobby and Traci out of millions. Don't you think that's motive for murder?'

'Probably chump change to a couple of big celebs like those two. Besides,' said the chief with a twinkle in his eye, 'Bobby and Traci both have alibis for the time of death.'

'Such as?' Kitty asked.

'They were having dinner in town, at Café St-Pierre. There were dozens of witnesses.'

'He or she,' Kitty added rather pointedly – after all, maybe Traci Nelson had done the deed herself – 'might have sneaked out.'

'I expect that's pretty hard to do when your face is as well-known as those two.'

'But not impossible.' Kitty wasn't about to let go. After all, somebody had killed Victor Cornwall and it had not been Fran.

The chief shrugged. 'Tell me what happened up in the mountains, Ms Karlyle.'

Kitty took a breath and explained to the chief how she'd heard about the trails and decided to take a hike up one of them with her dog in her free time. 'It was Mr Atchison who told me about them.'

'So he knew you were going to be up there?'

'Not exactly, no. Like I said, he told me about them in passing and suggested I might enjoy them, but I never told him I was going or when. I never told anyone. It wasn't until I was at the edge of the property and the manager—'

'Ruggiero?'

'Yes, that's right. He told me a little about each trail and suggested I might try the Matterhorn.'

'I see.'

What did he see? Did he think Rick Ruggiero might have set her up? Could he have been the one who'd pushed her off the

trail? 'Do you think he might have pushed me?' He had told her
that was the hike he would take if it was him.

Chief Mulisch shook his head in the negative. 'No. He was
on the property the whole time.'

'What makes you so sure?' asked Fran. She pushed a few
éclair crumbs around her spot at the table.

'He was in a staff meeting with eight other people.' He fixed
his eyes on Fran. 'What about you?'

'What about me?'

'Where were you when your friend had her accident?'

'It wasn't an accident,' Kitty said. 'Somebody pushed me,
Chief.'

'Are you certain?' he replied maddeningly. 'Maybe you
slipped, lost your balance, weren't watching where you were
going? Those trails can be treacherous. Accidents happen out
there all the time. Busted legs, arms, you name it.' He played
with the small woven banana leaf basket on the table that held
the diminished supply of sugar packets and artificial sweeteners.
He wasn't contemplating adding another, was he? 'Maybe,' he
said, 'it was your dog.'

Fran scoffed. 'You think her dog pushed her? That's a hoot.'

'Fran—' Kitty's voice held a warning.

'No, no.' Fran shook her head. 'What was I thinking? Hoots
are for owls. That's a woof, that's what I meant to say.'

Kitty closed her eyes, waiting for the boom of the gunshot.
But instead of death there were several moments of nearly as
deadly silence.

Finally Chief Mulisch spoke. 'No, I'm thinking dogs are
playful. Maybe he jumped up on you when your back was turned,
you know, all playful like and—' He pantomimed her fall by
walking his fingers to the edge of the table and then letting his
hand plunge toward the ground. 'Over you go.' He looked back
at Kitty. 'Nobody's fault at all.'

'Except that it didn't happen that way,' Kitty argued. 'I was
pushed.'

'Did you get a look at this reported assailant? Can you describe
him or her?'

'No, but I do remember seeing a hiking boot or shoe or something as I first started to go down.'

'Is there anything specific that you recall about this so-called hiking boot or shoe? Was it a man's boot? A woman's? A child's?'

'It was brown.'

'Great. Thanks for narrowing the suspects down for me.'

Kitty had to ask, 'A child's?'

'There are plenty of kids out there on the trails, especially on mountain bikes this time of year.' The chief had stuck his head under the table.

'What are you doing down there?' Fran demanded indignantly.

'Seeing what kind of shoes you're wearing.'

Kitty glanced down. Fran was wearing tan ankle-high boots.

'You never did tell me where you were during Ms Karlyle's near-death experience,' Chief Mulisch said.

Kitty wondered if the chief was making fun of them now. She couldn't believe that he could even consider that Fran might have been the one to push her. 'You don't have to answer him, Fran.'

'I was shopping,' Fran replied, ignoring Kitty's advice. 'Right here in town. I went to the Swiss Miss clothing store just up the street, then I went to that place with the watches and jewelry, Swiss Tinkers and Treasures, I think it's called.' She folded her arms in triumph. 'After that, I went back to the resort. I was in Lily's Boutique, which is located right there off the lobby, when I got the call from Steve – that's our producer – that Kitty had been hurt and was in the hospital. Before you ask, Chief, yes, I have plenty of witnesses who can back me up. In fact, that security guard—'

'Howie?' asked Kitty.

'Yeah, Howie. He chased down a valet to carry all my packages to our room and gave me the keys to the resort's hospitality van so I could get to the medical center as fast as possible.'

She turned to Kitty. 'Oh, Kitty, wait till you see the dress I bought. Yellow chiffon with a slit up the left side that goes on forever. Know what I mean? It's going to go great with that little coat I've got. You know, that one I bought that time at Macy's when we—'

Chief Mulisch cleared his throat and they gave him their attention. Once he'd gotten it, he nodded. 'Witnesses, huh?'

Fran nodded back, though her nod included a decided smirk.

'OK.' He sighed. 'I suppose that means you're not guilty.' He brought his cup to his lips. 'Of this particular crime.' He took a swallow. 'If there was a crime.'

Kitty felt her ears growing hotter than the lattes the café served up. This guy was making her madder by the minute. The cruller had been delicious but the conversation had not.

'I'm not guilty of *any* crime,' replied Fran.

That probably wasn't strictly speaking true. She and Fran had some things that might not always have been completely above board but Kitty wasn't about to say that to an officer of the law. 'Will that be all, Chief? I'm really not feeling well. I'd like to get my prescription filled and go back to my room and get some rest.'

He seemed to think for a moment then nodded. 'I think getting some rest is a good idea, Ms Karlyle, a very good idea.'

Fran slid out of the booth. Kitty picked up her purse and joined Fran at the door.

'Speaking of rooms.' Chief Mulisch turned to look at them.

'Yes?' asked Kitty.

'Did you notice anything funny when you went to Eliza's room?'

Kitty froze. Did the chief know that she had gone back to Eliza's room to snoop around? 'Funny? What do you mean?'

He spoke in slow, metered words. 'When you went to return the dog collars to Mrs Cornwall, did you notice anything odd about her room?'

Kitty breathed a sigh of relief. He didn't know she'd gone back to search Eliza's room. And she could never tell him. Not only would she be in hot water, but Howie would too. 'No, nothing at all.' Kitty waited but the chief said nothing. 'Why?'

'Because when my deputies went there this morning to check the room out, they tell me it looked like it had been tossed.'

'Tossed? You mean ransacked?'

He nodded.

'But it wasn't like that when I—'

'When you what?' he asked with a controlled yet scary voice.

Kitty cleared her throat. 'When I was there with Eliza. I mean, I would have noticed that, don't you think?' She batted her lashes.

Chief Mulisch's stony expression gave no indication what he was thinking. They felt his eyes on them the whole time they were crossing the street to the pharmacy. They were jaywalking and Kitty hoped he didn't come running after them to give them a ticket for the infraction.

When they got back to the prescription counter, it was Nickels' assistant who handed Kitty her pills. 'Where's Mr Nickels?' Kitty asked.

The girl shrugged as she swiped Kitty's credit card. 'He took off. I've never seen anything like it. His shift wasn't even over. He left me to fill in.'

Kitty looked up and down the street as Fran unlocked the door to the van. The late-afternoon sun stuck to the mountaintops like a bright red balloon. Nickels was nowhere to be found.

What was that all about?

THIRTY-THREE

Fran cranked the engine. 'I don't know about you but I'm beat.'

Kitty nodded, settling back in the passenger seat.

'What do you say we head straight to the lounge when we get back and have a glass of Napa merlot, maybe see if the spa can squeeze us in for a massage apiece?'

Kitty nodded again.

Fran pulled into traffic. 'And if we see any sign of the crew, we tell them to buzz off.'

Kitty grunted.

'Except for Steve, of course. If that sexy hunk of man is there I'm going to wrap my arms around his big ole chest, squeeze the bejeezus out of him and plant a big kiss on those irresistible lips. Hmm, girl.'

'Sounds good,' Kitty said.

Fran slammed on the brakes.

'Ouch!' Kitty shot forward and back. 'What's wrong with you?' She rubbed her shoulder. 'Watch what you're doing, Fran.'

'What's wrong with me?' Fran said, hands squeezing the steering wheel. The car behind her honked thrice and Fran lifted her foot off the brake. 'What's wrong with you?'

'What do you mean?'

'I mean you're not listening to a word I say.'

Kitty frowned. 'Sorry. It's Victor's murder. I can't help wondering what's going on and who is in on it.' She smoothed her skirt. 'What were you saying?'

'I was saying we should go back to the resort and get some rest. Pamper ourselves for a change. Give this whole murder thing a rest.'

'That sounds good,' Kitty said, 'but I have a better idea.'

Fran cocked her eyebrow but kept her eyes on the road. 'And what is that?'

'I want to go examine the Matterhorn.'

Fran shot her a quick look as she rounded the intersection and headed up the hill toward the Little Switzerland Resort and Spa. 'If by Matterhorn you mean the ride at Disneyland, I'm all for it.' She was forced to slow up behind a slow-moving flatbed loaded down with bales of hay. 'If you mean the trail on which you just today almost met your maker—' She looked Kitty squarely in the eyes. 'No way.'

'We've got to,' said Kitty.

'Oh, no we don't.' She pulled into the resort's long circular drive heading for the valet station. 'You're not dressed for it. And after the tumble you took today I dare say you are in no shape for it. Forget it. We'll do it tomorrow.'

'Tomorrow may be too late. Come on, it's going to be getting dark soon. Let's go now,' implored Kitty. 'Whoever tried to kill me may have dropped something or left some kind of evidence behind.'

'Like what?'

'I don't know, a clue, a footprint.' She looked at Fran. 'This could be important.'

'You do realize that whoever tried to kill you could still be out there.' Fran jumped out of the van and tossed the keys to the valet. 'And might try to kill you again,' she added.

'I know.' Kitty grinned as she patted her friend's arm. 'That's why I need you to come with me.'

Fran groaned as Kitty started up the twisted path leading to the edge of the resort and the trailhead.

'Wait!' cried Fran. 'At least let me change my shoes.' She clattered after Kitty. 'These boots aren't made for hiking,' she grumbled to the tune of an old Nancy Sinatra song.

'No time.' Kitty turned back and waved. 'Come on!' Fran reluctantly followed.

'If you ask me, this is a complete waste of time,' Fran said some time later. They'd been hiking for what seemed like forever and Fran stopped to lean against a large gray rock. 'It's getting dark.'

Kitty's eyes followed the direction of Fran's raised arm. The sun did seem to be sinking fast. It really wouldn't be wise to be out on the trail after dark.

'Look out!' warned Fran.

Kitty looked back. Two kids on mountain bikes screamed down the trail, passing her so close she could feel their wake. The one on the left shouted, 'On your left!' as he passed.

'Thanks, that was close.' Kitty shivered. Without the sun above, the mountains got cold at night. She took a few steps further. 'This is the spot.' She walked in a small circle. The ground was littered with footprints, human and animal. And the animal appeared to be dog. Unless there were wolves or coyotes around here. Not an impossibility. But most likely the prints had been made by Fred, the Corgis and Sheila's pack of dogs.

Kitty pointed. 'That's the tree where I was leaning. And,' she turned, 'yes,' she stooped over, pointing again, 'this is where I went down.'

Fran joined her. 'Wow, that's a long way down. You're lucky to be alive.'

Kitty had to agree. Things could have ended much more badly. She could have bashed her head on one of those big boulders as she fell. That could have been the end of her.

She leaned over.

'Careful,' admonished Fran. 'What are you trying to do, fall again?'

'What's this?' She picked up a crumpled cigarette butt and examined it. It looked fresh.

'Eww, gross,' said Fran. 'What's wrong with you?'

'This could be evidence.' Both John Jameson and Henri Moutarde smoked. Jameson had admitted as much and she'd spotted an open pack on the chef's desk.

Fran frowned. 'Yeah? There's a used tissue and an empty beer can over there.' She pointed a little further down the steep embankment. 'You want to collect those too?'

Kitty shook her head no. 'Not the can. But I'll take that tissue.' The beer can looked like it had been exposed to the sun and elements for ages. The can was faded and dusty, showing signs of decomposition. It certainly hadn't been dropped there today.

The white tissue looked disgusting but she didn't need carbon dating to recognize that it wasn't ancient. Some creep had tossed it recently. Kitty hated litter bugs. She stretched out her arm, grabbed the tissue and folded the cigarette butt inside. The police may be interested in this. Had she really just picked up the snotty thing? She handed it to Fran.

'What are you giving it to me for?'

Kitty patted the sides of her skirt. 'No pockets.'

'I don't want it.'

Kitty made pouty eyes. 'It could be evidence.' She stuck the soiled tissue under Fran's nose. 'It could lead to the real killer of Victor Cornwall.' She pushed it closer again. 'It could,' she said, 'exonerate you.'

Fran winced as she dropped the soiled tissue in her purse. 'You so owe me. Wait until we get home. I'm gonna want—' Fran stopped at the sound of heavy footsteps approaching from up around the bend. The trail rose quickly and turned sharply to the right just up from where they stood. Someone or *someones* were coming. The trail was now half in shadow and soon to be in darkness.

Kitty didn't like the idea of being out on the trail in the dark. There was no telling what kind of dangerous animals might be out here. A sudden sense of fear overcame her. Who was this person coming down the mountain? They were two women alone in the woods. 'Quick!' she whispered, grabbing Fran's arm and pulling her into the trees. 'Let's hide.'

Fran nodded and followed. The trees were broad but there were few of them in this spot. They snuggled up together behind a Douglas fir and held their breaths.

The steps came closer, slip-sliding over the loose, gravelly path. Kitty dropped to the ground, twigs digging into her knees. A man had stopped on the trail in the same spot where they had just stood. He stooped over, his hand brushing the ground. With his back to them, Kitty had no idea who it was. The dog with him sniffed the ground relentlessly.

'Well?' hissed Fran.

'I can't tell.'

Fran braced a hand on Kitty's shoulder and peeked out. 'It's Ted.'

Kitty gasped. 'Shhh.' She made quiet down motions with her hands and stole a second look around the other side of their hiding spot. Too late to be shushing Fran now. Ted had straightened and stood on the trail, unmoving. The dog with him was Chloe from the shelter, not Cucamonga or wherever he said he was from. The dog pulled at her leash.

He was looking toward the Douglas fir. 'Who's there?' They held their breaths. Kitty hoped he would assume he'd heard a squirrel or some other forest creature and simply start moving down the trail. After he had gone they'd follow at a safe distance. Instead, he took a couple of steps closer. 'Who's there?' he repeated.

Kitty looked at Fran. The proverbial jig was up. They were going to have to take their chances with Ted.

Kitty rose, dusted the sticks and assorted forest debris off her knees and stepped forward. 'Hi, Ted.' Kitty managed a half-hearted wave from the hip.

'Kitty? What are you doing here?' Ted told Chloe to heel. The dog ignored him and he let her drag him closer to the tree. 'Fran?'

Fran grinned and stepped out. 'Hi, Ted. Fancy meeting you here.'

He scratched his head. 'What were you two doing back there?'

'You know how it is,' Kitty said quickly. 'When nature calls you've got to answer.'

His eyebrows shot up. 'The two of you?' He shook his head. 'I've heard of women going to the ladies' room together in restaurants but never sharing a tree in the woods.'

Kitty blushed. She hadn't quite thought of it that way. Now that she did, it sounded kind of weird. Time to change the subject. 'Out for a hike?'

Ted said yes.

Duh, of course he was out for a hike. Two middle-aged men on mountain bikes and wearing way too much spandex thundered past them, heading down the trail. Their bike helmets looked like props from a sci-fi movie.

'We should get moving,' Ted suggested. 'It's getting dark.'

'I agree,' Fran said. 'You ready, Kitty?'

Kitty turned slowly. Ted could be a killer but it wasn't that far back to the resort. They were on a fairly open and exposed stretch of the trail with other people about. Besides, she and Fran were tough cookies; surely between them they could handle one Ted Atchison.

But what about his dog, Chloe? And since when did Ted have two Chloes?

And why were they looking so fuzzy?

'You OK?' Fran grabbed Kitty's forearm and looked into her eyes.

'I-I think so,' Kitty said. The day's trials and tribulations, not to mention the fall down a mountainside, had finally caught up with her. 'Fran, I don't feel so good.'

Fran held her more firmly. 'Maybe you'd better take one of those pain pills Doctor Peter gave you.'

Kitty shook her head. 'I can't. Left them in the van.'

'Then we've really got to get you back to the resort. Come on,' she said to Ted, 'you grab the other side.'

Once again Kitty was ignominiously helped down the Matterhorn Trail, this time half-dragged, half-shuffling her feet as Ted and Fran pulled her along, both bearing a portion of her weight on their shoulders as she wrapped an arm around each of them with Chloe, or rather, both Chloes, tagging along. Ted had unclipped Chloe's leash and let her run free.

It was embarrassing to be dragged back to the resort and through the lobby to their suite and would have been even more so if Kitty had not been so woozy. Fran pulled back the covers and Ted helped her settle Kitty down, her head nesting against the pillow. She grabbed a blanket from the closet and laid it over Kitty. 'I'll go get your pills,' Fran said. 'Be right back.'

'I'll stay here and keep an eye on her,' Ted promised.

A frisson of fear raced up Kitty's arms. Did she really want to be left alone in her room with a known liar and possible murderer? But how was she going to say that to Fran now? He might kill them both if he knew that Kitty was on to him.

While she debated what to do, she heard the sound of the door. Fran had gone. She was alone with Ted. He smiled down at her. Chloe rested her head on the covers, looking at her too. Barney was asleep on the dresser. He wasn't going to be any help if Atchison decided to strangle her next. As sore as she was, she doubted she could put up much of a struggle herself.

'Care for a smoke?' Kitty made a show of reaching for the bedside table drawer.

'No, thanks. I never developed the habit. Besides,' he said, looking around the room, 'I don't think smoking is allowed in the rooms.'

'Of course. What was I thinking? Guess I'm just tired.' Kitty settled back down. So, Ted either wasn't a smoker – and it hadn't been his tossed cigarette butt out on the trail – or was a very good liar. He sure seemed to be looking for something out there.

Kitty breathed heavily. It was a good thing Ted had said no. What would she have done if he'd said yes? The drawer probably contained nothing more than a Gideon's Bible. Would he be interested in smoking that?

'I'll get you a glass of water,' Ted said. 'You're going to need it.'

Kitty furrowed her brow. 'Why?'

'I don't know about you but I need something to wash down my pills.'

'Oh, right.' Kitty nodded.

Ted padded off to the bathroom. 'And I'll get you a cool compress for your forehead. I'll wet down one of these face-cloths.' His voice carried through the wall.

The phone on the bedside table rang and with a groan Kitty stretched out a tentative arm, searching for the receiver.

'Hello?'

She let her hand fall back to the sheets. Ted must have picked up the extension in the bathroom. Kitty could hear his end of the conversation.

'Who?' Short pause. 'I'm afraid she's zonked out in bed at

the moment. She's pretty worn out, know what I mean?' Long pause. 'I'll tell her you called.'

Kitty lifted her head from the pillow as Ted returned. 'Who was that on the phone?'

'Some detective.' Ted set the water on the nightstand as Kitty indicated.

Kitty's eyes dilated. 'Detective?' It wasn't Jack, was it? 'Did he give his name?'

Ted chewed the side of his lip a moment. 'Young or something like that.'

'Jack Young?'

'Yeah, that was it.' Ted scratched Chloe's snout.

Kitty groaned and laid her head back on the pillow. What must Jack be thinking? She knew what she'd be thinking if some woman kept answering the phone every time she called his room.

Ted sat at the edge of Fran's bed. 'Feeling better?'

Kitty nodded. 'I was a little lightheaded. I feel better already.' Still, it might not hurt, no pun intended, to take one of Dr Peter's prescribed pain pills. Chloe rested her head against Ted's knee. Kitty wished Fran would hurry back. What was taking her so long? How long did the woman expect her to be alone in a hotel room entertaining a possible killer? Her eyes drifted to the desk. 'There was a pad,' she said. 'You know, one of those little writing pads that hotels give you, on the desk this morning.'

'Oh?'

'Yes. I'd been making some notes.' She watched him carefully. 'About Victor Cornwall's murder. Possible suspects and potential motives.'

Ted smiled. 'You're a gourmet pet chef *and* a detective?'

'The pad was there when you came in this morning and brought the coffee and pastries. It was missing after you left.' She noticed he was rubbing his thumb and forefinger against each other nervously. 'You took it. Why?'

'Huh?' He scratched Chloe's nose, appearing confused, and was silent a moment before speaking. 'I remember now.' He shook his head as he smiled and explained. 'Sorry about that. I didn't realize it contained anything important. I have a terrible short-term memory.' He laughed, ostensibly at himself. 'Ask anybody. I remembered I needed to pick up a couple of things in town and didn't want to forget. I jotted them down on the pad.'

'Like needing allergy medication?'

He looked surprised. 'You know about that?'

She knew that she'd heard a sneeze or a cough the night they'd discovered Victor's body. She knew that could have been the killer hiding out on Victor's balcony. Kitty had thought it might have been John. He did have a smoker's cough. But it could just as easily have been Ted Atchison. And it was beginning to look like she was right. Right now, all signs pointed to Ted.

Ted clamped his hands down over his knees. 'I'll replace the pad if you like. I didn't take your pen, too, did I?'

There was that boyish charm of his, but Kitty wasn't buying it. She glanced at the door. Where the devil was Fran? 'I also know about Chloe, Ted.'

He visibly paled. Kitty clutched at the blanket and pulled it up to her chest as if it might protect her.

'You do?'

Kitty nodded slowly. 'I know you got her the other day from the Little Switzerland Pet Shelter. You haven't had her as long as you say and you did not adopt her from some place in San Juan Capistrano.'

Ted sighed heavily. 'I'm so sorry about this, Kitty.' He rose, towering over her, flexing and unflexing his hands.

Was this it? Had Kitty gone too far? Was she about to be strangled like the late Victor Cornwall?

THIRTY-FOUR

Kitty held her breath as Ted approached her bed. He was so close now that his knees pushed against her mattress. Kitty shot mental emergency signals to Fran. She always claimed to be psychic, so where was she now?

Pools of tears suddenly welled up in Ted's eyes. What, so now he was Mr Sensitive? What was he about to do, tell her how sorry he was that he was going to have to strangle her to

death? Tell her it was her own fault that he was being forced
to do it?

Kitty bit her lip. Why oh why hadn't she kept her mouth shut
until Fran got back?

Ted's hands went up. Kitty held her breath. It might be her
last.

Ted leaned forward. A moment later he was convulsing, heart-
rending, tearful sobs escaping from his downturned mouth while
the tears fell from his face leaving dark splotches on the blanket.
Kitty watched in stunned silence as Ted fell back onto Fran's
bed, holding himself up with his hands behind for support. She
watched as he cried, unsure what was going on. 'Are you OK?'

Ted wiped his nose with the back of his sleeve and sniffled.
His eyes were bloodshot and his nostrils inflamed. 'Kitty, I—'

Fran burst through the door waving the little white bag from
the Little Switzerland Market and Pharmacy. She came to an
abrupt stop. 'What's going on?' She looked from one to the other.
'What did you do to Ted?'

Kitty turned her attention to Fran. 'Nothing,' she said. 'And
what took you so long?'

Fran waved the bag. 'Your pills, remember? You left them in
the courtesy van and I'd given the keys back to the valet. I had
to track him down and then wait for the van to get back from a
trip into town to pick up hotel guests.' She dropped the bag in
Kitty's lap. 'What did I miss?'

'Ted was explaining to me why he lied about how long he's
had Chloe.'

Fran rolled the desk chair over between the beds. 'Oh, this has
got to be good. I want to hear this. Glad I didn't miss anything.'
She folded her arms, crossed her legs and waited.

Ted sighed heavily and rubbed his nose once more. 'You're
right,' he admitted as he scratched Chloe's side. 'I only got Chloe
a couple of days ago.' His lips flattened. 'You see, I lost my old
dog, King – my German shepherd – a few weeks ago.'

'Oh.' Kitty lowered her eyes. She felt like a heel. 'What
happened?'

Ted shrugged and wiped the newly formed pools from his
eyes. 'Old age. You know how it is.' He patted Chloe more firmly.
'These guys, and gals, can't last forever.'

Kitty nodded in understanding.

'I still can't fathom what this has to do with lying about this dog.' Fran pointed at Chloe who took it as an opportunity to lick her fingers. Fran rolled her eyes. 'Geez, is there anything or anybody a dog won't lick?'

'After King passed away I didn't know what to do. I'd made reservations to come here with him.' He looked from woman to woman. 'I knew he might not live much longer. This was going to be our last trip together. A time for just the two of us.'

Kitty felt tears pooling up in her own eyes and soaked them up with the edge of the blanket. Probably a bazillion bacteria on the thing but what choice did she have?

'King passed away before we could come.' Ted was silent a moment. 'Maybe I shouldn't have but, in the end, I decided to make the trip anyway. In King's honor.'

Kitty could see that even Fran was beginning to get teary-eyed.

Ted smiled sadly. 'I guess I also wanted to impress you. I wanted you to think well of me so I made up another dog.'

Kitty nodded. It wouldn't be the first time a man had lied to impress a woman. Lord knew it wouldn't be the last.

'That is so sad,' Fran said, swiveling idly in the desk chair. 'Heartbreaking, just heartbreaking. I understand how you feel.'

Kitty looked at Fran. She did? Fran had never had a pet.

'You know, I was reading only this morning that Victor Cornwall – the great weasel himself – was all broken up about the death of his dog.'

'You were?' Kitty asked. 'What dog was that?' She'd seen the two poodles and they were definitely alive and kicking the last she'd heard.

'Yeah,' explained Fran. 'There was a whole article on the guy in the *Little Switzerland Gazette*. A bit too flattering, if you ask me, but there was this section where it talked about how his dog, Manchester, had taken first place at the Boston Kennel Association Show and then died before they could place a ribbon on the poor puppy's chest.'

Fran wiped at the corner of her eye. 'I'm no Victor Cornwall fan, as you know, but that got me right here.' Fran thumped her heart with her fist. 'Know what I mean?'

Kitty knew. Even a lout like Vic seemed to have a good side. 'Boston Kennel Association. BKA.'

'Oh, the ring, right?' Fran said.

'Yes,' said Kitty. No wonder it held special meaning to him. 'I thought Vic lived in Sedona?'

'Now,' answered Fran. 'I believe the article said he was from Boston.'

Something niggled in a fuzzy corner of Kitty's mind. What was it? Henri Moutarde was from Boston. He'd once owned a restaurant there. She had seen the pictures and the magazine cover. Very interesting.

Kitty ripped open the bag from the pharmacy and unscrewed the cap from the bottle. The directions said to take two. She took one and washed it down with water. Too late, she realized that Nickels might have replaced her prescribed medication with some sort of deadly poison. Her eyes widened as she pictured an agonizing death.

'You OK?' Fran asked.

'I was thinking,' Kitty said. No point worrying Fran. If Nickels had taken the opportunity to poison her, Fran would know soon enough. They both would. Besides, even if he wanted her dead, would he do something that would so obviously point back to himself?

'You need to stop thinking.' Fran rose and laid a hand on Kitty's forehead. 'You feel clammy.' A knock sounded at the door and Fran went to answer.

'I should get going,' Ted said, rising from the edge of the bed. He called for Chloe to come then stood over Kitty for a moment. He patted her arm through the blanket. 'I hope you can forgive me, Kitty.'

Kitty said she did. He hadn't strangled her when he had the chance, so what choice did she have?

Rick Ruggiero strode into the room like he owned it. Of course, he practically did. The manager, in gray trousers and a dark charcoal camel's hair blazer, nodded to Ted as he departed. He was clutching a tall bouquet of flowers. 'Why all the long faces? Are you all right, Ms Karlyle?'

Kitty rose and accepted the flowers while assuring him that she was. Kitty read the card. The flowers had come from Alpine

4U. The shop was doing a booming business of late. The natural brown basket was packed with yellow lilies, gerberas, roses, button spray chrysanthemums, carnations and delicate green leaves. Kitty took a sniff.

'I also have this.' He extended his other hand. It held a green plastic bag with the resort's logo on it.

Kitty took the bag and opened it. 'What's all this?'

'Some complimentary lotions and potions from the spa,' explained Rick.

Fran peered into the bag. 'Nice.'

'Ms Dolofino asked me to bring them to you.' He rolled his eyes. 'She says they are, to use her words, beneficial to the body and the soul.' He watched as Kitty plucked a bottle called Aromatherapy Magic from the bag and unscrewed the lid. 'She says the ointments are good for aches and pains.' He shrugged. 'I wouldn't know about that. Frankly, I think she's a little goofy. But she's great with the pets and the guests love her.'

Kitty hugged the manager and thanked him once again. He said he had to be going and started for the door. 'Wait a minute,' called Kitty.

'Yes?'

'Have you heard anything new about Mr Cornwall's murder? Have the police made any progress finding his killer?' He might know something. He seemed to be chummy-chummy with Chief Mulisch.

He shook his head. 'Not that I know of. Don't worry, I'm sure they'll catch him.'

'Did you know Victor Cornwall?'

'Ever invest in one of his money-making schemes?' added Fran.

Lines appeared on Rick's forehead. 'Never invested. Never even met the man. I was in the military for twenty-seven years. I like to tell folks that I went from an inhospitable business to the hospitality business.'

'How well do you know John Jameson?'

'Who?'

'You know, Victor's friend. Eliza Cornwall's ex.'

'I don't know him at all. Why do you ask?'

'He asked Fran out on a date.' Kitty smiled. 'I'm trying to get some references.'

Rick laughed. 'You won't get them from me. Not to say there's anything wrong with the guy, but this is a big resort.' He swung his arms. 'Lots of people coming and going all the time. I can't know them all. Goodnight, ladies. I hope you feel better soon, Ms Karlyle.' He hesitated, his left hand on the door handle. 'You know, I can't help feeling that your accident today was all my fault.'

'Oh?' She wasn't about it say it but the thought had crossed her mind. Multiple times.

'I was the one who suggested you take the Matterhorn.' He paused. 'I'm glad you're OK.'

'Me, too.'

The manager nodded. 'You let me know if I can assist you further in any way.'

Kitty and Fran shared raised eyebrows as the door clicked shut behind him. Fran went to retrieve Fred from the doggie daycare while Kitty shuffled back to bed.

What about Rick Ruggiero? Could he be the mastermind of whatever was going on around here? He did run the resort. He appeared to be best buddies with Henri Moutarde, a man with plenty of secrets and a reason for wanting Vic dead. Did Ruggiero have secrets of his own? Might he have wanted Victor Cornwall dead too?

THIRTY-FIVE

K itty and Fran hit the dining room early. As the doctor had warned her, Kitty had awoken tired and bruised.

And famished.

She wolfed down a stack of buttermilk pancakes smothered in real Vermont maple syrup then attacked what was left of Fran's blueberry crêpes, which had been coated with powdered sugar. That fall down the mountain had left Kitty in need of a sugar refill. She licked sticky syrup off her upper lip. Chef Moutarde may be a jerk but he knew his way around the kitchen, at least when it came to breakfast. She even made a grab for Fred's breakfast biscuit – a corn fritter shaped like a foot-long dog bone

– but the Lab had growled as her hand hovered over his plate. The nerve of some people, er, dogs.

'When are you going out with John again?'

'I'm not,' said Fran, motioning for a refill on her coffee.

'You've got to.'

Fran put up her hand like a stop sign. 'No way!'

'Fran, this is important.'

'Forget it.' The waitress refilled her cup. Kitty declined.

'Calm down. I'm not asking you to get in bed with the guy. Just go out on a date with him today. The earlier the better.'

Fran shook her head. 'No way, girl. I saw the way he was carrying on with Eliza at the hospital. Why would I want to go out with John again?' She folded her arms across her chest. 'I am so over that man.'

'Fran, I need to get a look in his room.'

Fran's eyes drew together. 'What for?'

Kitty shrugged. 'I don't know.' Her voice betrayed her exasperation. Everyone was a suspect to her and leads seemed hard to find. 'Clues, anything. There has to be something that we're missing. Somebody killed Victor Cornwall and they must have had a good reason to want him dead. You don't kill a person for nothing.' She counted on her fingers. 'Money. Revenge. Sex.' By her count, John Jameson qualified for all three categories.

Kitty hesitated. 'Self-defense, I suppose.' It was possible that whoever had killed him had felt threatened. Maybe Vic had been the attacker and whomever he was attacking had managed to turn the tables on Victor. That was an angle she hadn't considered yet but was certainly worth considering.

'You can put me in the revenge category,' quipped Fran sourly. 'If I wasn't a suspect I wouldn't give a hoot who killed Victor Cornwall.'

Kitty leaned forward. 'I am trying to help clear you. As I recall, you did ask me, beg me, to help you find Victor Cornwall's real murderer and keep you out of jail.'

Fran harrumphed and bit into the last bit of cold whole wheat toast after slathering on some strawberry jam. 'How are you planning on getting in his room, anyway? Steal a housekeeper's uniform and feather duster?'

'No, smarty pants. I've got it all figured out.'

Fran looked dubious.

Kitty pulled a keycard from her purse and held it up. 'With this.'

Fran cocked an eyebrow. 'What is that exactly? I mean, I know it's a keycard, but whose – John's?'

Kitty shook her head and looked around to be sure no one could overhear. 'Everybody's.'

'Everybody's?'

'Everybody's.'

Fran leaned in, obviously intrigued. 'Where did you get it?'

Kitty couldn't hide her smug satisfaction. 'Remember last night when the manager came to the room?'

'Yeah, so?'

'I picked his pocket.'

'You what?' Fran said loudly, then lowered her voice, her eyes nervously bouncing around the tables. 'You stole it? How?'

'When he hugged me,' Kitty explained. 'I've noticed that he always keeps his master keycard in the front right pocket of his blazer.' Kitty made a dipping motion with her hand, wiggling her fingers. 'It was a cinch.'

Fran grinned. 'Girl, I am so proud of you.' She slammed her hand against the table. 'I'll do it.'

'Great. The sooner the better. Once Rick's noticed the card is missing who knows what will happen.' As manager, he may have some way of neutralizing it or something and then the plastic card would be useless to her.

Filled on coffee and carbs and with a plan of action, they signed for breakfast and left. Passing through the lobby, Kitty caught sight of Eliza Cornwall at the front desk. 'It looks like she's checking out.' Kitty grabbed Fran's arm. 'You go on ahead. Try to reach John. I wonder if he's checking out, too.' What would she do if all her suspects left town? She couldn't possibly follow them all.

Fran left with Fred and agreed to check in with her later.

A heap of soft-sided Louis Vuitton bags filled a chrome luggage rack from top to bottom. A valet stood behind Eliza as she conducted her transaction with the hotel clerk. Kitty waited until she'd turned in her keycard, then approached. 'Mrs Cornwall, Eliza, I see they let you out of the hospital. I'm glad you're feeling better.'

Eliza placed the back of her wrist against her forehead.

What a ham, thought Kitty.

'I'm a bit tired but a little rest at home and I should be back to health.' Eliza waved for the valet to continue.

They followed slowly behind. 'You're checking out?'

'Yes.'

'But what about your husband? What about the service?'

'Victor's remains will be shipped back to Sedona once the police release them.'

'What about the police? Are you sure you should be leaving?' Kitty stepped in front of Eliza, blocking her way. 'They may have more questions for you.'

Eliza shrugged. 'If they want me, they know where to find me.' She laid a hand on Kitty's shoulder and nudged her aside. 'If you'll excuse me . . .'

Kitty had no choice but to let her go. She double-timed it back to the dining room where she'd seen Deputy Mulisch, the chief's son, sitting alone at one of the tables. She stopped in front of him and he lowered his coffee mug and his newspaper. 'Can I help you?'

'Um.' Kitty wondered what she should say. 'I thought you might want to know that Eliza Cornwall, Victor's widow, is checking out of the resort. I believe she's going home.'

Deputy Mulisch wiped his mouth with his napkin. 'Well, woop-dee-doo.' A waiter breezed by and set an omelet with home fries and a small bowl of fruit in front of him. The deputy asked for a bottle of ketchup.

'Aren't you going to stop her?'

'Why would I do that? I'm trying to eat my breakfast.'

'She could be the killer.'

'You know something I don't?'

Kitty figured she knew a lot of things he didn't but wasn't sure how to say so without getting cuffs slapped over her wrists. 'What about Jerry Lee Nickels?'

'What about him?' He scratched his nose.

'Is he a suspect?'

Deputy Mulisch's eyes darkened. 'Jerry is an officer of the court, Ms Karlyle.' He snapped his white linen napkin then settled it on his lap. 'You'd best be careful what you say. I don't like what you're implying.'

'I wasn't trying to imply anything. I'm simply pointing out that since he lost money following one of Victor Cornwall's schemes, Deputy Nickels might have a good reason to want him dead.'

'Ms Karlyle, we've got plenty of motives for people wanting the victim dead, but,' he said, his eyes boring into her, 'we've only got one woman who was in the right place at the right time,' he drawled, 'to do the deed.'

'Wrong,' countered Kitty. 'Fran was in the wrong place at the wrong time and I'm going to prove it.'

'Stay out of police business, Ms Karlyle. Not only is it against the law, it could get you hurt.'

'What's that supposed to mean? Is that a threat? There's nothing wrong with me wanting to help my friend.'

'No,' he shook his head, 'there's nothing wrong with that at all.' He pointed his butter knife at her nose. 'But somebody doesn't like it. And I think them pushing you off a mountain is their way of letting you know.' He dropped the knife and snatched up his fork. 'Now, if you'll excuse me, my breakfast is getting cold.' He turned his attention to his omelet.

Kitty spun on her heels. She'd gotten all she could from the deputy. Should she call Chief Mulisch? Would the father be any more helpful? Probably not. Apparently, she was the only one who was really interested in solving Victor Cornwall's murder.

'Wait a minute!'

Kitty smiled and turned around. The deputy had obviously changed his mind. 'Yes?'

'If you must know, Miss Nosey,' he said rather snidely, 'Chief mentioned that Mrs Cornwall is going to be staying with friends up in Santa Barbara for a couple of days. Said the hotel was giving her bad memories.'

'Santa Barbara? Why, that's where—'

He eyed her suspiciously. 'Where what?'

No point telling him that she knew about the speeding ticket. He'd probably accuse her of interfering again. Kitty flung her arms out with a laugh. 'That's where she's going. Well,' she threw him a wave, 'see ya.' Kitty made a beeline for the kitchen. She'd spotted Chef Moutarde through the swinging doors and wanted to have a quick word with him.

In front of witnesses. That way he couldn't kill her.

As she passed through from the dining room into the kitchen, she stopped suddenly. What about the dogs? Where were Mercedes and Benz? Had Eliza left without them?

A waiter crashed into her back, sending a tray laden with dirty dishes and silverware bouncing off the floor. 'Excuse me.' Kitty bent to help pick up the mess she'd created. 'I am so sorry.' She wiped her hands on an apron lying atop one of the prep tables and pressed on. A search for the chef, including his office, turned up nothing. One of the sous chefs told her she could find him outside the delivery doors catching a smoke.

She hoped he wasn't alone. Her phone rang. She glanced at the screen. It was Fran. 'Hello?'

Fran let her know that she had arranged, much against her better judgment, a rendezvous with John in an hour. 'And an hour's all I'm giving you!' Fran yelled into the phone before disconnecting.

Perfect. She patted her front pocket. A few questions for the *bon chef* and she'd have plenty of time to get to John's room and search it.

Interesting that Eliza Cornwall had checked out and yet John had remained behind.

Interesting too that John Jameson apparently had no qualms about going out with Fran when he appeared to want to get back with Eliza. Kitty had half-expected Fran to fail. Was he OK with two-timing his ex-wife?

What could it all mean?

THIRTY-SIX

Chef Moutarde tossed down his cigarette and ground the butt under his heel, leaving a gray smudge on the sidewalk. 'What are you doing in my kitchen?'

Kitty put one hand over her forehead to shield her eyes from the piercing yellow morning sun. 'I wanted to have a word with you, Henri.'

He didn't look at all interested. 'About what?'

'I heard you had a very successful restaurant in Boston.'

'So?' He pulled out a pack of Camels, tapped the side of the pack and withdrew another cigarette.

Kitty watched him light up. 'So, it must have made you angry when you lost your business – all because of Victor Cornwall.'

Moutarde glared at her frostily. He sucked on the cigarette, creating a bright orange mini-sun, then exhaled. Kitty held her nose. Hadn't this guy heard of the ill effects of secondhand smoke?

She waved a hand in front of her face and turned sidewise to get out of the direct light of the sun. Tears were welling up in the corners of her eyes. 'Now you're here at the resort working for someone else. No longer your own boss. That's got to hurt.'

The chef mashed the cigarette in his fingers. 'Not at all. I quite enjoy my position. I must go now.' He pushed past Kitty and whipped open the door. He paused at the threshold, propping the door open with his left shoulder. Cool air spilled out invitingly. 'If you are thinking that I might have killed Victor Cornwall, think again, mademoiselle.'

He smirked and adjusted the top button of his chef's jacket. 'I'm betting it was his friend, Mr Jameson.' He paused as if to let his words sink into Kitty's skull. 'Or his widow. Or both.'

'Why do you say that?'

'I've seen the way the two of them carry on.'

Kitty raised an eyebrow. 'Carry on?' Sort of like she had seen at the hospital?

'What you Americans call monkey business.'

Yep, that's what he meant.

'They had dinner together here after the murder. They seemed quite cozy.' The chef sneered. 'Perhaps they are in cahoots, no?'

'Did you tell the police this?'

He shrugged. 'Why would I do this? Victor Cornwall is dead. Even if I was certain who did this thing, I would not turn them in.' He pulled away from the door. 'I'd pin a medal on them.' The door fell shut behind him.

Kitty looked at her watch. She'd have to hurry if she wanted to get to John Jameson's room in time to give it a thorough search. She took the elevator up to the second floor. A maid stood up in the hall beside her cart. Fran had given Kitty John's room number and she watched the numbers on the doors as she slowly made her way up the hall.

The room she wanted was right beside the cleaning cart. That figured. Acting as casual as possible, Kitty pulled out the keycard, smiled at the housekeeper and swiped the card in the lock. The light turned green and Kitty smothered a sigh of relief.

'Have a nice day,' said the young woman, snatching up a stack of fresh towels and heading into the room next door.

'You too,' said Kitty as she grabbed the handle and pushed open the door. 'Hello?' She let the door close silently behind her. There was no answer. Kitty glanced in the bathroom. Empty. Only a couple of dirty towels on the floor and a lingering aroma of cologne.

Jameson's bed was unmade. A cursory look at his suitcases told her that they were empty. All his clothes had been put away in drawers. She opened each one and riffled through his things, careful not to leave any trace of her having been there.

It didn't appear that he was leaving any time soon.

Too late, she realized that she should have brought gloves, like a pair of those disposal ones they used in the kitchen. Kitty figured she was going to have to make a checklist of all the things she was going to need if she was going to keep snooping around like this. Maybe she should order up a lock-picking kit as well.

She discovered an open pack of cigarettes and a pack of Nicorette in the night-table drawer. A small disposable lighter lay between them. She thought back to the night of the murder. That noise she'd heard on the balcony. It could have been John coughing.

He was a likely suspect. As far as she knew, no one had seen him go to his room like he claimed he had. She wondered if the police considered him as strong a suspect as she did. Jameson and Victor could have gone back to Victor's room together, struggled and Jameson had killed him. They were equally matched in size and muscle but Victor had been drunk and his friend could probably have easily overpowered him. Then she and Fran had come in and John had had no choice but to go out through the balcony.

Kitty was deep in thought, one hand clutching John's cigarette lighter, as she ran through all the permutations of Victor Cornwall's murder. She didn't hear the suite's door open.

'What are you doing here?'

'Eliza!' Kitty dropped the lighter. 'I-I was—'

'Snooping,' she shouted angrily, her face turning purple with outrage. 'That's what you're doing.'

'No, I—' Kitty couldn't think fast enough.

'I'm calling security.' She dug into her bag and pulled out her cell phone.

'No, wait.'

Eliza glared at her.

'Fine, I was snooping.' Kitty hoped a little truth would earn her some time. And sympathy. 'I'm trying to figure out who killed your husband.'

'What business is it of yours?' demanded the widow. She held the cell phone out like a threat.

'Because my friend is one of Chief Mulisch's main suspects and I'm trying to clear her name.'

Eliza said nothing for a moment. She slid her phone back in her purse and laughed. 'And you think John did it?' She laughed once more. 'That's delicious.' She shook her head. 'John wouldn't hurt a fly.'

Yeah, but would he hurt his ex-business partner and the man who stole his wife from him? Kitty said, 'Are you sure?'

Eliza pulled a face. 'I ought to be. I've known the man since college.'

'People change,' said Kitty.

Eliza sighed. 'Not John. He'll never change.'

What did that mean? 'What are you doing here? How did you get in?'

Eliza crossed to the window and looked out. 'John and I had some unfinished business.' She spun to face Kitty. 'Business that's none of your business.'

Kitty gulped. What was this unfinished business? Eliza's face had turned to stone. Had Eliza murdered her husband? Who knew what kind of twisted relationship she and Victor had had? She could have been furious at him for any number of reasons: brutish behavior, money, adultery – Victor had more flaws than a cheap diamond.

Eliza stepped toward her. 'Do you know where I can find John?'

Kitty shook her head no.

Eliza frowned and bit her lip. 'Fine, I'll find him myself.' She high-heeled it to the door, then turned around. 'Whatever it is you're looking for, Ms Karlyle—'

'Yes?'

Eliza Cornwall smiled supremely, confidently. 'You aren't going to find it.'

Kitty trembled as the door closed. She'd been pretty sure Eliza had been about to attack. While Eliza looked harmless enough – for a barracuda – if she had strangled her husband she could probably do the same thing to Kitty with no trouble at all.

Kitty put her hands on the table beside the sliding glass door for support and gazed out the window. It was a beautiful day, so why did everything seem so ugly and complicated?

About to turn around and leave, defeated once again, she noticed Ted Atchison in the distance. He was alone and moving furtively from tree to tree along one of the many trails that snaked along the perimeter of the resort's property.

She pressed her nose against the glass. What was that man up to now?

Kitty held her breath, listening to the sound of her own heart beating. Her eyes traced the path as it slid in and out of the trees and up toward the first low hills. Several resort properties dotted the landscape.

The pool area was sparsely occupied. A man in white shorts and a pink tank top was skimming leaves from the surface of the turquoise water with a long-poled net. Howie was shuffling near the edge of the property, hands in his pockets – a one-man crime-stopper. A man and woman were pushing red rental bicycles along the paved section of the path.

Kitty swiveled her head to the left and spotted a woman walking two dogs further up. The woman looked familiar. Come to think of it, so did the dogs. Kitty squinted, wishing she'd had a pair of binoculars like the ones she'd seen Ted with the other day. The woman looked like Lina. The dogs looked like Mercedes and Benz. Apparently Eliza had given the dogs to Lina after all. Kitty smiled. Good for Lina. Better for the dogs.

Unbelievably generous for Eliza.

Once again, Kitty turned to leave, then froze. Suddenly, the scene before her came together. None of it made sense, but she had to be right. Ted Atchison was following Lina. When Lina moved, he moved. When she and the dogs stopped, he stopped.

Why was he stalking her?

Kitty's heart revved into second gear. This could only mean one thing. Ted Atchison, the man of many lies, had murdered Victor Cornwall. She didn't know why but she was certain she had found Victor's killer. Kitty's heart revved into third gear. Poor Lina must have seen something – something incriminating that could lead to Ted's arrest for the murder of Victor Cornwall.

Why hadn't Lina told the police? Was she afraid? Was she blackmailing Atchison?

Could it be that she didn't realize what she had seen?

Kitty's blood turned cold. She watched as Lina moved on. Ted, stooping low, jumping from tree to tree, followed at a distance. But the killer realized what Lina had seen even if she didn't. And he was after her now – to prevent her from talking!

Ted was probably waiting until Lina got far enough away from the resort before attacking. There'd be no witnesses to whatever he had planned for her. Out in the woods he could make it look like an accident and no one would be any the wiser.

Kitty shuddered. That was exactly what he had done when he'd shoved her down the mountainside. She darted from the room and down the hall. She had to reach Lina before it was too late.

THIRTY-SEVEN

K itty flew through the resort mindless of the confused and bemused stares that followed her. She surged out the revolving door, paused long enough to get her sense of direction then charged up the walk to her left. Her muscles and bones ached but she didn't have time to worry about that now – she had to warn Lina.

The valet scratched his head and asked her if she needed any help, but she barely paid him any notice. 'Can't talk. Get help!' she panted without breaking pace.

The valet scratched his temple and shrugged, turning back to his mate.

By the time Kitty reached the edge of the property where the furthest rooms and bungalows were located she was panting like a lead sled dog at the end of the Iditarod. It hadn't seemed like much of an incline but running up it at full speed had left her breathless and seeing stars.

She paused at a fork in the road. To the left, the pathway was paved and led back around to the employees' quarters and tennis facilities. The path to the right was unpaved. While this wasn't the way she'd come the other day, this had to lead to the trails.

Kitty pushed on, wiping the sweat from her forehead with the back of her hand as she twisted first left, then right. She was tempted to call out to warn Lina but that would only give Ted warning, too. She didn't want that to happen. Who knew what that might precipitate?

He could strike sooner.

Mercedes and Benz might come to Lina's aid but it was doubtful. The dogs had been useless when their master was killed so what use might they be to Lina if Ted attacked?

Probably none.

A large wooden sign popped into Kitty's vision as she rounded a bend in the path. Like the one she'd seen the other day, it gave the names of the three nearest trails, each mapped out in different colored squiggles. Kitty glanced up at the glow of the sun, half-hidden behind tall gray clouds. If she had her directions straight, Lina and Ted were following the Wendenhorn Trail. That was the one that wrapped around the lake like a necklace.

Kitty leaned over, hands over her knees as she raked in breath after breath. Hadn't Rick said that the Wendenhorn was the easiest of the three? Thank goodness for that. Kitty forced herself to run on, telling her brain to ignore the pain that fought for her attention, willing her to stop and rest.

The trail broadened. The lake stood before her. Its deep blue water glistened, alive with the motion of the light waves that the wind running over its surface kicked up. Under other circumstances, this would have been a beautiful site. Someplace to sit and have a quiet picnic with Jack and the dogs.

But not now.

Perspiration rained from her brow and stung her eyes. Ted was loping toward Lina. The groomer had her back to him. Without skipping a step, Kitty yelled, 'Lina, look out behind you!'

Lina stopped at the edge of the lake and was standing on a small boulder that jutted out into the water. Her arm moved and Kitty saw a small splash as something struck the water and sunk. The groomer turned too late. Ted was on her, though she must have heard his steps pounding up the path at the last second. She dropped her arms and faced him. Ted had come to a stop a few feet shy of her.

The dogs glanced at Ted then went back to sniffing the grass.

Kitty jogged on, her view of the two unobstructed now. She waved her arms as she ran, trying to get Lina's attention, but the groomer's eyes were on Ted. The two appeared to be talking. Lina hopped down from the rocks. What was she doing? What were they saying? Why was she getting closer to Ted instead of running away? Kitty silently urged Lina to jump in the lake and swim to safety on the other side.

Couldn't Lina swim?

Kitty opened her mouth to call out a warning then froze, her mouth hanging open. What on earth? Lina was approaching Ted. Had she lost her mind? Ted crossed his arms and said something. In the next instant, Lina had crouched and her arms and legs swung out with murderous intensity. Ted fell like a stone to the ground. Meek and mild Lina had some serious self-defense chops!

Kitty once more pushed on. She wasn't more than a minute or two away now. Ted was lying in a fetal position trying to fend off Lina's blistering attack. Kitty couldn't resist a smirk. That would teach him.

Still, she couldn't let Lina kill the guy. She had to reach her and help. Kitty was only a couple hundred feet away now. She could hear Mercedes and Benz barking like crazy but taking no sides in the fight. From her left, Kitty caught a blur of motion. It was Howie. 'Howie!' Her voice came out like a harsh whisper.

Howie had broken through the trees only a few feet from Lina and Ted. He shouted and both Lina and Ted looked up. Ted's hair was tousled and his nose bloodied. Lina waved to her co-worker. Thank goodness this was all over. Kitty slowed to a walk. Howie and Lina could handle things from here on in. She dragged her phone out of her purse and hit 911. Thank goodness she had reception. 'Come quick,' she said, 'we've caught a murderer!'

She pulled in a breath as the dispatcher spoke. 'That's right,' answered Kitty. 'Wendenhorn Trail, out by the lake.' She waved her phone in the air in Lina and Howie's direction but they still didn't seem to notice her, too occupied with their own problem – Ted – at the moment. 'Don't worry, guys, I—'

Kitty dropped her phone as Lina's right fist lashed out, striking Howie in the neck. Howie blurted out in pain and fell to his knees, choking for breath. Lina leapt on him, clawing at his back, looking like a wild animal about to make a kill. Ted struggled to his knees and was grappling for Lina's thrashing legs.

Kitty ran as fast as she could. What was going on? Had everybody gone crazy?

Kitty leapt on Lina's back, grabbing her shoulders. 'Lina, stop!' She tried to pull Lina off Howie but the woman was too strong. What had gotten into the mild, animal-loving woman?

Then it hit her. Lina was from Boston too, or thereabouts. She had to be. It was Olivier that had given her away. The Northern red-bellied cooter. They were an endangered species. And one of the few places where they could be found was in one small section of Massachusetts, in Plymouth, if Kitty remembered correctly.

Lina drew back her arm and punched Kitty in the head. Kitty saw stars and screamed. Howie was barely moving and Ted was holding onto Lina's legs as if he meant to weigh her down.

Lina swung again, a glancing blow, as Kitty twisted away. She grabbed a fistful of Lina's hair and pulled with all her might. Lina shrieked like a mad lioness and turned toward her, all three bodies tangled together as one.

Kitty panted. She was losing strength fast. She knew there was no way she was ever going to win a hand-to-hand battle with the woman. Especially since Howie and Ted were already down for the count.

Howie. The tranquilizer gun. The one he said he carried at all times. Kitty couldn't remember if it had been on his belt when he broke into the clearing. She could only hope so. Ignoring the rain of blows falling on her back like softball-sized hail, she worked her way down Howie's side, clutching at the security guard's pants for grip. Lina's torso was blocking her view. Kitty patted Howie's midriff and legs. Where are you, tranquilizer gun?

Then she felt it, clipped securely in its holster.

'Stop fighting and I promise this will all be over quickly,' grunted Lina.

Kitty shouted something rather unladylike as her hands fumbled with the holster snap. She had it! Her hand trembled as she slid the gun from its holster. Lina's elbow smashed into her ribs and the gun fell from her grasp. Kitty cried out in frustration. Her hands fumbled blindly for the gun.

And found it.

But Lina had found the gun too. Their hands fought over the grip. Kitty gritted her teeth and sunk her nails into the back of Lina's hand with every ounce of energy she had left. Lina hollered and lost her hold on the gun. Kitty wrapped her fingers around the handle. There was no time to lose. Lina could knock her out or kill her at any moment or wrestle the gun away and use it on her.

Kitty winced. She'd never shot anyone before but it was now or never. She felt the barrel of the gun hit soft flesh and flinched as she squeezed the trigger. There was a small bang and Lina grunted.

Please let that be Lina's leg and not mine, Howie's or Ted's, was all she could think as she fought off Lina's attempt to wrestle her onto her back like a helpless turtle. Lina was still coming. Had she missed her mark?

Lina's hands wrapped around Kitty's neck, squeezing like an unstoppable vice. The day was turning to black as Lina choked what little breath she had left out of her. Kitty was gathering herself up for one last rally when Lina suddenly stopped. The groomer rose, her eyes glazing over, as she looked down on Kitty.

Kitty held her breath, her heart beating madly. Lina abruptly fell to her side and dropped into the lake with a dull splash. Kitty twisted, holding herself up on her right elbow. She hadn't realized how close they had all come to the water's edge in their thrashing.

Howie lay moaning on his side. Ted appeared to be out cold. Kitty crawled to the edge of the boulder. Lina was lying face down in the shallows. With a giant groan, Kitty managed to rise to her knees. She reached out, struggling to grab Lina by the arms. But Lina was too wet, too heavy.

And Kitty was just too plain tired.

Still, despite everything Lina might have done, she couldn't let her drown like this. Kitty waded into the shallows, sinking into the muck all the way to the tops of her ankles. Mustering up all her reserves of will and energy, Kitty plunged further into the lake and hissed as the glacial water hit her skin. She lifted and dragged Lina's still form up out of the frigid lake and onto the black rocks then fell down shivering on the boulder beside Lina, arms and legs akimbo. Kitty had lost her shoes in the mud. The dogs had stopped yapping and were sniffing at Lina's unmoving form. Kitty stared at the dark clouds above. This was all Steve's fault.

After all, whose bloody idea had this trip been away?

THIRTY-EIGHT

K itty had run out of steam. And words.

Jack sat on the edge of her hospital bed. 'That's OK.' He patted her hand. 'Take it easy.'

Kitty had been talking nonstop since Jack's surprise arrival, trying to explain everything that had been going on during her stay in Little Switzerland. It hadn't exactly been the relaxing getaway with her pets that it had been promised to be.

'If I'd known things were going to get this crazy I would have stayed home, Jack.' She was so glad he was here. He'd come in after breakfast and hadn't left her side since. Elin Nordstrom wasn't with him. The lieutenant had dropped him off and was driving back to LA. Jack was going to take Kitty home in the Volvo once the doctor released her.

'And missed all the excitement?'

'The only excitement I'd like now is to curl up on the sofa with you and watch TV.'

'I think we can arrange that. Especially since Fran's got the guys.' Fran had caught a ride back to Los Angeles with Greg and the crew. She had wanted to stay with Kitty but Kitty had insisted she go. She wanted Fred and Barney back home.

They deserved a break from their vacation.

'I can't believe Doctor Peter made me spend the night here.' Kitty shook her head and pulled at the stiff sheets. 'I'm fine. Really,' she added, seeing the look on her fiancé's face. 'Keeping me overnight for quote unquote observation.' She made accompanying quotation signs with her fingers. 'What a waste of a perfectly good hospital bed.'

Jack snickered.

'What?'

Jack tapped her chin. Then her temple. 'I think Doctor Peter might have been more concerned with your mental stability than your physical one.'

Kitty huffed. 'I don't know what you're talking about.'

Jack stood and paced alongside her hospital bed. 'Oh, I don't know.' He started counting on his fingers. 'Let's start with how you decided to play detective and investigate a brutal murder and ended up here,' he said, spreading his arms, 'in a hospital bed, bruised and scraped, for the second time, I might add – but still beautiful,' he said with a grin, 'after chasing down the killer, wrestling her to the ground, shooting her with a tran-quilizer gun and then jumping in an ice-cold lake to save her from drowning.' He stopped there, their eyes locked in a dueling match.

Kitty pouted. 'I suppose when you put it that way . . .'

Jack snorted. She wanted to be mad at him but she was just so happy to see him. And when he laughed like that, something inside her simply glowed with warmth and affection.

'Did I tell you about the ring?'

Jack nodded. 'Victor Cornwall's ring.'

'That's what it had all been about. Well, not the ring, but what it represented.' She'd already told the police all this – and some to Jack – but felt a need to repeat it. 'Victor Cornwall's dog, Manchester, had won best of breed at the Boston Kennel Association annual show one year. Lina Dolofino had been working at the event. She'd seen the way Victor treated that dog and was appalled. When the dog died immediately after the show, Lina blamed Victor for his death.'

'Why didn't she try to kill Vic then?'

'Who knows? But when their paths crossed here, Lina's anger at his treatment of his pets came raging back. She couldn't stand what he'd done to Manchester and didn't want the same thing to happen to the poodles.'

'So she confronted him.'

Kitty nodded. 'In his room. She wanted the ring, which he adored, and his promise that he would give up the dogs. Lina says Victor laughed in her face. He offered her money.'

'But Lina didn't want money,' Jack said. 'She wanted justice and, finally, she wanted revenge.'

Kitty shivered. 'Lina admitted strangling Victor. She wore a pair of those disposable latex gloves she used when bathing pets in the salon.' She'd told the police she hadn't gone to Vic's room to kill him but Kitty figured she was going to have a hard time convincing a jury of that considering how she'd happened to have a pair of those gloves with her at the time. 'The ring hadn't been on Victor's finger, though. Lina had searched the room and been unable to find it. What she didn't know was that Victor's ring was lying on the lobby floor.'

'Where you found it,' said Jack. 'Which is how you ended up in this mess and in this hospital bed.'

Kitty ignored the comment. 'But Lina found something else. Something that only Victor, John and Eliza were aware of: Victor kept a pile of money with him. He was so fearful that the feds would take it all away again, like they had when he'd been convicted of swindling, that he kept a large stash of cash with him at all times.'

Jack whistled.

'When Lina heard me knocking on Victor's door she stuffed the cash in a pillow case and rushed out to the terrace. That's who I heard sneezing.' Despite her love of animals, the groomer had a severe allergy to dog and cat dander. Kitty had noticed her sniffles now and again but hadn't managed to put two and two together.

'I heard Lina put the peanut oil in Eliza Cornwall's perfume.'

Kitty said she'd heard the same. 'She hadn't intended to

murder Eliza, only to scare her. Lina wanted Victor's dogs. She was sure Eliza couldn't care for them properly and wouldn't even try.'

Jack sat at the edge of the bed. 'So Lina found the money stuffed inside the dogs' beds and took it. Then she used the money as leverage with Eliza – that and the fact that she'd nearly killed the woman – to get Eliza to turn the dogs over to her?'

'In exchange, Lina gave the money back to Eliza, minus the fifty thousand dollars that she'd already given to the Little Switzerland Pet Shelter.' Lina said she'd done it to prove to Eliza and John that she wasn't bluffing about having the money. Apparently she had threatened to give it all away if Eliza didn't give her custody of Mercedes and Benz. Eliza agreed to the deal. That's why Kitty had seen the groomer with the dogs. It was their old dog IDs that Lina had tossed in the lake. The tissue Kitty had found in the mountains had been a dead end.

'How did Lina know Eliza was allergic to peanuts?' asked Jack. 'It's not all that common.'

'Eliza had mentioned it when Lina was describing to her the various lotions and ointments she used on the pets that came in the salon. Eliza insisted that she use nothing with peanut oil in it. She was deathly afraid of it remaining on the dogs' hair and then transferring to her.' Not that Kitty had actually ever seen the woman pet the dogs.

Lina had given Kitty some of that same ointment after her tumble down the mountain; Rick had brought it for her. Odd, considering that she'd been the one who had shoved Kitty down the mountainside and was the reason for her pain and suffering. All because she thought Kitty was getting too close to the truth. Lina claimed she had panicked and felt guilty afterward. The liniment contained peanut oil. Lina had explained that peanut oil was very good for joint pain and used it herself. Her hands had taken a lot of abuse bathing and grooming dogs over the years. The police had discovered two bottles of peanut oil in the salon, hiding in plain sight.

'Get this, Jack. It turns out that John and Eliza weren't a couple at all – not that John hadn't wanted them to get back together, at least, according to Eliza's version of the story. All they shared was a greed for Vic's cash.'

'And it looks like Eliza is going to get to keep it,' Jack said.
'What?'

'It wasn't ill-gotten gains, just a chunk of loose cash, and it appeared that Eliza had every right to the money.'

'John ransacked my room and broke into Victor's car in a search for that loot. Eliza was in on it. She's an accessory. She must have telephoned from the movie to say that I was occupied.' That had been their chance to search her room. They must have believed that she had Victor's cash. She hadn't, of course, but since she and Fran were the last people to be seen in Victor's room, they were convinced that Kitty and Fran were holding out on them. 'Now she gets to keep it?'

'I've seen worse,' Jack replied. 'At least she doesn't have the dogs.'

Sheila, from the pet shelter, had already found a lovely home for the two poodles. Lina wasn't going to be caring for them from her jail cell and Eliza had not wanted them back.

Lina had asked to see Kitty before she was hauled off to the county jail and Kitty had agreed to meet her. The groomer had been escorted into her room in handcuffs. She expressed some remorse over practically killing her, Ted and Howie but said she hadn't planned on harming any of them. She'd only wanted to disable them long enough to make her getaway with the dogs. Start a new life in a new town. Lina asked Kitty to look after Olivier, her turtle. Kitty had agreed. Olivier was sunning himself in a cardboard box near the hospital room window now. Kitty could only hope he got along with Fred and Barney otherwise she'd be in for another session with Dr Newhart. But who can't get along with a turtle?

Kitty glanced at a vase of yellow daffodils on the dresser, a gift from Ted Atchison for saving his life, and found herself lost in her thoughts. They'd come from the Alpine 4U Card and Gift Shoppe, of course. It turned out that Ted was a reporter. He'd been sent to the resort to cover the New-Age/New-Pet Festival and do a fluff piece on the resort. After the murder he'd decided to do a little investigating himself. That's why Fran had seen him exiting the police station. He'd been trying to gather some information on the victim and see if the police had any suspects.

That was why he'd lied about his background and the dog.

He hadn't wanted to blow his cover. Besides, Rick had made it his mission after the murder to keep reporters out. Ted couldn't let that happen. That also explained what he'd been doing when Kitty had spotted him outside her room with binoculars the other day. He'd thought she might be involved too and was spying on her.

Ted had been hoping that finding Victor Cornwall's killer and breaking the story would be his big break, his way out of the lifestyle pages and onto the front page. Instead, it had almost gotten him killed. He'd been snooping on all the guests, including John and Eliza. He explained that he had seen Eliza and Lina in a heated argument after which Lina handed Eliza a small bag and Eliza, in exchange, handed over the dogs.

Intrigued, he had started keeping tabs on Lina, too. When he saw her hurrying from her room with the dogs he had decided to follow. John was with Fran and Eliza had driven off. He'd figured she was the only suspect worth following at that point.

Ted was now bandaged up and on his way back to San Juan Capistrano. The good news was that he was keeping Chloe. He had lied about having a dog before. Kitty wasn't real fond of Ted Atchison's somewhat devious character. Maybe that was what made him a good reporter, so he just might make the front pages one day yet.

Ted was lucky to be alive – lucky that Howie had shown up when he did. Lina was an expert at Krav Maga, a self-defense system used by the Israeli Defense Forces. She had spent seven years in the Israel military where she had become skilled at hand-to-hand combat. Vic had never stood a chance.

After his own near-death experience, Howie was now grumbling about getting a real gun but Kitty was certain Rick would never allow it.

Kitty herself vowed to work on her gullible nature. She'd actually bought Ted's tale about grieving over his previous dog. She couldn't believe how easily she had fallen for the story and how sorry she had felt for him. Of course, she also thought at one point that he might be a killer – especially when she'd seen him stalking Lina on the trail.

At least Jack had understood when Kitty explained why every time he happened to call her room, Ted picked up the phone.

That could have been a disaster.

As for Chef Moutarde, he'd simply turned out to be a jerk. What was the word Lina had used? Oh, yeah, shmendrik. If Victor Cornwall was the king of all jerks then Henri Moutarde was the prince of all jerks. She'd be glad to leave them all behind. That included Deputy Nickels, who she'd heard was still trying to get Chief Mulisch to charge her with interfering with a police investigation. That guy had real problems. With all the medications at his disposal as a part-time pharmacist, maybe he should write himself a prescription or two for something to stabilize his mood.

Steve burst through the door and into her thoughts. He took one look at Kitty and clapped his hands to his face. 'Kitty, look at you!'

'Hi, Steve.' She waved toward her fiancé. 'You remember Jack.' Jack rose.

'Of course.' He pushed Jack out of the way and leaned over the hospital bed. 'Tsk-tsk.' He shook his head. 'You're a mess. This won't do. It won't do at all.'

Kitty frowned. 'Gee, thanks.' She could see Jack smothering a laugh over Steve's shoulder and shot him a dirty look.

'No, really. You look like . . . like . . .'

Kitty sat straighter. 'Like I fell off a mountain? Wrestled a crazed killer to the ground?'

Steve twisted his neck and tapped his index finger against his cheek. 'I was going to say like a train wreck.' He took a step back and assessed her for a moment. 'But, yes!'

'Maybe it would be best to let Kitty rest, Steve,' said Jack, laying a hand on Steve's shoulder.

Apparently he'd finally gotten those *get this guy out of here* signals that Kitty had been shooting him. Maybe she was getting the hang of this psychic stuff after all. But her signal sending must be still in need of some fine tuning, otherwise Jack would have punched Steve in the nose by now.

'Of course. Rest is what you need.' Steve stopped at the door. 'You've got to be in the studio tomorrow to film two new shows. And a new promo for the network.'

'What?' Kitty jumped from the bed and Jack pushed her back down. 'No way,' she said, her arms folded.

'Of course, with all those cuts and bruises . . .' Steve was shaking his head and didn't appear to be listening to a word Kitty was saying.

His eyes narrowed as he seemed to study her face.

Kitty squirmed, feeling like she was under a microscope.

'Say what you will about Fran but she does know her way around a makeup brush.' He often had lots to say about Fran. None of it good. 'I'm sure she can make you—' He paused, one hand on the door. 'Presentable?'

Kitty gaped. Had he really just used the word *presentable*? 'I'm not ready to go back to work, Steve.' She refolded her arms over her chest as if preparing for battle. 'I need at least a week off.' She looked to Jack for support.

'I agree.' Jack nodded. 'At least a week.'

Steve didn't even pause to consider. 'Impossible,' he said, snapping his fingers. 'Time is money and the network is waiting for product.'

'One week,' said Kitty ominously, 'or I tell everyone, and that includes the crew, that you take a needlepoint class with a bunch of old ladies every Sunday morning.' She had recently been made aware of Steve's predilection for needlepoint but hadn't realized how she might be able to use that bit of juicy knowledge to her advantage. Until now.

'But—' Steve was actually blushing. He turned to Jack and pointed his finger. 'You heard her. That's blackmail, isn't it?'

Jack shrugged.

'But you're a police officer. Can't you do something?'

A trace of a smile showed across Jack's lips. 'What can I do? There's no crime in Kitty telling everybody you do needlepoint. It does seem a little odd, though.' He winked at Kitty. 'I mean, a grown man and all . . .'

Steve chewed his lower lip. 'Fine.' He raised his hand. 'Three days.'

'Seven.'

'Four.'

'Five,' said Kitty, running her hand over the bed sheets. 'And that's my final offer.'

Steve sighed heavily. 'Fine. I don't have all day to argue with you. Roger's waiting in the car with the babies.' He pointed his finger at her once more. 'You've got five days.' He seemed to do some mental math. 'Dad's not going to be happy.'

Kitty didn't care. She'd finally be getting a real vacation and some time alone with Jack. She'd deal with Steve's dad when the time came. Until then, she was on vacation. She fluffed her pillow and looked at the plastic cup of banana pudding the nurse had brought her with renewed interest. She picked up her spoon. 'Want some?' she asked Steve and Jack. Both declined.

Jack walked Steve to the door and held it open.

'I'll call you in a couple of days,' Steve said.

'Nice try,' replied Kitty. 'I've got five days off. You'll see me day six.'

'Fine,' Steve relented. 'Day six.'

Her neck twisted and her lips turned up at the corners. The spoon hovered near her lips. 'There is one more thing.'

'Yes?' said Steve, his voice flat.

'I want a dressing room for me and Fran.'

Steve glared at her but she didn't back down. When Steve looked at Jack he merely shrugged again. 'Consider it done. Are we finished here?'

'Yes,' replied Kitty, fluffing her pillow.

'Good luck,' Steve said.

'Thanks,' Kitty replied.

One of Steve's brows went up. 'I was talking to your fiancé. He's going to need it.'

Kitty grabbed the water pitcher beside the bed with both hands and took aim. Steve ran from the room.

Jack snatched the pitcher from Kitty's hand. 'Careful with that,' he said, setting it down out of reach. 'You could hurt somebody.'

'I wasn't really going to throw it, Jack.' Kitty kissed him hard. 'But don't ever tell Steve that.'